KILL BROTHERS

a novel

STEVEN D. MOSCOVITZ

TORTIE POINTE PRESS

Copyright © 2023 by Steven D. Moscovitz
All rights reserved. No part of this book may be used or reproduced in any manner whatsoever without written permission except in the case of brief quotations embodied in critical articles or reviews.

Published by Tortie Pointe Press

ISBN: 979-8-9863472-8-8

Produced by GMK Writing and Editing, Inc.
Managing Editor: Katie Benoit
Development Editor: Randy Ladenheim-Gil
Copyedited by Joshua Rosenberg
Proofread by Kelly Clody
Text design and composition by Libby Kingsbury
Cover design by Libby Kingsbury
Printed by IngramSpark

Although this work is based on historical facts pertaining to World War II and the Holocaust, the story, characters, and events depicted herein are the product of the author's imagination. Any similarity to living persons past or present is purely coincidental.

For Michele, My Belle

PROLOGUE

BERLIN, GERMANY

June 7, 1942

The woman in the parlor rose to the relentless fist-pounding on the front door. If she didn't know better, she would have thought it was a medieval battering ram intended to send the door crashing down. She carefully placed her unfinished cup of tea on the saucer on the sideboard. Smoothing her dress, she walked in measured paces to the foyer, then pushed the curtain to the side of the window to identify the visitor. She took a deep breath and said, loud enough to be heard, "Just one moment please."

From his study, to which he'd left the door slightly ajar, her husband said, "Trude, dear, who is it?"

Without emotion, she replied, "It's the Gestapo, Heinz."

"You may let them in. I've been expecting them." He sighed, his voice filled more with resignation than trepidation.

Trude opened the door, and a uniformed man with a colonel's SS insignia, accompanied by another officer of somewhat lower rank holding a large leather satchel, stepped inside. "I am Standartenführer Hoenig and this is Hauptsturmführer Müller. May we see Obersturmführer Heydrich?"

Heinz was already making his way to the foyer. Seeing him, both men saluted. "Heil Hitler, Obersturmführer Heydrich."

Heinz responded, "Heil Hitler!"

Hoenig continued, "Obersturmführer Heydrich, first, please accept my most heartfelt condolences for the untimely death of your beloved brother, Obergruppenführer Heydrich. I served under your brother's command and am disconsolate at his death. Rest assured, it will be avenged!"

"Thank you, Standartenführer Hoenig. This has been a most painful and trying time for our family. Reinhard was my idol as well as my brother. It is both a personal loss of the greatest magnitude and, of course, an even greater loss for the Reich."

Müller stepped forward, removing a large package from the leather satchel, and Hoenig explained, "This contains Obergruppenführer Heydrich's personal papers. Reichsführer Himmler himself requested we bring them to you. I know the funeral is in two days, but he wanted you to have them before they were misplaced." Müller handed the packet to Heinz, who nodded in appreciation. Hoenig finished, "Again, please accept our most heartfelt condolences. May your great brother's memory live on forever. Heil Hitler!"

Obergruppenführer Reinhard Heydrich, who Hitler referred to as "the man with the iron heart," had succumbed to injuries suffered three days before, following an assassination attempt in Czechoslovakia. Heydrich had reported directly to Himmler and was one of the most feared men in the Third Reich.

"Heil Hitler," Heinz replied, and Trude nodded as the Gestapo officers showed themselves to the door.

"Trude, dearest, could you bring a cup of tea to my study? I wish to review Reinhard's papers in private."

Trude Heydrich prepared a cup of tea and a saucer from the silver serving tray and placed them on the table in Heinz's study.

"Thank you, Trude. I would like to be alone now, if you do not mind. Please close the door, and tell the children I do not wish to be disturbed," he said. He held the package in front of him with both hands, not unlike the way a father would hold a newborn child.

"I understand, Heinz…I am so sorry." Quietly, she left the study, closing the door behind her.

Reinhard had always seemed larger than life to Heinz. In their youth, and even into adulthood, he was Heinz's protector. Now he was gone. While Heinz held a respectable rank in the SS and was a well-known journalist and the publisher of *Die Panzerfaust*, the soldier's newspaper, his brother was like no other. No one was as driven to perfection, no one as determined, no one as strong-willed or more devoted to the Reich than his brother. He was the embodiment of an Aryan god: tall, blond, blue-eyed, and handsome.

An elaborate funeral service was held in Prague, where Reinhard was murdered, but Heinz would have to endure a second, official ceremony in the new Reich Chancellery in Berlin on June 9. Hundreds of thousands of good Germans would line the streets, saluting their fallen hero. Hitler himself would attend, and Himmler was scheduled to give the eulogy. Heinz shuddered at the thought of the fanfare, the attention and limelight he himself eschewed. It would be difficult to remain composed in public, so, for the next several hours at least, he would lose himself in his brother's personal papers.

Heinz turned on the Tiffany lamp on his desk, raised the glass of hot liquid to his lips, and sipped. The tea was hot and strong, just as he liked it.

The meticulously arranged documents were comprehensive and scrupulously detailed, in the true German spirit. If he didn't know better, he would have thought it a dossier prepared by an intelligence operative to be used against an adversary. In chronological order, Reinhard's entire life's story unfolded: born in March 1904, the first son of Richard Bruno Heydrich, who sang opera and founded a music conservatory in Halle, where Reinhard, Heinz, and their older sister, Maria, all were born and raised. Their mother,

Elisabeth Anna Maria Amalia Krantz Heydrich, was the daughter of Eugen Krantz, director of the Dresden Royal Conservatory, and taught piano. Richard was Protestant, Elisabeth, Catholic. Before the Great War, the family was well-off financially.

Heinz thumbed through papers detailing Reinhard's early years. He was an excellent student, highly disciplined, a talented violinist, and an accomplished swimmer and fencer. Heinz rubbed his eyes, wistfully remembering the mock fencing contests with his older brother, which Reinhard won handily. He was extremely competitive, regardless of the opponent. Reinhard never cared to lose.

Heinz winced at the entry that resurrected one of the most painful episodes of his brother's youth: being harassed and bullied by classmates who called him "Moses Handel." This was in connection with a rumor—unfounded of course—that Reinhard had Jewish roots, due at least in part to their mother's Jewish-sounding maiden name. Heinz well-remembered witnessing the rage exploding, the vows his brother made to make those boys "pay." There was a small notation in hastily scribbled graphite beside this entry that, Heinz assumed, was added by some SS functionary, indicating that the issue had been investigated. Obviously, this nonsense was untrue, but the humiliation always stuck in Reinhard's craw... perhaps contributing to his rabid anti-Semitism.

Following Germany's defeat in 1918, things changed dramatically for the Heydrich family: indeed, for Germany itself. Violent clashes erupted between communist and anti-communist groups in Halle. At fifteen, Reinhard joined the Maerckers' Volunteer Rifles, a paramilitary group against the communists, and subsequently joined the Deutschvölkischer Schutz- und Trutzbund (German Nationalist Protection and Defiance Federation), an anti-Semitic organization.

The postwar years were very hard on the Heydrichs financially. The Treaty of Versailles rendered much of Germany poor and broken. Inflation was rampant. Many Germans became impoverished, with few people able to afford the luxury of music lessons for their children. Herr Heydrich struggled to maintain his school, and his wife gave private piano lessons to help make ends meet.

Heinz held his breath for a moment. The files were very thorough indeed. But, much to his relief, the file moved ahead, going on to discuss Reinhard's service with the Reichsmarine, the German navy, beginning in 1922. Perhaps, the Gestapo had not cataloged every detail of Reinhard's life. Heinz wiped the sweat from his brow with his handkerchief. His brother's legacy would not, after all, be ruined by an unfortunate youthful indiscretion.

By April 1924, Reinhard was promoted to senior midshipman, *oberfähnrich*, and enrolled in officer training at the Naval Academy Murwik. His intensity and hard work saw him promoted to *leutnant*, ensign, and signals officer on the battleship *MS Schleswig-Holstein*. His superiors recognized his no-nonsense attitude and almost maniacal discipline. He was promoted to sub-lieutenant, *oberleutnant*, and now the six-foot-three, handsome, twenty-four-year-old found the world was his oyster.

To Heinz's surprise, considering what he hadn't found a moment before, the next several entries were not expunged from Reinhard's records. They referenced personal episodes that were a great source of pain and embarrassment for his stolid, conservative father and his strict, Catholic mother. Reinhard was afflicted with an insatiable sexual appetite and a total lack of judgment when it came to women. For someone who seemed so disciplined, his physical desires could not be contained. Sexual liaisons, affair after affair, girls' names and addresses…they were there in black and white…his sexual cravings ultimately leading to his dismissal from the navy, dismantling everything he had worked so hard to attain.

PART I

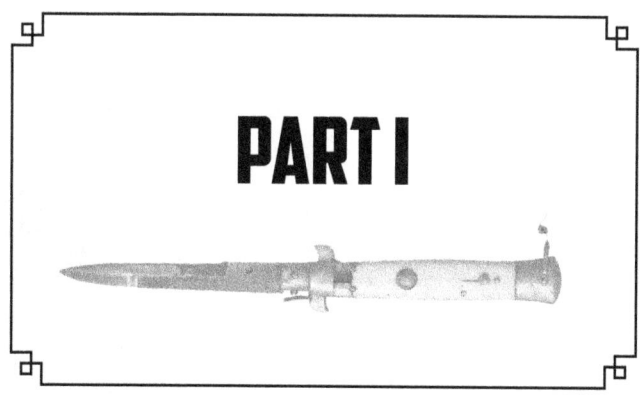

1

HALLE, GERMANY

1921

"Play that a bit more slowly, my dear," the teacher said to the young girl at the piano. "Beethoven meant the first movement in the Moonlight Sonata to be lyrical, soft, and relaxing, not a horse race."

The girl smiled slightly, knowing the critique was not meant to be mean-spirited. Her piano teacher was never truly critical or hard on Greta. While she did not suffer fools, Miss Elisabeth, as her students referred to her, was fully aware of the limitations of Greta Weber, who was not a prodigy, didn't possess perfect pitch.

To be sure, the teacher could be brutal to students who showed no aptitude for piano, and even more ghastly to those who were capable but ill-prepared. Greta was neither. The girl practiced constantly, never tired of repeating bars of music, and was exceedingly respectful and dedicated. But Elisabeth Heydrich knew this student was not immensely gifted. She simply loved to play the piano. Elisabeth sensed the girl's joy and encouraged her...Greta would never be a professional pianist like some of her other students, but she felt it was her duty to perpetuate the girl's love of the instrument.

Besides, Greta's father, Helmut Weber, who owned a local bookstore, always paid on time, and in cash. Word had it that his late wife, Sophia, was somehow related to the fabulously wealthy and renowned Warburg banking family, so it was no wonder. The Jews always succeeded where others could scarcely manage.

"That will be all for today, Greta," she said, looking at the stately Howard Miller grandfather clock behind the piano, which had just chimed. "It is five o'clock."

"Thank you, Miss Elisabeth," the girl, always polite, replied.

Elisabeth, who had once taught many gifted students at her husband's music conservatory, now gave private piano lessons to students, regardless of talent, so long as the parents were capable of paying. The once-flourishing conservatory had fallen victim to the recession visited upon Germany after the Great War.

"It is always my pleasure, my dear. Just one moment and I will see if Reinhard is available to walk you home." Elisabeth approached the staircase and called up, "Reinhard, are you free to take Greta home?"

The response was immediate. "Yes, Mother. I will be right down."

Reinhard knew that Greta's lessons ended at five o'clock every Thursday afternoon, and he relished the opportunity to walk her home. Greta was nearly two years younger than he. Yet even at fifteen, she was tall, had the most riveting sea-blue eyes, a slightly turned-up nose, high cheekbones, wavy blond hair, and the figure of a movie star. He was completely enamored of her and eager to flirt with her on their walks.

He assisted Greta with her coat and they left the house. "I will be back shortly, Mother," he said, smiling as he closed the door behind him. They turned the corner, and when he knew they were no longer in view of his mother's curious eyes, put his arm around her shoulders.

"Greta, I have decided to enlist in the Reichsmarine. My father is unhappy, but I am determined. I start next January."

"Why are you telling me this now, Reinhard? January is such a long way off."

"I think you know I care about you deeply…Heinz thinks we're in love…I just thought," he stammered, "that you and I should be steadies."

"Oh, Reinhard, you are so sweet." She reached up and kissed him on the cheek.

His face was ablaze. He took her by her shoulders and attempted to kiss her, but she pushed back ever so slightly. "Reinhard," she whispered, "gently…slowly…"

He pulled back and apologetically whispered, "I am so sorry, Greta. Please forgive me."

"There is nothing to forgive, dear Reinhard…slowly…a little at a time."

"Yes, Greta…I am sorry…but you are so beautiful and I like you so much…I don't know what came over me."

She replied, "I like you too, Reinhard. You are sweet and handsome," as they stopped in front of her home. "I will see you next week."

"I will count the minutes." He reached into his coat pocket and removed a small, waxed paper envelope with "Yours Truly, RH" written on it in smudged blue ink. "Would you please take this?"

"What is it?"

His words were sheepish. "It is a lock of my hair for you to keep, so you will think of me. I wanted so much to give you a gift, but I have no money…I am sorry."

She smiled, making his heart soar, and said, "Do not be sorry, dear Reinhard. I will hold it close to my heart," and she climbed the steps to her front door, then turned and blew him a kiss.

January 1922

Resplendent in his Reichsmarine sailor's hat and double-breasted frock coat, Reinhard knocked on Greta's front door. It was opened by Helmut Weber.

"Good afternoon, Reinhard. Greta is still not herself, I'm afraid…"

Before he could finish the sentence, Greta interrupted from somewhere behind her father. "Reinhard, give me a moment and I will walk with you."

"Are you certain you are up to it, Greta?" Helmut asked.

"Just for a few moments, Papa." She donned her warm wool winter coat and cashmere scarf and left the house with Reinhard.

When they had turned the corner, he began to put his arms around Greta, but she pushed back. "Reinhard, I have something to tell you," she said, shaking.

"What's wrong? You have missed your last few lessons with my mother, and she said you were not well." Reinhard was not the most observant young man, but even he noticed that Greta's eyes were cloudy, her lips held tight. And could she have somehow aged in just a few weeks?

"I have been sick every day. I am pregnant," she blurted out.

"What?" he stammered in shock. "Can that be possible? Are you sure?"

She nodded stiffly. "It has been three months since I had my days. Soon, I will have a belly. I will have to tell my father…what can I do?" Tears were streaming down her face.

"You must do something…I begin my service this week. I don't know what I can do."

Greta sighed and struggled to regain her composure. She looked into Reinhard's icy blue eyes. "I will have to tell my father."

"But Greta, he will want to kill me! I cannot…I…I…am leaving."

All emotion gone now, Greta's words were cold, distant. "Do not worry, Reinhard. I will wait until after you go. Since my momma died, I am all Papa has. He is sensible and forgiving…I can only hope and pray he will forgive me." She turned away and began to walk back home, alone.

Reinhard stood dumbfounded. He watched her walk away, doing nothing to stop her. She disappeared around the corner, and his mind was still racing. He began to walk in the opposite direction, faster and faster, a car just missing him as he crossed the street without looking, drawing the ire of the driver.

He thought, *I cannot be a father…Mr. Weber…oh Jesus…what will he say? What will my father say? What will my mother say?* He shuddered, then walked in circles for an hour before going home.

"How is Greta, Reinhard?" his mother asked, sounding worried.

"She is all right, Mother." He rushed up the stairs to his room without saying another word.

That night, he could not sleep. He was unable to think things through. He could not be a father. Now, he wasn't sure if he loved Greta. If he had ever loved her at all. His desire for her, he decided, was physical. It had never been anything more. He could not marry her. Her mother was a Jew. He was going to have a career in the Reichsmarine. Nothing could stand in the way of that.

"Where are you going, Papa?"

"I have an appointment with Reinhard's parents, my dear." His words were emotionless.

"What are you going to say?"

"I am certain the Heavenly Father will give me the right words."

Greta's once-stoic father, who had lost his beloved wife only a few years earlier, had aged considerably since. His wavy shock of dark hair was now graying and receding noticeably, his tall frame bent, his broad shoulders narrowing. He was in his early fifties but looked far older.

Time had battered the soul of the kindhearted Helmut Weber. After a long, agonizing battle, his precious Sophia was lost to the cancer that had riddled her body, ravaged her beauty, and stolen her last breath. Greta loved her mother and still mourned her, but her father remained inconsolable. One could plainly see half his being had died with Sophia. And if his grief for his late wife was not stifling enough, the economic slump that followed the Great War, crippling the entire country, had left his beloved bookstore on the brink of insolvency.

Greta never truly felt the economic hardships that forced the families of her classmates to wear secondhand clothes and ration their meals. Her momma's parents were always there to lend a hand financially. She was aware how fortunate she was, how spoiled and doted upon by her parents and grandparents, and here she had betrayed her father by becoming pregnant at fifteen, adding to his misery. Could he ever forgive his thoughtless daughter, who had allowed herself to fall into such a predicament? How had she behaved so foolishly, so recklessly?

Growing up, Greta never tired of hearing the story of how her parents met. Helmut Weber had fallen head over heels for the beautiful blond girl he met in a local bookstore. Their eyes met, looking up simultaneously, in the small section dedicated to biographies of classical music composers. They sat there for hours, discussing Beethoven, Mozart, and Handel, until the manager began less than subtly shooing them toward the door so he could close the store.

Sophia Kaufman had long blond hair, hazel eyes, high cheekbones, and sumptuous lips. She was of medium height, but the six-foot-two Helmut towered over her. She admired his thoughtful blue eyes, wavy black hair, and dimples that were on full display when he smiled.

From that first meeting at the bookstore, they were inseparable. Where Helmut was serious and careful, Sophia was playful and carefree. They were in some ways opposites but somehow perfectly matched. Yet their romance did not come without its complications. Helmut was raised in a Catholic family, while Sophia was of nonobservant Jewish stock, raised in Hamburg. When they met, Sophia was visiting her aunt, who had married and moved to Halle before the war.

While neither of them were themselves especially religious, Helmut's parents were devout Catholics and, at first, objected to the relationship. After months of trying to dissuade their son, they gave in. His parents died within a year of each other, two years after Helmut and Sophia married, his father succumbing from complications following a stroke, his mother suddenly from a heart attack. Helmut reasoned that his mother, who had been so devoted to his father, died of a broken heart.

Sophia's family was quite wealthy, her mother's parents were cousins of banker Moritz Warburg. Her father, Samuel Kaufman, worked in the "family business." Sophia grew up with servants, among them a butler, a nanny, a cook, and a chauffeur. She frequented the Philharmoniker Hamburg and the Staatsoper Hamburg. Their home had a large library with books from floor to ceiling, the great room adorned with artwork by the likes of Manet, Renoir, Monet, and Degas. The Warburgs and the Kaufmans had acquired their wonderful art collections over the years with the advice of French art dealer Alexandre Rosenberg, whose business was now managed by his sons, Léonce and Paul. When Sophia and Helmut married, her parents bought Helmut the bookstore in Halle where the young couple met, to provide the groom a career, and rented them a modest flat above the store. As a wedding gift for Sophia, her generous parents gave her a precious Renoir, "Young Girl Bathing," hoping the walls of her home would come to glow with the beauty and sophistication to which she was accustomed. The flat was too small to properly display the Renoir, so they placed it in storage until they eventually moved into a larger flat or house.

"I will see you later for dinner, Greta," Helmut said as matter-of-factly as if this were any other day, buttoning his black wool greatcoat, then absentmindedly angling his dark gray fedora to the right. "I have told Frau Schwarz that she may leave early tonight, after she prepares supper. You and I will talk when I return."

As he opened the door to leave, he turned to see his child, his only child, who looked so much like his beloved Sophia, with tears streaming down her face. "Greta, you and I have cried enough I think, yes?" he said tenderly. She nodded her head, and Helmut closed the door behind him.

As he walked slowly to the Heydrich residence, Helmet pondered what he would say. When Greta initially broke the shocking news of her pregnancy to him, he experienced many feelings all at once. He was irate, angry to the point of wanting to exact violent revenge on the Heydrich boy. Then, fighting through his tearful disbelief, he understood it was not young Heydrich alone but also a willing Greta who consummated the act together. Greta was merely fifteen and the Heydrich boy still only seventeen. It was preposterous to believe they could marry, even more so that these children could successfully raise a child. At that point he found himself so enervated as to be completely and utterly exhausted. When all was said and done, he could not abandon his one and only child. And, in accord with the Catholic upbringing he had never forgotten, he could not see harm brought to an unborn baby. He was certain that the solution he would propose to the Heydrichs today would be the only possible one for either child, for either family.

Helmut arrived at the Heydrich home precisely at the agreed upon time and knocked twice on the door.

Frau Heydrich opened it and smiled pleasantly. "Please come in, Herr Weber. May I take your hat and coat?"

"Thank you," he said, removing both and handing them to her.

"To what do we owe this pleasure, Herr Weber? I have missed Greta so much. She is a joy to teach and loves her music so. I hope she is feeling better," she said with true concern.

"Ah, yes, Frau Heydrich, Greta loves the piano. Is Herr Heydrich at home?"

"I am sorry, Herr Weber, my husband is still at work. I told him you would be here promptly at five, but he had a number of lessons to teach and won't be home for several hours. Oh, Herr Weber, forgive my manners; come into the living room and please sit down. May I bring you some tea?" she asked.

Helmut took a seat on a high-backed, upholstered chair. "Thank you, Frau Heydrich, I would like some."

Elisabeth brought cups of tea for both of them and placed one in Helmut's outstretched hand. "Would you like some sugar or cream?"

"No, thank you, this will be fine." Helmut held the glass in his hand without drinking. "Frau Heydrich, I have not come to speak to you about Greta's piano lessons. Allow me to explain."

Helmut put down the tea on the coffee table before continuing. Rather than meeting the woman's eyes, he looked down at his shoes. "Frau Heydrich, it seems that my daughter, Greta, is pregnant and your son, Reinhard, is the father."

Elisabeth gasped. "It is not possible…you must be mistaken." She was breathless, pale, so close to fainting as a rushing sound filled her ears, and so she did not hear the sound of something dropping to the floor in another room. For the moment, she had forgotten that she was not alone with Greta's father in the apartment; Reinhard's younger brother, Heinz, was in his bedroom.

Helmut sighed. "I am afraid it is true, Frau Heydrich. I know that Reinhard has left already to join the Reichsmarine. But you may confirm it with him. According to Greta, he may have left you a note."

Elisabeth stammered, "I…I don't know what to say. Please forgive me. I…I am in a complete state of shock. Please excuse me for a moment." She stood and quickly went to the bathroom, where she vomited into the toilet. Helmut heard her retching and instantly felt sorry for her.

Elisabeth wiped her lips, washed her hands, and stared into

STEVEN D. MOSCOVITZ   17

the mirror...her eyes were bloodshot. She allowed herself a few moments, attempting to pull herself together, before returning to the living room.

"Herr Weber, I am bereft of words. If I may, I would like to see if such a note exists...if you wouldn't mind, I will excuse myself and go to Reinhard's bedroom and look for a moment," she said.

"By all means...I know this is impossible...I have been living with it for several days now, hoping I would awaken, as if from a bad dream."

Elisabeth, feeling like a suddenly old woman, climbed the stairs and walked slowly to the bedroom her sons had so recently shared.

She knocked before opening the door and waited politely for Heinz's quiet "Come in." She did not even look in his direction. If she had, she would surely have noticed the shocked expression on his face, where he lay on his bed, pretending to read a book.

Elisabeth went to stand over Reinhard's neatly made bed. Sure enough, under the pillow was a plain white envelope. She took it and left the room, closing the door behind her. She stopped before reaching the staircase and read the handwritten note she found inside.

Dear Mother and Father,

By the time you read this letter, I will be away in the Reichsmarine. I am heavyhearted and ashamed to tell you that I am responsible for making Greta Weber pregnant. I have given the matter a great deal of thought and come to the conclusion that I am not equipped to be a father or a husband at this moment in my life, but if you insist, to clear the family name, I will come home, absent without leave if necessary, and marry her. Perhaps it was cowardice to leave for the Reichsmarine as I did, without saying a word to you first, but I did not know what was the proper thing to do. I was so scared. Greta said her father would know how to handle things and that I should leave as scheduled. I do not believe I love her. But I will return to marry her if that is what you wish. I am sorry for the pain I have caused you.

Your loving son,
Reinhard

She grasped the banister to steady herself and slowly descended the stairs. Then she crossed the hallway into the living room without a word and handed the letter to Helmut.

Greta's father removed his glasses from the case in the inside pocket of his gray tweed suit jacket. He read the note slowly, then returned it to Elisabeth with a sigh.

"Herr Weber, I have no words. I apologize to you from deep within my heart for the horrendous conduct of…"

Helmut stopped her. "Frau Heydrich, I am sorry for interrupting you, but I must. Ever since Greta told me of this predicament, I have wrestled with every emotion that has ever coursed through my mind. But casting blame is of no use. I have come to you with a solution I think merits your consideration," he said bluntly.

Helmut motioned for her to sit, then continued. "Greta and Reinhard cannot raise a child, so there is no point in their marrying. Nor can we. They are too young and, meaning no disrespect, you and your husband and I are too old." He paused for a moment, looking down at his clenched hands, nearly overcome with emotion.

"Please, continue," she said. Helmut could read on her face pain and embarrassment. She was, he recalled, a devout Catholic.

"Thank you, Frau Heydrich…I am sorry. At present, my bookshop is having great financial difficulties. To be frank, I have decided to sell it. Greta and I will move to Berlin, to live in an apartment owned by my in-laws, who are relocating to London. I had actually decided this before I learned of Greta's condition. At any rate, my in-laws have always been more than kind and generous. In fact, they offered to have us join them in London. But Germany is our home, and Greta and I had already decided to decline their offer. We will live in a small flat above a commercial space that is currently empty. I may open a small bookshop, or even subdivide it to see if we can earn some rental income." He paused for a moment, again looking down at his hands. "I have already explained my decision to Herr Remer, my head clerk, and that I will be forced to terminate his employment. This came as no surprise to him. We have always been very close, and he was aware of the problems with the business. He and his wife, Paula, have been our good friends for many years. When my wife was ill, they supported my family in every way imaginable. They are aware of virtually every aspect of my personal and business life…and herein lies the solution."

Elisabeth seemed to unconsciously lean forward, her hands clasped on top of her knees as she listened to Helmut intently.

"The Remers are both in their late forties and have always wanted to have children. They have tried over the years, but she could not conceive. I shared with them in confidence that Greta was pregnant without divulging the name of the father. They made some inquiries with cousins who live in New York City, and who indicated that there, unlike here, jobs are plentiful. America is prospering while Germany is floundering. To the victor go the spoils, as they say. The Remers are very excited at the prospect of moving to America. Both have studied English and are looking forward to making a fresh start. They are intent upon getting their affairs in order and moving toward the end of the summer. After I explained Greta's predicament and our plans to move to Berlin, they expressed great interest in adopting the baby and leaving for New York with it as soon as is practicable. Suffice it to say, I was elated to hear this but felt it was my duty to discuss the matter with you and Herr Heydrich first."

Elisabeth was silent for a few moments, clearly contemplating the ramifications and gravity of the situation. "Well, Herr Weber, it most certainly seems to be an elegant solution. I will have to discuss this with my husband, of course, before—" As she was about to complete the sentence, they heard the front door open, and a moment later, Richard Heydrich walked into the room. As the living room door closed, Helmut caught sight of a young man—perhaps Reinhard's brother—standing in the hallway.

"Good evening, Herr Weber," Richard said. "I am so sorry to be late. I hope Elisabeth has offered you some tea. To what do we owe the pleasure of your company this evening?"

Elisabeth gestured for her husband to sit down on the ottoman beside her chair, then held out Reinhard's note and asked him to read it.

Richard shook with disbelief and shock and remained silent while Helmut repeated the solution he had just suggested to Elisabeth. Richard's words were slow and careful when he was able to speak. "Perhaps an adoption is best for everyone, and a new start in a new environment is in everyone's best interest—especially the baby."

"I was hoping you would agree. Of course, I will make it clear to Greta that this is the best thing we can do for the baby. Truthfully, I think she already knows. I am almost certain she overheard me talking on the telephone yesterday with a midwife in Berlin about delivering the baby. I specifically inquired what happens when a baby is to be adopted immediately after childbirth. It seems, under usual circumstances, the baby is whisked away to an adoption agency or clinic. That will be what Greta will expect. In this case, the baby will be taken by the midwife to Frau Remer's parents' flat in Berlin. So, Greta will not have any contact with the child, nor will she know who is adopting it. The midwife said it is much easier that way.

"I will make sure Greta understands that the adoption is

designed to protect the anonymity of the couple adopting the baby. And I will assure her that the child will be raised by a responsible, loving couple who will be wonderful parents. She will not know the Remers are involved. The midwife has connected me with a wet nurse who will stay with Frau Remer's parents until they are ready to sail to New York, and then travel with them there. I will make financial arrangements accordingly."

Silence permeated the room. Elisabeth looked at her husband, and the couple spoke to each other with their eyes, the same way long-married couples were capable of finishing each other's sentences. The two of them then turned to Helmut, and Richard spoke. "Herr Weber, I know I speak for Elisabeth when I say we give you our blessing to proceed with the adoption. I agree, it is the only solution. We will notify Reinhard when we think the time is right. Please let us know what contribution we may make financially. We will find the means to pay for our portion as you see fit. It is our obligation. May I ask when the baby is due?"

"Ah, yes." Helmut sighed. "The due date is June 16, and the Remers are hoping to leave for America in mid-to-late-August. The midwife in Berlin tells me a newborn shouldn't travel for at least a month or two after birth." He continued, "I appreciate your offer for assistance, but with great respect, I have access to sufficient funds, so there will be no need for you to provide anything additional." Helmut was well aware the proud Heydriches were barely making ends meet.

Heydrich bowed his head. "You are very gracious and generous, Herr Weber. But I insist."

"You are very kind, Herr Heydrich. But I will manage and be in touch if there is anything we need. I am closing the shop next week so we can focus on packing and moving to Berlin shortly thereafter. Coincidentally, the Remers' lease is up at the end of January, and they will move in temporarily with Herr Remer's in-laws, who also live in Berlin."

Helmut rose. "Thank you for your time, Herr Heydrich, Frau

Heydrich. I appreciate you being so agreeable and helpful."

"We thank you for making this as painless as possible for us all," said Elisabeth. "I am grateful for your thoughtfulness and kindness." She went to the closet and retrieved Helmut's hat and coat.

Richard shook Helmut's hand. "Herr Weber, we thank you from the bottom of our hearts. We are deeply indebted to you for not shaming my son or our family. You are a fine man. If you ever need anything at all, ever, we swear to you, you can call on us."

"Thank you, Herr Heydrich. I will be on my way now."

Elisabeth opened the front door for him, and Helmut slowly walked home.

When he arrived, Greta was waiting for him. She gave her father a hug as if she would never let him go. "There, there, dear child," Helmut said, "everything is going to be all right, I promise."

Frau Schwarz had left a roasted chicken and two baked potatoes in the oven. As Helmut sat down at the dinner table, already set for their supper, Greta donned oven mitts to remove the warm food. They ate in silence.

After clearing the table, Greta washed the dishes and Helmut dried them. When they finished, Greta brewed tea and they sat down at the table again.

Helmut, to Greta's great relief, spoke at last. "Herr and Frau Heydrich were, of course, shocked at the news. Indeed, as you had suggested, Reinhard left them a note taking responsibility for his actions, offering to leave the Navy, marry you, and raise the child to uphold their family honor. I recommended, as you and I agreed, that it would be best if the baby were adopted by a mature couple who would be better prepared to raise a child. So, that is that. I informed them that I am selling the bookshop and that you and I will soon be moving to Berlin."

Greta looked down at her tea glass, fingering the saucer, tears beginning to run down her cheeks.

"Greta, please. No more tears. This makes the most sense for us all. The movers will be coming in a few days to help us pack."

"Oh, Papa, it is all my fault. I am so sorry."

"No, no, my dear child. Indeed, we all make mistakes. Perhaps if your mother was alive, or if I were a better father, this pregnancy wouldn't have happened."

"No, Papa. You are a wonderful father. I failed you," she insisted.

"Greta, dear. You could never fail me. You are young and for some time have had no mother to guide you. And our move to Berlin has nothing to do with the child. These are difficult times for Germany. The war rendered many powerless and poor. Perhaps we deserve our fate as a people. But regardless, we are fortunate that your grandparents have been generous to us and given us the opportunity for a new start in Berlin. We will have a roof over our heads where we can live rent free. I might even be able to open a small bookshop downstairs."

Greta looked forlorn as she wiped the tears from her cheeks with a cotton napkin. "Papa," she said, "is the new apartment very small? I mean, will we be taking all our belongings?"

She alluded not just to their possessions but to the furnishings and especially her beloved piano, and her father understood her immediately.

"Yes, my dear. The apartment is quite spacious. We will, of course, be taking everything. Now, I suggest you go to sleep and try to awaken refreshed for school tomorrow. No one will suspect by looking at you that there's a child on the way, and I have explained to the school that we are leaving Halle, so no one here will ever need to know. With the help of your grandparents, I will hire a tutor to continue your education once we are settled in Berlin, and I have also made arrangements for a midwife and the adoption. Everything will be taken care of. So, you have nothing to worry about."

Greta got up from her chair and gave Helmut a fierce embrace. "Papa, I love you so much. Thank you for not hating me."

With tears welling up in the corners of his eyes—something Greta had seen only when her mother passed away—Helmut said softly, "Silly talk, my Greta. I love you...go to sleep."

She left the dining room and repaired to her bedroom, closing the door behind her.

As soon as he was alone, tears flowed down Helmut's face like a hydrant that had just been opened to douse a fire. He mopped his cheeks with a napkin and then put his head in his hands.

The next morning, after Greta left for school, Helmut arrived at the bookstore, where Herbert Remer was taking inventory and packing books.

"Good morning, Herbert. I met with the Heydriches and everything will be arranged. I have some work to do at home now. But I wanted you to know that Greta and the Heydriches fully understand that adoption is the best course. I made it clear to Greta that the process will be discreet and assured her that the baby will be given a wonderful home. While I arranged for the midwife in Berlin, I also contacted a wet nurse who will travel with you to America and stay with you as long as you need her services."

"Oh, Helmut, that isn't necessary. Paula and I are happy to pay these expenses," Herbert said with the utmost sincerity, "You and Greta are giving us a priceless gift, for which we will be eternally grateful."

"I can think of no one better to raise the child. It is as if my own brother and sister will be the parents."

When Helmut returned home, Frau Schwarz had a message for him. "Please contact Paul Rosenberg as soon as possible."

"Thank you, Lily." Helmut smiled, closing the door to the small room he used as an office.

Lily Weiss was hired by the Kaufmans when she was just sixteen years old to take care of their newborn. She stayed with the family until Sophia married Helmut and continued to work with them as their housekeeper. She married a career soldier, Arthur Schwarz, who was awarded the Iron Cross for uncommon valor in the Battle of Verdun. Although he made it home following several difficult field surgeries, his injuries led to repeated hospitalizations before he eventually succumbed to his wounds. In a way, it was a blessing in disguise. Arthur had lost his left leg. Worse, a botched bowel resection had left him in unbearable pain.

Frau Schwarz was loyal, loving, and not especially strict with Greta. If she were shocked or disappointed when she learned that the young girl was pregnant, she didn't show it. Frau Schwarz was like Greta's second mother. Other than her own momma, there was no one closer or kinder to Greta than Frau Schwarz. In fact, before she told Helmut she was pregnant, Greta confided in Lily, seeking her advice and counsel on how to break the news to her father.

When Helmut broke the news to Frau Schwarz that they would be selling the bookstore and moving to Berlin, she didn't blink. Of course she would move with them. She was now in her fifties, and her life revolved around taking care of Greta and Helmut. They were her only family.

Helmut dialed Paul Rosenberg in Paris. He and his brother, Léonce, were arguably the most renowned art dealers in Europe. Helmut knew he could count on them to be fair and discreet.

"Good afternoon, Monsieur Weber. We have decided to agree to your terms for the Renoir. I will be in Berlin on business next Wednesday. I will deliver a draft for US $100,000, as you requested, and bring the appropriate paperwork."

"Thank you, Monsieur Rosenberg. I appreciate your handling this purchase so expeditiously. I will have the company that is handling our move to Berlin prepare a crate for the Renoir. I have the provenance and will have everything ready for your inspection on Wednesday."

Helmut had made the calculations. In his small, antique, leather-bound planner, he had estimated the cost of the move to Berlin, including the home furnishings and inventory from the store, as well as the funds required for at least ten years' living expenses. He assumed no rental income would be earned from the ground-floor space. He made a Helmut-like, extremely conservative assumption that the economic downturn would last forever, and he would be unable to rent the retail space for years to come. He also put aside funds for a dowry for Greta, and fees for the midwife and the full cost of the wet nurse, including her ticket across the Atlantic and back. Of equal if not greater importance from his perspective, Helmut deposited, through Warburg banking connections, $50,000 in the Bank of New York in the name of Herbert and Paula so they could comfortably raise their new child in the United States. This enormous sum would assure the Remers would be able to raise the baby without worry. They could give their son or daughter the finest upbringing. Helmut's intention was simple. He wanted the Remers and their child to live the American dream Europeans heard so much about. He did not intend to mention a word of it to them until they were safely ensconced in their apartment in New York.

As much as Helmut and Sophia had been appreciative of the wedding gift of the Renoir, it had been in storage throughout their marriage, a life without financial worry for his Greta and the Remers and their adopted baby—his grandchild—was something he deemed of incalculable worth.

BERLIN June 1922

"Papa," Greta screamed. Lily came running, with Helmut a few steps behind her. The floor was wet where Greta stood, sobbing. "Something is wrong, Papa…oh my."

"Greta, nothing is wrong," Lily Schwarz said calmly. "Your water has broken. Helmut, please call the midwife to come. You may also want to contact Dr. Steiner so he is aware that Greta is in labor. It will be hours yet, but good to let him know. I will get the room ready. I have clean rags, clean towels, rubbing alcohol, and a couple of sterilized pots. Relax, young lady, everything will be fine."

"I am so afraid, Lily!" Greta cried.

"Hush, my girl!" Lily's voice was tender. "Everything will be all right...you will have the baby in a few hours."

Frau Stern, the midwife, a beefy woman with gray hair piled on her head in a bun that gave the appearance of a helmet, was in her mid-fifties. She was highly experienced and sought-after. She arrived in less than thirty-five minutes and instructed Helmut to leave them at once and make himself comfortable elsewhere. This would be a long evening.

"Herr Weber, call the wet nurse and let her know your daughter is in labor. It could be several hours yet, but I will want her to come shortly after the baby arrives. She knows what to expect."

After Helmut left, Frau Stern opened her bag and laid out her tools on the crisp, clean sheet Lily spread on the table in Greta's room.

"Make sure there is plenty of clean cotton, rags, and soapy water. Do you have some rubbing alcohol, Frau Schwarz?" Frau Stern asked. She briefly examined Greta as she was speaking to Lily, then sighed, "Hmm."

Trying to look unconcerned, at least to Greta, Lily asked, "What is it?"

"Ach. The baby is still breech. I was hoping the position would change. Never mind; I am prepared." She extracted a forceps from her bag and laid it on the table. "Let us douse this with alcohol, please."

Greta's face instantly turned pale, "What is happening? Is the baby all right?" Tears continued to stream down her face.

"There, there, child," Lily consoled her, holding her hand.

Sensing the young girl's escalating fear, Frau Stern explained, almost nonchalantly, "Greta, the baby is in the breech position, which means the legs will come out first. I have delivered my share of them. Everything will be fine."

Greta looked up at Lily, whose concerned expression betrayed her. "This is a bad thing?" she wept. "I am so frightened."

"Usually, the head comes out first, and the mother pushes when it appears, to help the baby be born. This is a little more complicated. You and I will work together when the time comes. You will be pushing and I will be pulling," the midwife said, smiling to allay the girl's fear.

"Is that what the tool is for?" Greta asked, pointing to the forceps.

Frau Stern nodded. "Yes, but don't let it worry you, young lady," she said.

Lily added, "I will be here the whole time, don't worry about a thing."

Greta screamed with each contraction. She had never felt such pain before. The contractions started out slowly, reached a crescendo, and then subsided. At each peak, Greta gripped the side of the bed with one hand and, with the other, grasped Lily's hand like a vise. This continued for hours, with the pains gradually coming closer.

The midwife stood up for a moment and said, "I will be right back. I am going to ask your father to call Dr. Steiner and the wet nurse. The baby will be here soon." She left the room to find Helmut, who would also call the Remers, whom he had spoken with several hours earlier.

Frau Stern returned to Greta's bedroom, and shortly after that, Dr. Steiner arrived. "Hello, Greta," he said pleasantly. His reassuring voice and familiar face gave Greta momentary comfort, before the next contraction began.

Frau Stern worked deftly with the forceps as Dr. Steiner assisted. Lily held Greta's hand as the girl, now sixteen years old, writhed in pain.

Not without difficulty, the child came. Dr. Steiner cut the umbilical cord, raised the baby, patting its back to clear its lungs, and everyone sighed with relief when they heard a cry. As planned, Dr. Steiner immediately carried the baby from the room so Greta would not see him.

Frau Stern excused herself as well. "I will be right back, young lady."

An exhausted Greta looked up at Lily. "I know you are not supposed to say, but you must tell me: Is it a boy or a girl?"

"It will have to be our secret forever. It is a little boy. You mustn't tell anyone I told you, my Greta." Lily scanned the girl's face, wondering why she wanted to know.

"I promise, Lily." Greta lay back against the pillow and closed her eyes.

❖ ❖ ❖

Dr. Steiner took the baby to Helmut's study, where he and the wet nurse, Bella Ginzburg, waited. The taxi driver that brought the woman to the Weber residence was told to wait until it was time to take her to Mrs. Remer's parents' home.

Helmut, the midwife, and the nurse stood while Dr. Steiner examined the baby, Frau Stern looking on silently.

It was a very difficult birth. While the baby was otherwise healthy, Dr. Steiner knew that Frau Stern had had to pull a little harder on one of his legs with the forceps than one would have wished. It was likely that leg would be somewhat longer than the other, and possibly the boy would suffer hip pain as he grew. The wet nurse deftly swaddled the baby and held him to her breast so he could suckle.

HAMBURG September 1922

The *SS Resolute*, a twenty-thousand-ton steamship, stood at the Port of Hamburg as stevedores moved quickly up and down the gangplank to load the belongings of the people who had booked passage to sail to New York. The *Resolute* and her sister ship, *Reliance*, formerly German-owned, were now part of the fleet of United American Lines, known for their excellent service and unsurpassed beauty. Each luxurious ship had a swimming pool, a gymnasium, hairdressing and manicure facilities, a botanical garden, and passenger elevators. The first-class staterooms were equipped with large beds, not berths, porcelain washstands with running water, wardrobes, dressing tables, and writing desks. There were 338 first-class and 280 second-class passengers on the ship when it left Hamburg. Sixteen would disembark at Southampton, England, and one couple at Cherbourg, France, before the ship sailed on to reach New York's Ellis Island.

Paula and Herbert Remer were sailing with their almost three-month old son, Walter. The Remers and their wet nurse, Bella Ginzburg, stared at the magnificent ship in awe. Paula's and Herbert's mothers thanked the workers who carried the trunks and suitcases to the first-class stateroom, as the fathers argued quietly about how much to tip them.

Helmut Weber had booked a first-class suite for the Remers and the wet nurse and would not accept a single mark from Herbert or his parents or in-laws in repayment despite their protestations. It was his gift to them, he said, for taking this most precious cargo to a new life—a better life—in America. Helmut had given an envelope to Herbert the day they shuttered the bookstore in Halle, making him promise not to open it until they arrived in New York. It contained the information Herbert and Paula would need to access the money awaiting them in their name at the Bank of New York.

There were tearful goodbyes, embraces, and promises to visit soon. Paula's parents were reasonably well-off—her father a furrier in Berlin who occasionally traveled to New York on business, wholesaling Russian sables to upscale stores—and were able to assure their daughter they would visit either the next summer or the one after that, during the slow season. The elder Remers, pensioners, would have to scrimp and save and perhaps sail in steerage if they hoped to visit their children in America, though they promised to make every effort to come. "Whatever it takes, Herbert, to see our grandson, we will do it," his father said, sounding less than confident, hoping to cheer his wife, who was crying inconsolably.

Herbert held baby Walter as they boarded the ship. When they arrived at the top of the gangplank, they turned and waved to their parents. They were off to America, where the streets were paved with gold.

2

BERLIN

September 1928

"Do you have a hot date tonight, Greta?" joked Lily Schwarz, admiring her fashionable coiffure, much the same as Marlene Dietrich's short, layered cut and stylish bob. She was wearing an exquisite true navy, low-cut, ankle-length silk dress. "I haven't seen you this dolled up since you dated that short fellow with the mustache... what was his name?" While Lily was not Greta's mother, she had helped to raise her and knew precisely which buttons to press to get a reaction from her.

Greta frowned. "If you must know, dear Lily, I have a date tonight with Papa. We have been invited to the Liebermanns' to see some new impressionistic works Max recently added to his collection...and by the way, that 'short fellow' you referred to was Heinrich Wertheim—his family owns Wertheim's! But he doesn't appeal to me, if you must know, though it has nothing to do with his height, or his mustache either. Your description sounds more like that crazy Hitler." Greta shuddered, thinking of Adolf Hitler and his fringe Nazi party, which had won twelve seats in the Reichstag in the election in May.

The game would now commence. Lily would pursue Greta nearly to the point of annoyance, and Greta would parry deftly to the inevitable standoff.

"You know, neither of us is getting any younger. I want to see you married before I can't see anymore! A beautiful girl like you…I hate to break it to you, but you won't find your Märchenprinz if you're so picky. A Wertheim—short or tall, horizontal or vertical—would be good enough for me!"

"My dear Lily, when I meet Mr. Right, you will be the second to know, and I shall be the first."

They were both quiet for a moment. Then Greta added, "You know you are my second momma. I want you to be happy, but this is my life to live as I choose. I would do anything for you, but if it is meant to be, it is; if not, then not."

Greta knew Lily had never even considered marrying again after her husband died. Lily had assumed the role of Greta's mother and Helmut Weber's caretaker after Sophia died, and their well-being became her reason for living.

Lily replied almost wistfully, "You know, Greta, I don't think you gave him a chance."

"Who, Hitler or Heinrich Wertheim?" Greta responded with a smile.

"Funny girl you are. It is not my place to be a mother hen, but you haven't had a second date with any young man in the last three years, if memory serves me right. My math would suggest that you have dated less than half a boy each year!" she said jokingly. "This is 1928, dear. Young people go out every night, from party to party and nightclub to nightclub. They meet, fall in love, and get married…Greta, you are a truly stunning, special girl. Any boy would be lucky to even talk to you. You can't meet your Prince Charming if all you do is traipse over to the old Liebermanns' castle and chat with some blue, red, and green boys in paintings on the wall. Go to a cabaret and dance the night away."

Greta rolled her eyes, yet with a kind smile. "You never know who will be there, Lily. There might be some nice, ninety-year-old bachelor acquaintance of the Liebermanns who will sweep me off my feet," and they both laughed. The game ended…again, battled to a standstill.

Helmut called out, "Greta, are you ready? It's already 8:20 and Max and Martha are expecting us in ten minutes. It's a beautiful night. Shall we walk there?"

"Saved by your papa once again, dear girl," Lily said.

"I will be right there, Papa," Greta replied to her father, grinning.

He met Greta and Lily at the front door, dressed in a cream-colored linen suit, a crisp white cotton shirt, and a navy-blue silk tie. He donned a straw boater, then reached out to his daughter, his hands gently holding hers, and looked her up and down. "Ah, you look beautiful, my dear Greta…the spitting image of your momma. If he's smart, Max will make you the subject of his next painting!"

"Oh, Papa. Herr Liebermann probably has many more interesting subjects to paint than me. Shall we go?"

Greta smiled at Lily and Helmut tipped his boater. "Good night, Lily."

Greta and her father strolled from their flat at Unterlinden 35 to the Liebermanns' mansion at Pariser Platz 7, near the Tiergarten, in less than five minutes.

As they arrived, the massive door slowly opened and the butler greeted them. "Herr Weber, welcome. Fraulein Weber, good evening. Herr Weber, may I take your hat?"

"So nice to see you, Helmut," said Martha Liebermann, who was standing behind the butler. Her smile was grand, sincere. "Greta, you are a vision. If I didn't know better, I would swear you were Marlene Dietrich!"

"It is a great pleasure, Martha," Helmut responded, while Greta blushed, remembering what Lily had said to her earlier.

"Come this way. Max is holding court." Martha led them to the great room, where her husband, cocktail in hand, was surrounded by more than a dozen well-dressed men and women, discussing his latest acquisition, a Manet. Aside from being a world-famous impressionist himself, having just been recognized the year before, at age eighty, with a large exhibition and proclaimed an honorary citizen of Berlin, Max Liebermann was a renowned art collector, possessing one of the greatest impressionist collections in Germany.

Out of the corner of his eye, Max saw Helmut, Greta, and Martha and interrupted himself, pausing in midsentence to turn to his newest guests with a flourish. "Helmut, Greta…so good to see you," he said as others turned in their direction. With well-practiced self-deprecation, he added, "I was just forcing everyone to admire my latest acquisition! A Manet! Now, *he was a great artist!*"

The guests were an esteemed group: Paul Rosenberg, who had just facilitated the acquisition of the Manet, and whom Helmut knew well from the disposition of the Renoir several years earlier; the former German interior minister Walter von Keudell; the physicist Albert Einstein and his wife, Elsa; the businessman and race car driver Adolf Rosenberger; the conductor and composer Otto Klemperer and his wife, Johanna; the lyricist Bertolt Brecht and his lover, the composer Elizabeth Hauptmann; and Kurt Weill and his wife, the actress Lotte Lenya. While no stranger to such luminaries given her grandparents' and Helmut's friends, Greta was still awestruck by Lotte Lenya, who was starring in *Die Dreigroschenopera*, *The Threepenny Opera*, with music by her husband and lyrics by Brecht, which had opened just a week before at the Theater am Schiffbauerdamm. Greta had seen it with her father and loved it.

As Max turned back to his illustrious guests, the door opened again and the butler escorted a young man into the great room. He was of medium height, slim, an inch or so shorter than Greta, but had piercing, light blue-gray eyes, dirty blond, wavy hair, and a clean-shaven, square jaw. He wore a light blue poplin suit, a crisp white shirt, and a dark tie. "Ah," Max said, again interrupting his own chain of thought, "welcome, Alfred! Good to see you, my boy. Are your parents in tow?"

With a deep yet controlled baritone and the ease of a man

self-confident, yet not cocky, Alfred Sternlicht replied, "I am afraid not. There is a wedding tomorrow, and my father and mother are working overtime on the bridesmaids' dresses. It seems at the last minute, Anna Siegfried had to have one more bridesmaid in the wedding party, 'lest she die,'" he said lightly, mimicking a feminine voice.

Max couldn't help but smile. Anna Siegfried's wedding was a major social event and the wealthy Siegfrieds practically wrote the book on ostentatiousness, so Sternlicht & Company, one of Berlin's most exquisite couture boutiques, would do the impossible to satisfy the bride and her parents with delivery of the dresses in time for the ceremony.

Greta, who was engaged in conversation with Lotte Lenya, turned her head in the direction of the baritone voice and momentarily stopped speaking, holding her breath. Lenya immediately saw her reaction and smiled. She whispered the obvious to Greta: "Handsome, yes?"

Max was speaking again. "How uncivil of me. Let me introduce you." He put his hand on Alfred's shoulder and proceeded to introduce him to everyone in the room. "And this is Helmut Weber's daughter, Greta."

Alfred, his eyes meeting Greta's, took her hand in his, raised it to his lips, and said, "Enchanted."

Greta, her hand lingering in his perhaps a bit too long, her eyes affixed on his for what seemed an eternity, tried to reply, but no words would come. Her cheeks flushed like a schoolgirl's.

Lenya, sensing the moment—that love-at-first-sight moment—spoke just loudly enough to divert everyone's attention. "Max, you were saying about the Manet…"

"Ah yes," Max picked up his cue, "the boldness of color is striking, don't you agree?" And he continued to comment on the painting, while Paul Rosenberg added some professional commentary.

One server offered the guests hors d'oeuvres and another

poured from a bottle of 1925 Château Mouton Rothschild red Bordeaux. Greta gratefully accepted a glass and Alfred did the same. The two spoke for what felt like hours, until Helmut tugged at his daughter's elbow and said, "I am sorry to interrupt, but it is getting late, Greta…it is time to go."

Helmut turned to Alfred. "It is a pleasure to have met you, Herr Sternlicht." He said something about finding the butler to retrieve his hat and say good evening to the Liebermanns to give the young people sufficient time to say good night. He had seen the look in their eyes. He had been a romantic once, after all, and had hoped for happiness for his beloved daughter for many years. And Alfred Sternlicht was of fine stock.

"You know something, Greta?" Alfred declared. "My family has been close to the Liebermanns for many years, so I didn't want to disappoint Max when he invited us to this party. I almost convinced my parents to allow me to work on the dresses tonight, but they insisted I come here in their stead. Suffice it to say, I am not nearly as skilled with a needle as they. But I am most fortunate that I came this evening. I do love Max's collection, but there is no work of art I could conceive of as exquisite as you. Would you allow me to call on you?"

Greta felt her face flush, "Of course, Alfred. Please do."

❖ ❖ ❖

Theirs was a storybook romance. Alfred and Greta were inseparable. They attended the theater, gallery openings, and traveled the countryside, enjoying dinners in the finest restaurants from Berlin to Paris and the coast of the French Riviera. And, of course, it culminated in the "wedding of the century," or at least that was what Lily called it. The beautiful, blond daughter of Helmut and the late Sophia Weber was dressed in a showstopping silk wedding gown, handcrafted by the gifted hands of the groom's parents at

Sternlicht & Co. The head piece was accented by a diamond-studded tiara, lent to Greta by Goldberg and Sons Jewelers, and the heavy silk train was roughly eleven feet in length. The groom, the son of Josef and Bette Sternlicht, was attired in tie and tails, lovingly custom-made by his father.

The magnificent wedding was attended by a who's who of Berlin high society and took place at the Liebermanns' home at Pariser Platz 7 in the summer of 1929. The bridal party included Lotte Lenya, Kurt Weill, Elizabeth Hauptmann, and, of course, Max and Martha Liebermann. Surprising to some and known by few, the *trauzeugin*, Greta's maid of honor, was one Lily Schwarz. Helmut escorted his beloved daughter to stand beside Alfred, placing her hand in his with tears in his eyes, so very happy to give her over to a man he could trust and care for as much as he did Greta. If only Sophia had lived to see this day.

For just a moment, as Greta exchanged her vows with the man she adored, she closed her eyes and pictured her son—a handsome, bright boy of seven—the boy she had never seen, watching her curiously, holding the waxed paper envelope containing a lock of his father's hair, which she had hidden away. Then she looked at Alfred, her Märchenprinz, and smiled.

3

THE BRONX, NEW YORK

September 1928

In 1928, in New York City, the melting pot of the United States, the Jewish population was over 1.7 million. Approximately one-third of the city's Jewish population lived in the Bronx, which comprised roughly 45 percent of the borough's residents. Three of those residents, the Remers, Herbert, Paula, and little Walter, were among the first tenants of a magnificent, spacious, high-ceilinged, four-bedroom, three-bathroom apartment at 960 Grand Concourse, a few blocks from Yankee Stadium. The building, completed in 1927, boasted an art deco exterior with a beautiful, gated courtyard and garden. The wide, multilaned and tree-lined Grand Concourse reminded Herbert and Paula of Berlin's lovely Unterlinden.

Upon arrival from Germany in 1922, Herbert's cousin, Frederick, had secured an apartment for Herbert, Paula, Walter, and the wet nurse, Bella, in the same building his family rented at 945 Aldus Street, not far from Southern Boulevard. Frederick lived there with his wife and their infant son. Frederick also helped his cousin get started in a small retail fruit and vegetable market next to his candy store. The landlord had offered Herbert a one-year lease, waiving the month's security on Frederick's word that his cousin was of some means and would guarantee the rent for the year. Herbert could pay the rent up front if necessary.

A friend of Frederick's late father and Herbert's uncle, Sam Sonnenschein, a successful fruit and vegetable wholesaler in the Hunts Point section of the Bronx, supplied the Remers inventory and, more importantly, precious advice on running the business. Herbert hit it off with Sam right away, and he ensured a supply of excellent produce at a fair price and thirty-day net payment terms.

Sam was a chubby, balding man in his late sixties whose wife had died during the 1918 influenza epidemic. The Sonnenscheins had no children, so, for all practical purposes, Sonnenschein Produce was Sam's baby. He had started as a fruit peddler in Harlem at the turn of the century. Seeing greener pastures in the up-and-coming Bronx, he established a storefront off 169th Street and later expanded operations as a fresh fruit and vegetable wholesaler in Hunts Point. He enjoyed Herbert and Paula's company, their erudition and, of course, their precocious baby son. Sam bonded with Walter, almost considering him a grandson.

Moving to the upscale Grand Concourse was both proof of the Remers' financial success, generated by their now-thriving fruit and vegetable business, and the booming economy in the South Bronx. This was, after all, the Roaring Twenties. Their new neighborhood, to which they easily acclimated, was a friendly, comfortable area populated with well-off people like them, the majority of whom were Europeans, many of them of German Jewish descent. And there were a fair number of families with young children, potential playmates for Walter.

Herbert was a natural when it came to retailing. He had a knack for numbers and seemed to have a perpetual smile on his face. In Helmut's bookstore, he had acquired an understanding of inventory control and customer preferences. His pleasant manner and generous spirit endeared him to his customers. To mothers shopping with young children, he would almost always offer an extra orange or apple..."for the road," he would say with a laugh, gesturing with a pretend glass in his hand. He knew these gifts were good for business.

Years later, Herbert would regale his customers with the story of how, when he first opened the shop, a young, rough-looking, barrel-chested man would pass the store in an old, beaten-up truck on Tuesday and Thursday mornings at 11:00, like clockwork. He would leave the truck with the motor still running, jump out, grab an apple or whatever fruit was on special in the crates in front of the store, hop back in the truck, and take off.

One day, having gotten wise to the petty larcenist, Herbert came out to stand in the doorway of his cousin's candy store, next door, as soon as he heard the unmistakable backfire of the unmuffled truck. He stepped back to his own store just as the young man grabbed a Macintosh apple.

"May I help you, young man?"

The young driver said gruffly, "Get lost."

Herbert said gently, "Young man, I see you take a piece of fruit from my stand twice a week. I consider it a great compliment to my produce! I don't know how far you've come to get here, but I must have the best apples in the Bronx if you make sure you always pass by my store to take my fruit."

The tough-looking driver laughed out loud and walked back to the driver's side of his truck.

Herbert followed him, and just as the man closed the door, he handed him two more apples. He said kindly, "Look, if you are hungry, take two apples. Here…I insist."

The truck driver took the apples without a word and drove off.

The next Tuesday, the young man appeared again, precisely at 11:00 a.m. He stopped the truck and shut off the motor. In anticipation, Herbert had put several apples in a brown paper bag and written on the front, "For my friend, the Tuesday and Thursday truck driver," which he placed on top of the produce outside. The driver laughed, grabbed the bag, and went inside.

"Hey, mister," he shouted, "thanks for the apples! Here, take this," and he offered Herbert twenty-five cents, although each apple cost only a penny.

Herbert smiled. "Ah, I see you found them! Good. Please keep your money." Herbert spoke in a serious tone. "Young man, if you are ever hungry, you are welcome to take as many apples or plums or oranges as you want. If you have mouths to feed at home, or if your loved ones are hungry, take what you need. I mean that. No charge. So, what's your name? Mine is Herb Remer." He extended his hand.

The young man hesitantly shook Herbert's hand and replied, "Arthur Flegenheimer."

"Well, Arthur, remember, you are always welcome to take an apple or two. Just stop in and say 'hello' when you do."

The young man walked out of the store, and he continued to show up at precisely 11:00 a.m. on Tuesdays and Thursdays for another six months or so, occasionally conversing with Herbert, usually about the Yankees. Then, abruptly, he ceased coming to Herbert's store. Not a word or a goodbye. Herbert, who had taken a liking to the young tough, who had started his career as a petty thief, a bouncer, and a truck driver before he partnered with Joey Noe, a bootlegger and gangster, was sad to have lost contact with him. The young man Herbert knew as Arthur Flegenheimer would one day be more familiar as Dutch Schultz.

Herbert enjoyed recanting the story of his brush with a young tough who eventually became a notorious mobster. Depending on his audience, he was known to embellish the story a bit. Sometimes, he would go so far as to describe how, on their initial encounter, Herb confronted the thieving thug with almost superhuman strength and grappled with the man as the biblical Jacob did with a more powerful angel, preventing the theft of his prized apples. Most who heard this version of the story would double over with laughter, recognizing the storyteller's inability to keep a straight face while weaving the yarn and simultaneously considering the savage reputation of Dutch Schultz.

What Herbert never knew was that Schultz never forgot Herbert Remer's acts of kindness. He would issue an edict that should anyone ever shake down or lay a hand on Herbert Remer or anyone in his family, that poor soul would have to answer to Schultz personally—and such a confrontation was sure to end badly.

Herbert Remer was a man of medium height. He had a light complexion, an aquiline nose, and a full head of dark, curly hair. So, too, it seemed, did many other Jewish residents of this South Bronx neighborhood. Paula, a short, slim woman with always stylishly coiffed salt-and-pepper hair, occasionally helped at the shop but preferred to spend most of her waking hours raising Walter. Shortly after he was seven months old, Paula dismissed Bella Ginzburg, the wet nurse. It was an amicable parting, with the Remers offering to pay Bella's fare back to Germany or help her get settled in America. Without hesitation, she elected to stay in New York. The Remers helped Bella find an apartment in prosperous Washington Heights in Manhattan, which also had a large German Jewish population, and paid her rent and expenses until she secured a job. Within a few months, she found work as a secretary in a hat manufacturer and quickly settled into her own version of the American Dream, frequenting the speakeasies that emerged during Prohibition and discovering the uninhibited world of the Roaring Twenties. She was in love…with America.

Perhaps because she could not have children of her own, after hoping and praying to conceive for so many years, Paula doted on young Walter relentlessly. Actually, "doting" didn't do justice to the term. Paula's "nurturing," as she called it, would likely make a mother bear feel inadequate when defending her cubs against predators. It seemed Paula's every waking moment was consumed by taking care of Walter. Herbert would often joke that "it is a miracle Walter learned to walk because Paula didn't let his feet touch the ground."

When not reading stories to him, Paula took little Walter in his carriage to Central Park, rather than to one closer to home, so he could hear the unaccented English a successful American citizen would require to prosper in the *Goldene Medina*. Nothing was too difficult for her son!

Paula's great love was music. As a girl growing up in Berlin, her parents often took her to the opera and symphony. They indulged her, going so far as to rent a piano and arrange for lessons. Sadly, she hadn't the aptitude for playing, barely able to master "Flohwalzer," which she later came to know was called "Chopsticks" in America. However, she reveled in the sights and sounds of the symphony and immersed herself in the glory of classical music. Now, in New York, Paula extended her love of music to jazz, swing, and ragtime. On Saturdays, she unfailingly tuned into NBC's *Music Appreciation Hour* and occasionally trekked to Broadway for a live performance with young Walter. Herbert more often than not was unable to join them, being tethered to the store and, admittedly, his love of music was nowhere as keen as Paula's.

The first Broadway show Walter saw, at the ripe old age of five, was *Show Boat*, produced by the great showman Florenz Ziegfeld, with music by Jerome Kern and Oscar Hammerstein. Walter hummed each song repeatedly for days afterward, to his mother's delight.

When any music began to play, regardless of genre, Walter's excitement was palpable. He would bounce up and down and squeal with delight. At times, he would even furrow his youthful brow in what appeared to be mock concentration, as if he were conducting an orchestra, like Arturo Toscanini. As an infant he seemed enthralled by music. By the age of six, he was absolutely mesmerized by it.

The Remers anxiously awaited the delivery of the grand piano they had purchased from Krakauer Brothers, one of several highly regarded piano manufacturers located in the South Bronx, the "piano manufacturing capital" of the United States, or so claimed the proud residents of the Port Morris neighborhood. Seizing on

Walter's love of music—or, more precisely, Paula's interpretation of his love of music—she'd decided the boy would be a virtuoso and had ordered the piano. Herbert, who had difficulty saying no to Paula, was at a loss to rein in his wife, especially when she enlisted the aid of Sam Sonnenschein to select the appropriate instrument. Sam's late wife had been a pianist and quite discriminating when it came to her pianos. So, they agreed on a Krakauer. The massive instrument was delivered to the Remers' third-floor apartment shortly after they moved in.

At first, Paula and Sam encouraged Walter to sit on the bench between them as they attempted to play "Chopsticks." Walter imitated them, striking the keys as they did. Then, after watching his mother and Uncle Sam endeavor to play, he began to play "Chopsticks"—perfectly. Paula and Sam looked at each other. Then they both stood up and watched the boy. The six-year-old tested additional keys, seemingly without rhyme or reason, but with great concentration.

After a few minutes, Walter's indiscriminate key strokes evolved into music—beautiful music. He began playing Beethoven's Moonlight Sonata, continuing for a good five or six minutes, and abruptly stopped. He looked up for a moment with that furrowed brow, as if pondering a difficult Talmudic question, then went back to playing. Paula and Sam recognized "Maple Leaf Rag" as if it were Scott Joplin himself at the piano. Herbert walked in, assuming Paula and Sam were listening to the radio. He stopped and stood still, dumbfounded. Paula and Sam were speechless.

When Walter concluded the piece, the adults stood in stunned silence. Paula began to cry. Herbert and Sam looked at each other, smiled broadly, and began to applaud. Walter pushed back the bench and bowed, just as he recalled the orchestra leader had done at the end of *Show Boat*. He said, "Momma, why are you crying?"

"They are tears of joy, Walter, tears of joy," she responded.

The next day, Sonnenschein placed a call to his late wife's friend

Janet Schenck, the founder of the Neighborhood Music School. Arrangements were made to audition young Walter. The school's original building on 238 East 105th Street in Harlem had recently been razed to make way for a new one under construction in its place, so Mrs. Schenck and a recent graduate and piano teacher at the school, Dora Zaslavsky, agreed to visit the Remers in their apartment.

Introductions were made, and the kindly Mrs. Schenck sat down on the piano bench next to the blond little boy who had entered the room with a noticeable limp. She asked, "Walter, would you mind if I played something on your piano?"

Walter nodded and politely said, "Yes, thank you, Mrs. Schenck."

Janet Schenck proceeded to play parts of Rachmaninoff's Piano Concerto No. 2. Her slim, practiced fingers danced on the keys with grace and certainty. Walter listened intently. She played on for about three minutes, stopped, and repeated the music. Then she made room on the bench and motioned for Walter to join her.

"Would you like to play, Walter?"

The boy sat down and said, "Yes, may I, Mrs. Schenck?"

She nodded, and Walter concentrated on the ivory keys for a few moments before he permitted his hands to stroke them. And Walter began to play. Note for note, key stroke for key stroke, Rachmaninoff's music came to life.

As he played, Paula cupped her face with her hands, tears rolling down her cheeks. Herbert and Sam both stood with arms akimbo, wearing broad smiles. Janet Schenck and Dora Zaslavsky exchanged numerous glances as the boy played.

When he concluded the concerto, Mrs. Schenck exclaimed, "Bravo, Walter. Lovely, just lovely. Can you read music?"

The boy looked at her quizzically, and Paula answered, "Mrs. Schenck, Walter just began kindergarten recently. He does not read yet."

Mrs. Schenck smiled. "Yes, I understand. I meant, can he read sheet music or musical notes?"

Paula shook her head, and Dora said, "He has a marvelous ear. We can certainly teach him to read music."

Mrs. Schenck added, "Of course. Walter, would you like to play anything else?"

"Yes, I would like to play the rag song? Is that OK?"

The woman nodded, and Walter began to play the "Maple Leaf Rag."

When he finished, everyone smiled and applauded, and Walter made what was becoming his signature bow and said, "It was nice to meet you, Mrs. Schenck and Miss Dora. May I be excused now? Uncle Sam and Papa said they would take me to the playground after I played."

"Yes, of course," Paula said, and Sam, Herbert, and Walter left the parlor.

Janet Schenck said, "Mrs. Remer, your son is very gifted. If you are amenable, we would love to have him attend the Neighborhood Music School. We can arrange for him to come after school or on Saturdays. We know it would be a rather long trip each day for such a young child, but I think he has special talents and would thrive with us. I would like to have Miss Zaslavsky work closely with him. Not to embarrass her, but she is one of our first graduates, an accomplished pianist, and a wonderful teacher. Our school has a comprehensive curriculum and a very dedicated board. Harold Bauer and Pablo Casals are not only board members but take an active interest in our students. Would you be interested?"

Paula gathered herself together and said, "Of course I will have to discuss it with my husband, but I think he will be very excited."

Mrs. Schenck and Miss Zaslavsky stood, and Schenck said, "Then we look forward to hearing from you. It has truly been a joy listening to your son."

"Thank you!"

Dora added, "Thank you so much for inviting us, Mrs. Remer. Walter will be a wonderful pianist, I am sure. I was wondering…I noticed his limp. Has he hurt himself playing outside? I hope he is all right."

Paula whispered, even though they were the only ones in the room, "Walter's birth was a difficult one—he was a breech baby—and the doctor told us he would always have a limp."

"Oh, I am so sorry. I didn't mean to pry," Dora said sheepishly. "A little limp will never get in the way of such a talent, Mrs. Remer. You can be sure of that."

4

BERLIN

In the early 1920s, Germany's postwar Weimar Republic suffered from economic stagnation, high unemployment, and hyperinflation, largely due to the oppressive terms of the Treaty of Versailles. Throughout the country at the time, political fringe parties like the Communists and the relatively new Nazis gained ground as the economy suffered. Their followers confronted one another, often violently, endeavoring to reset a postwar Germany in their image. During the latter half of the decade, financial stability gradually returned, and fortunes improved, largely due to America's largesse in offering loans and support for German industry. Still, the Communist and Nazi parties mutual hatred simmered palpably just beneath the surface, lying in wait for the opportunity to pounce. Meanwhile, the German elite prospered.

The Sternlichts, who produced the finest, world-renowned bespoke wedding dresses and tuxedos, had become exceedingly wealthy. Revenue generated from New York, London, and Geneva far exceeded sales at home. Josef Sternlicht, Alfred's father, was not one to play the stock market. He didn't understand stocks and as he said frequently to his son, "If you can't hold it, you don't own it." He maintained numbered accounts in UBS Switzerland, where he kept several currencies in large denominations, partly for paying his foreign suppliers and partly for investment purposes. His foreign currency holdings seemed certain to appreciate in value versus the almost always shrinking German mark. He kept roughly equal sums of US dollars, Swiss francs, and British pounds sterling. With a constantly collapsing mark, he was making a fortune. He kept accounts in his, Bette's, and Alfred's names.

Josef was also a savvy art collector. In addition to purchasing his friend Max Liebermann's works, he owned pieces by Monet, Renoir, Picasso, Matisse, and Degas. He kept a stash of gold bars in UBS safety deposit boxes. To a minority of their countrymen, the latter part of the 1920s in Germany became known as the "Golden Twenties." The Sternlichts were among them.

NEW YORK

In the United States in general, and New York City in particular, the postwar economy was booming, and many established residents who ran successful businesses enjoyed the excesses of a soaring stock market. Speculation was rampant. Consumers spent with abandon and stock market investors borrowed to enhance their gains. Affluent neighborhoods were buzzing with activity. New buildings seemed to go up every day. To be sure, there were also poor areas, unglamorous ghettos like the Lower East Side, teaming with impoverished, near-starving immigrants: Italians, Irish, European Jews. But, on the Grand Concourse, to the Remers and their neighbors, the most important decisions seemed to revolve around which automobile to purchase or which state-of-the-art icebox to buy.

On October 24, 1929, everything changed. It was referred to as Black Thursday on Wall Street. The stock market crashed. Stocks on the New York Stock Exchange dropped 11 percent at the opening of trading that day, and the market continued to decline for several weeks, eventually losing 90 percent of its value from the previous high point set on September 3, 1929. The market's savage decline led to the Great Depression. The market did not reach its nadir until almost three years later, on July 8, 1932. Fortunes were lost. Many speculators, who had financed their purchase of stocks with debt, lost everything and then some. The financial destruction bankrupted businesses, destroyed lives, and fostered an environment for political upheaval the likes of which the world had never seen. Roughly a quarter of the world's working-age population was unemployed. It would lead to incalculable pain and suffering and, ultimately, the rise of fascism. It would render the unimaginable, imaginable.

In the United States, industrial production was cut in half. Americans stood in bread lines and at soup kitchens. Homelessness and poverty abounded, while President Herbert Hoover assured the country not to worry, that the Depression would run its course. The American people would demand change. In 1932, with fifteen million unemployed and still no hope in sight, Franklin Delano Roosevelt, a Democrat, was elected president.

The Great Depression was a global financial debacle that left no economy unscathed. Germany was especially hard hit. As conditions worsened, public discontent soared and membership in the Nazi Party grew. In the September 1930 elections, it increased its representation in the Reichstag almost ten times, winning 107 seats. Just two years later, in November 1932, they won control of 230 seats, 33 percent of the Reichstag—the most won by any single party during the entire Weimar period. Still short of a majority, Adolf Hitler, the leader of the Nazi Party, agreed to a coalition with the Conservative Party in an effort to gain control of the government.

As Germany descended into the economic abyss, its people were seeking a savior. Hitler, a charismatic orator, promised to deliver economic prosperity to a desperate German people. On January 30, 1933, German President Paul von Hindenburg appointed him chancellor. Hitler moved quickly to assume full control of the government.

5

BERLIN

June 1942

It was well past midnight as Heinz Heydrich sat bleary-eyed, burrowing through his brother's papers. They revealed things about his brother that he would rather not come to light—especially Reinhard's womanizing. But Reinhard's "friends in high place" knew more about him than he realized.

SS-Oberführer Walter Schellenberg said, "Heydrich's only weakness was his ungovernable sexual appetite. To this he would surrender himself without inhibition or caution, and the calculated control which characterized him in everything he did left him completely."

Reinhard met Lina von Osten in December 1930 at a rowing club party. The two almost immediately became romantically involved. Lina, blond and svelte, was an early and rabid Nazi Party follower. The attraction was almost savage in its intensity. On May 30, 1931, Reinhard was dismissed from the Navy, charged with "conduct unbecoming an officer and a gentleman," when his affair with Lina was discovered. Reinhard was already engaged to marry another woman six months before—absolutely unacceptable behavior for an officer of the vaunted Reichsmarine. Admiral Erich Raeder himself relieved Heydrich of duty. Reinhard Heydrich would join the Nazi Party the next day. Six weeks later, on July 14, he joined the SS. He and Lina von Osten were married in December 1931.

Reinhard's rise through the Nazi ranks was legend. Heinrich Himmler selected him to assist in developing the counterintelligence division of the SS in 1931. Heydrich established a network of spies in Nazi Party headquarters in Munich with the express purpose of obtaining information on their internal enemies, mostly through blackmail and extortion. So pleased was Himmler with Reinhard's work that, as a wedding present, he promoted Heydrich to SS Sturmbannführer, as head of the newly named Sicherheitsdienst, or SD. To solidify their power, the SD attacked the police headquarters in Munich; and Himmler became the chief of the Munich police and Heydrich the commandant of the political police.

In 1933, the same year Adolf Hitler became the chancellor of Germany, the first concentration camps were established to incarcerate Hitler's political opponents. The infamous Dachau opened in March of that year. Hitler quickly consolidated power and issued a series of edicts and anti-Jewish laws, which Reinhard Heydrich was fanatically pleased to enforce. On April 1, 1933, the Nazis staged a boycott of Jewish shops and businesses. On April 11, a Nazi decree defined non-Aryans as "anyone descended from non-Aryans, especially Jewish parents or grandparents. One parent or grandparent classified the descendant as non-Aryan, especially if one parent or grandparent was of the Jewish faith."

❖ ❖ ❖

April 1933

Alfred and Greta stood in front of the large Renoir over the mantel in the Sternlichts' great room. Josef stood alongside Bette, Helmut Weber, and Lily Schwarz, while the butler handed each a glass of wine. Their presence was requested by the young couple for an announcement.

"So, Alfred," Josef began jokingly, "you came all the way downstairs to tell us something formally? You couldn't have just passed a note down the dumbwaiter?" Alfred and Greta lived in the flat just above his parents in the building at Unterlinden 67 that housed the Sternlicht & Co. showroom on the ground floor.

"Josef, you are such a silly goose," Bette chimed in. "Children, don't mind your father…one glass of wine is all it takes." Everyone, including Josef, laughed.

"Mother, Father, Herr Weber, and Lily, Greta and I wanted to give you the wonderful news that we are pregnant!" Alfred proclaimed.

Lily gave Greta a big hug, tears rolling down her cheeks. Helmut, ever the controlled, emotionless German father, brushed tears from his eyes, his bottom lip quivering, beaming at his daughter. Josef and Bette embraced Alfred, and then Greta.

Helmut could barely speak. Greta hugged him and said, "Oh, Papa!" They exchanged a glance…a special glance that only they, and of course Lily, understood.

Josef said, "This calls for a toast! To our grandson!"

Bette poked him playfully in the ribs. "You mean to our granddaughter!" And they all laughed.

Alfred clasped Greta's hand with one hand and raised his glass in the other. "To a healthy baby!"

"Hear, hear," Josef added.

"When is the baby due?" Lily inquired.

"The first week in October, the doctor said," Alfred answered.

Bette said, "Please, where are my manners? Everyone, sit and make yourselves comfortable." She pointed to the two large Louis XV sofas abutting each other.

"Lily, I don't want to put you on the spot, but would you do us the honor of helping us raise the baby?" Greta asked.

"My dear, I wouldn't let anyone else!" She smiled and then added diplomatically, "With Bette's approval, of course."

"I can't imagine anyone who could help raise a child any better than you, Lily. I have the evidence right here," Bette said, looking in Greta's direction.

Josef turned serious. "Not to put a damper on this wonderful news, but what do you make of Hitler's idiotic new edicts, Helmut, boycotting Jewish-owned stores and making himself the master of the Aryan race?"

"He and his crew are absolutely insane. But I am sure it will pass. He didn't even earn a majority in the Reichstag. The other parties won't stand for it," Helmut said. "It's just a matter of time before he and his crew of clowns are ousted."

"But he managed to have the Conservatives and the Catholic Center Party support his Enabling Act," Alfred interjected, referring to the legislation that would give Hitler's government the power to decree laws without a vote in the Reichstag for a four-year period. Many Socialist and Communist members were arrested before the vote to ensure the act's passage. Hitler soon followed that by outlawing political parties and trade unions. It was clear he was positioning himself and the Nazi Party to attain total control of the German Republic.

"One thing is for sure: He certainly hates the Jews." Josef shook his head. "Blames all of Germany's problems on them. Last week there were Nazi storm troopers holding up signs in front of Jewish businesses. 'Don't buy from Jews. Jews are our misfortune.' They were standing in front of my store! Incredible, in this day and age, in a democratic republic! Meanwhile, they are such fools. I'm not even a Jew. My father converted when I was a boy. Not that we are religious Protestants by any means. But Hitler and his minions are ignorant beyond words."

"The Nazis frighten me. I am half Jewish," Greta said softly. "My mother was Jewish, Mr. Sternlicht."

"Greta, my dear, not to worry. As your father says, Hitler and his scoundrels will be gone in a few months," Bette murmured.

Nevertheless, Alfred, on behalf of his father and the family business, went to the police and registered a formal complaint in regard to the one-day boycott. He indicated that it had cost them business and erred in boycotting a Protestant-owned business. The officer taking down the information gave a cursory glance at the complaint form and said, "Sternlicht. Isn't that a Jewish name?"

"It may sound like one, but it no longer is, sir."

The officer smirked. "Well, perhaps you should change your name." He dismissed Alfred with a wave of his hand. "Be on your way, Mr. Sternlicht. Next!"

Throughout 1933, the Nazis issued more anti-Semitic decrees. On April 7, laws for the Reestablishment of the Civil Service prevented Jews from holding civil service, university, or state jobs. On May 10, books authored by Jews and others not approved by the state were burned in public. On July 14, a law was passed stripping Eastern European Jewish immigrants of their German citizenship. Still, many Jews, veterans of the Great War and proud Germans, continued to believe that either they would not be more seriously impacted or that Hitler and his regime would soon be drummed out of the government.

Over the summer months, Greta's belly grew increasingly large. Alfred, when not working in the shop, was always by her side. They occasionally visited with the Liebermanns, mostly to cheer Max. Martha and Max were, of course, always happy to see Greta's ever-increasing belly, but Martha told them he reserved his smiles solely for them. Like other Jewish artists, his works had been removed from public view and he had become very depressed. In May he had resigned his honorary presidency, senatorial posts, and membership in the Prussian Academy of Arts. On the advice of his Swiss banker, he deposited the most important works in his art collection in their office in Zurich. He now was totally withdrawn from the public eye.

On September 24, just after Alfred and Greta retired for the evening, Greta's water broke. Lily called the midwife, who at first said, "I'll be there in an hour. No rush, I would imagine. She's two weeks early, yah?"

Lily countered, "This is Greta's second…the baby could come faster. I will explain later."

"Ah…I will be over shortly."

At 3:23 a.m. on September 25, 1933, after what seemed like myriad contractions, Greta pushed one more time at the midwife's direction and a head covered with a shock of matted blond hair, followed by the rest of a body emerged. The woman held a beautiful baby boy in her hands. She gently patted his back and he cried on cue. She wiped him quickly and expertly and handed him to Greta.

"My baby," she said. "Lily, my baby boy."

Lily beamed. "I will get Alfred!"

The midwife helped Greta get cleaned up. Then she introduced the new mother to the art of bonding with her infant son, getting him to suckle at her breast. Shortly thereafter, she allowed Lily to bring in Alfred and his parents and Helmut to meet their new grandson. Alfred kissed Greta's forehead and marveled at her and the baby, while the grandparents stood behind him with smiles broader than the Unterlinden on their faces.

Alfred said, "I want to introduce you to our son. Your new grandson, Hans Peter Sternlicht."

At last, Greta had all she had ever wanted—not only her prince, but their child to hold and love, forever.

6

THE BRONX

Herbert Remer's mind was swimming. So much was going on.

During the depths of the Great Depression, months after the stock market crash, he had come to Sam Sonnenschein's financial rescue. He, like many other successful businessmen during the Roaring Twenties, had taken to speculating in the market, making the cardinal sin of buying stock on margin, borrowing to enhance his "sure thing" gains. When it all came crashing down, he was forced to sell his stocks at a loss and was now $30,000 in the hole. An enormous sum.

Herbert, ever the bean-counting businessman, had never been enticed by the market. So, aside from the funds he had secreted away in the Bank of New York savings account Helmut had opened for the family, he had squirreled away a very substantial sum from the produce store and from a thriving fruit and vegetable distribution business. He offered to cover Sam's loans at no interest and insisted his friend take as long as he needed to repay him. Sam was enormously grateful, but he made Herbert a better offer. In exchange for paying off the loans, he made Herbert a full partner in Sonnenschein & Co.

As luck would have it, Herbert had landed a fairly large number of retail accounts in the Bronx and Manhattan, particularly with speakeasies, restaurants, and caterers, the beginning of his distribution business. He was somehow successful while others were not, even more so as the economy slowly began to show signs of life. Unbeknownst to him, his old friend, Arthur, now Dutch Schultz, one of history's most infamous, ruthless, and wealthy mobsters, had "convinced" Herbert's customers to use his produce—exclusively. Schultz made certain the boss of bosses, Charles Luciano, was all right with the deal.

"Lucky" Luciano, with the help of his longtime friend, Meyer Lansky, had established a group known as the Commission in 1931 and was effectively the head of organized crime in New York. Shaking down businesses like Herbert's was a mainstay for the network, but Luciano was a man of honor who agreed to the arrangement Schultz had set up for Herbert, which he continued to know nothing about.

Naturally, Herbert was grateful that business was so good. He saw the devastation wrought on many families all around him. He was truly blessed. But he worried about his elderly mother, who struggled at home after his father's death in 1929. He sent her money and continued to offer to bring her to America, but she refused to leave Berlin. With Hitler now in charge of Germany, he still hoped she would see reason and join them in America.

After the boycott of Jewish businesses in April, enforced by the Sturmabteilung or the SA, the Nazi Party's paramilitary organization, Paula's father was rattled. On the spot, he decided to move his business out of Germany and used his contacts to set up shop in France. He sent as many crates of his inventory and belongings to a friend's warehouse in a Paris suburb as he could during the next few days. When the last crate of furs was on its way, the Schmidts left via rail. They rented a flat in the Marais and left their Berlin landlord no forwarding address.

But these were not Herbert's only concerns. He was especially upset with twelve-year-old Walter's recent violent outbursts at school. Though he was a prodigy on the piano, he suffered from anger issues offstage. Herbert and Paula were certain the cause of Walter's anger was that they had recently had the conversation they had dreaded for so long. Walter now knew he was adopted. At first, he seemed to take it in stride. He even indicated that he himself had wondered where he came from, given his height, blond hair, and blue eyes.

Evidently, after several weeks of absorbing this bombshell, like many adopted children—or so said the doctor Herbert and Paula consulted—Walter experienced the anger, hurt, and denial considered common. It began to manifest in fits of rage directed at his mother. If she asked him to put away his clothes or even practice the piano, he would scream, throw the clothing at her, or kick or punch the nearest wall. But rather than receding over a period of weeks, as the doctor assured them would happen, no matter what his parents did or said, his anger seemed to grow.

Tall, muscular, and athletic, Walter loved playing basketball in gym class. However, two boys playing against him had recently made the error of ridiculing the boy for his limp. Without a moment's hesitation, Walter threw the ball at one boy's face, breaking his nose. Then, he slugged the other one in the mouth, chipping a tooth and knocking him down, bloody. He was sent to the principal's office and suspended from school for a week.

The principal called Herbert at the store, and he had to leave early to pick up Walter. He was urged to ensure his son apologized to both boys and their parents.

When they arrived home from school, Herbert pointed to a wooden chair in the kitchen. "Walter, please sit down," Herbert said, his voice unsteady, tinged with both anger and regret. "The principal said your anger got the better of you when these kids teased you. I know children can be cruel."

"They made fun of my limp."

"That was a nasty thing for them to do. But they were just words. Cruel words, I know. But now one boy has a broken nose and the other a cracked tooth, and he needed stitches. You have heard the saying, 'Sticks and stones may break your bones but words can never harm you.' My father had a better saying: 'If you hit somebody, they may hit you back even harder.' You are lucky these boys didn't. If someone says bad things to you, stop and take a deep breath before you do anything. Self-discipline comes with maturity. But violence should always be a last resort."

Herbert paused and then said softly, "Walter, Mama and I know how difficult this time has been for you. We understand you have a lot of anger, learning you were adopted. I know we explained this to you before, but I want to tell you again, we could not have children of our own and we jumped at the chance to adopt you when we had the opportunity. You were an infant. The woman who gave birth to you could not raise you. Circumstances would not allow it. But we hope in time you will come to love us again, as you did before we told you, as much as we have always loved you and wanted you more than any parent could ever love or want a child."

Walter nodded, suggesting he understood. Paula, who had been waiting outside the kitchen, wondering what had happened at school, bustled in and offered to make a snack for everyone.

She and Herbert took turns repeating variations of these words to Walter in the hope that he would come to believe them. But while his tendency toward physical violence and verbal rage subsided over time, Walter still harbored resentment toward the couple he now knew weren't his *real* parents. And he would always have difficulty controlling the impulse to lash out at anyone he thought betrayed him.

Dora Zaslavsky, Walter's piano teacher, saw him in a different light than most. She saw an extraordinarily gifted young pianist who could play the most difficult concerto with the ease of a Rachmaninoff or Rubinstein and was equally skilled "tickling the ivories" when playing a jazz set. Dora could overlook his occasional youthful indiscretions, as she thought of them. This was normal adolescent behavior from her perspective. She had, from time to time, witnessed other prodigies exhibiting extreme behaviors. They were just a little different. She was convinced he was bound for greatness.

7

GERMANY

1934-1938

Himmler had named Reinhard Heydrich the head of the Gestapo on April 22, 1934. The Gestapo's intent was simply to eliminate the political opposition. On Hitler's orders, Himmler and Heydrich conspired to bring down Ernst Roehm, head of the SA, which would enable Hitler to effectively control an army some three million men strong. Acting swiftly, on June 30, 1934, Heydrich's SS purged the SA, murdering some two hundred people, including Roehm, during what would become known as the Night of the Long Knives. Now, Hitler had virtually complete control of Germany's political and military apparatus. Through the Gestapo, Himmler and Heydrich had the authority to arrest, convict, and execute anyone perceived as an adversary. After President von Hindenburg's death on August 2, 1934, Hitler anointed himself the German führer, or leader, cementing his and the Nazi Party's complete control of Germany. And, on August 19, 1934, Hitler received 90 percent "yes" votes from Germans, approving his new and absolute power. This was the new Germany. Hitler's Germany. He would rescue the Fatherland from the subhumans—homosexuals, communists, gypsies, and Jews—and build an Aryan empire...the Third Reich. Reinhard Heydrich was now one of the most powerful, dangerous, and feared men in the entire country.

❖ ❖ ❖

Daily life proceeded to become increasingly difficult for German Jews during the next several years. In March 1935, Jews were barred from serving in the armed forces. In September, the Nuremberg Laws were passed. Jews were no longer considered German citizens. They could not marry Aryans. The Nazis defined a Jew as anyone with three Jewish grandparents or any one identifying himself as a Jew who had two Jewish grandparents. Jewish doctors were prohibited from practicing medicine in German hospitals.

The world was silent.

On March 31, 1938, the emboldened Nazis annexed Austria, immediately imposing the same anti-Jewish decrees there. On April 26, 1938, the Nazis ordered the mandatory registration of all property held by Jews. On October 28, seventeen thousand Polish Jews were expelled from Germany. Poland refused to take them in.

On November 7, Ernst vom Rath, a German diplomat in Paris, was assassinated by Herschel Grynszpan, a seventeen-year-old, German-born Polish Jew. Although the young man lived in Paris, his family was one of the thousands who had been expelled from Germany and were at present living in huge refugee camps on the border of Poland. The Nazis used the assassination of vom Rath to punish the Jews. In a secret telegram sent to Gestapo headquarters and local regional offices of the SD, SS-Gruppenführer Reinhard Heydrich gave detailed instructions on how to engage local "political authorities," Nazi thugs, to conduct seemingly spontaneous demonstrations against Jews. The objective was to terrorize the Jews while ostensibly making the retaliatory action appear a simultaneous expression of anger as a result of vom Rath's murder.

BERLIN November 10, 1938

"What is going on out there, Alfred?" Greta said, trying to keep her voice down so as not to awaken Hans.

"I don't know," he said, moving a curtain aside to peer out the window. "It looks like hooligans smashing windows. I will go down to see if Mama and Papa are all right."

"Be careful," she said as he closed the apartment door behind him.

"Momma, Momma, where did Papa go?" It was too late; the noise had woken little Hans, who stood in the foyer beside Lily.

"Don't worry. Papa went down to the store to check on Oma and Opa," she responded. After a few minutes passed, Greta dialed the phone in the store. There was no answer. She put on her long, gray wool coat and tied a silk scarf around her neck.

Lily, who had hastily put on a robe and slippers, came to her. "Where are you going, Greta?"

"Bette didn't answer the phone. I am going downstairs. Please watch Hans." Before Lily could protest, the door closed behind Greta.

When she arrived downstairs, she found the shop windows were broken. JUDEN was scrawled across what was left of them. Greta cautiously entered the bashed-in front door. "Alfred," she called out, "Alfred." He didn't answer.

The showroom was a mess. Battered mannequins lay sprawled, with filthy, shredded silk wedding gowns and broken displays littering the floor. She opened the small door in the back of the store that led to the office. Bette sat on a wooden chair in the corner, shaking uncontrollably.

Greta ran to her, knelt down next to her, and gently held her hands. "Bette, what happened? Where are Alfred and Josef?"

Bette continued to shake, though she slowly gained sufficient composure to answer in a trembling, monotonic stream of words.

"The Nazis came. They kicked in the door and broke all the windows. Josef and I ran to the office and locked the door. We heard them. Cursing, shouting, breaking things. Then they said, 'Open the door, Jew!' My Josef, my brave Josef, opened the door. He said to them, 'I am not a Jew. Why do you ruin my store?' That is when one of them hit him in the face, hard. He staggered, and they hit him again and dragged him to the front of the store. Alfred came down into the showroom. He screamed at the sight of his father, bleeding, 'Papa! Papa!' Another Nazi came from nowhere and hit Alfred on the head with a truncheon. He fell to the floor like a stone. They tied his hands behind him and dragged him away by his collar. And then they took Josef the same way...and they were gone."

"Oh my God, Bette. I will go to the police. I will—"

"Greta, the police were standing right outside. They let them do it."

"Come upstairs with me. I will call my papa. He will know what to do."

They went upstairs, opened the door, and Greta quickly locked it behind them. She motioned to Lily to help her. Together, they helped Bette to the couch.

Hans said, "Oma, are you all right? Where are Papa and Opa?"

Greta winced. "Papa and Opa had to go with some men. They will be back later. You must go back to bed, Hans." She hugged him, and Lily took his hand and walked him to his bedroom.

Greta picked up the phone and called Helmut, telling him what had happened. He already knew from the sound of breaking glass and the screams coming from the street that some sort of violent demonstration was taking place.

"I will be right over, Greta. Stay where you are. Keep the door locked."

She wanted to tell him not to go outside, but he had already hung up.

Helmut carefully walked the few blocks to the Sternlichts' building. Shards of broken glass littered the sidewalk. The so-called demonstrators were very methodical. They had vandalized only Jewish-owned businesses. Storefronts were defaced with the words "Jew" and "Jew Pig" or covered with the Jewish Star of David. The Nazi thugs were gone now, had moved on to the next neighborhood. He could smell fires burning. Berlin's synagogues were burning. Helmut knew one thing was certain: This was a well-organized pogrom.

Lily somehow had managed to get Hans back into bed, and when Helmut arrived, she made him and Bette some tea. Bette repeated for Helmut precisely what she had told Greta. She could not stop trembling. Helmut, nearing seventy now, suddenly looked a good deal older. He held his head in his hands, thought for a moment, and then said, "I will go to the Gestapo headquarters first thing tomorrow and find out where they took Josef and Alfred. In the meantime, I could use another glass of tea, Lily, to calm my nerves."

No one got any sleep that night, including, it seemed, five-year-old Hans. The little blond boy with the sea-blue eyes crept out of bed after Lily thought he had fallen asleep. He had put his ear to his door and listened to the adults, though he couldn't understand much of what he heard.

The next morning, despite Helmut's protestations, Greta insisted on accompanying him to Gestapo headquarters at Prinz-Albrecht-Strasse 8.

When they arrived, about two dozen people, some of whom they recognized from the neighborhood, had formed a line outside the building, ostensibly to get information on the fate of loved ones. The Gestapo sergeant at the front desk looked up at Helmut. "If you are here to find information about Jew relatives, get in line outside."

"Sergeant, my name is Helmut Weber. I am a German citizen. I am not a Jew," he said, in as harsh and superior a tone as he could muster. "I would like to speak to SS-Gruppenführer Reinhard Heydrich. He knows me well. Don't dally, man. I need to speak with him immediately on a matter of great urgency."

To Greta, the idea of seeing Reinhard after so many years, and to beg for assistance from him, especially when he had become such an important man, was frightening. Yet she was willing to do anything—*anything*—to bring Alfred home. Would he even recognize her? At that moment, she determined to carry the lock of hair he had given her when she was fifteen with her at all times. She never knew when she might need it.

The sergeant, not entirely sure what to make of Helmut, but realizing this matter might be above his pay grade, said, "Wait one moment." He picked up a telephone receiver. "Can you ask the lieutenant to come to the phone?" Then, while looking up at Helmut, he said, "Lieutenant, a Helmut Weber is demanding to see Gruppenführer Heydrich with an urgent matter. He says the gruppenführer knows him." He paused to listen to the response. "Thank you, Lieutenant." He hung up the phone. "Mr. Weber, the lieutenant will be out to see you shortly."

A door opened behind the sergeant and a bespectacled SS officer emerged. "Herr Weber, I am Lieutenant Franz Karl. Please be seated." He pointed to a small room to the right of the sergeant's desk, which contained an old wooden desk and a few metal chairs. "How may I help you?" His tone was that of a suspicious interrogator, not a friendly police officer.

"I would like to speak with Gruppenführer Heydrich on a matter of the utmost importance."

"Herr Weber," the lieutenant replied, "the Gruppenführer is a very important and a very busy man. Perhaps you can tell me what the issue is and I can discuss it with him for you."

"Lieutenant, I am sure you are a very competent and discreet man, but with all due respect, I must speak with Reinhard Heydrich directly."

The Gestapo man, though highly trained in interrogation and physical deportment, was having difficulty reading Helmut. "Why don't you give me your telephone number, Herr Weber, and I will get back to you."

"I'm afraid it can't wait."

The lieutenant's eye twitched slightly, betraying his irritation. Helmut was sure he had the upper hand in the conversation now. "I will be right back, Herr Weber." He stood up and left the small office.

Greta, who had followed her father in, began to speak, but Helmut shook his head almost imperceptibly. She understood. There could be a listening device somewhere in the room.

Helmut assumed the Gestapo man would try to ascertain exactly who Weber was. Was he some Jew here to cause trouble? Was he a crank? Or was he legitimate, a friend of the gruppenführer, as he insisted? The last thing this lieutenant would want to do at this point in his career was get on the bad side of Heydrich.

Karl returned almost twenty minutes later with several folders in his hand. "Herr Weber. And I apologize for not introducing myself to the young lady."

Greta replied stiffly, "I am Herr Weber's daughter."

"Ah, yes," he said sarcastically, "you are indeed Herr Weber's daughter. I see you lived in Halle and took music lessons from the mother of our gruppenführer. So, yes, Herr Weber, you clearly did know the gruppenführer. I see that you, Frau Sternlicht, are married to a Jew, Alfred Sternlicht. I see that you are also a Jew because your father married a Jew." Karl saw that Greta's hands were quivering. He smiled. Then he looked squarely in Helmut's eyes and said, "So, Herr Weber, what exactly is so urgent that you need to speak with Gruppenführer Heydrich at once?"

Helmut was filled with rage but contained himself. He took a breath and spoke in his usual mild tone. "My son-in-law and his father were beaten and abducted last night while the police looked on. We would like Gruppenführer Heydrich's assistance in ascertaining their whereabouts."

"I see." Karl smirked. "Well, I think I may be able to help you. It seems that Josef Sternlicht uttered some very uncomplimentary words about the Reich to the police officers who recovered him from his so-called abductors. The police decided to question him at a more practical location. The good news is that he will be released tomorrow. If you come back here at 10:00 a.m., he will be released into your custody."

Greta found it difficult to get the words out. "And what of my husband?"

"I am sorry, Frau Sternlicht, but I have not had as much success tracking him down. Rest assured, I will have our staff investigate and let you know as soon as we learn anything about his whereabouts. Have a good day." The lieutenant stood and abruptly left the room.

"Wait," Greta shouted, getting up from her chair. But Karl was gone.

Helmut got up quickly and took Greta's hand. "Let's go home, dear. There is nothing more we can do here."

She was in a fog as they walked home.

Helmut relayed what had happened to Bette and Lily. Greta, who was as enervated as if she had been in a boxing match, sat quietly beside him.

The next day, Helmut and Greta returned to Prinz-Albert-Strasse 8 precisely at 10:00 a.m. A beaming Lieutenant Karl met them, accompanied by two Gestapo officers and Josef, bruised and battered, his clothes in tatters, standing unsteadily between them. "Ah, Herr Weber and Frau Sternlicht. Here is Herr Sternlicht, as promised."

"And my husband?" Greta inquired.

"Yes, I have not forgotten him, Frau Sternlicht. I will be in touch with you as soon as I have more information. Good day."

Karl turned and walked away with the two officers behind him.

Josef did not speak as they slowly walked home. Greta was in tears and Helmut was quiet, pondering what he could do for Alfred next.

Lily and Hans were in the kitchen in Alfred and Greta's flat upstairs when they heard the door open in the apartment below. While Lily was drying the breakfast dishes, Hans sat on the floor, playing with his teddy bear in a pot. He cleverly positioned himself by the dumbwaiter, as he had done in the past, so he could hear the adults speaking downstairs.

Josef sat down on a chair in the kitchen as Bette brought him some strong tea. He seemed dazed and confused. "Bette," he asked, "where is Alfred?"

"We still do not know. Helmut and Greta inquired again, but the police claim they have not yet located him."

"I saw them bludgeon him, Bette. I saw them drag him away. I summoned all my strength, but I could not stop them." He could not have looked more forlorn. He took a sip of the tea before he continued. "The thugs who pulled me away from the store were somehow in cahoots with the police. The Gestapo took me to a place called Sachsenhausen, a prison camp of some sort. I told them that they had arrested the wrong person. I said, 'I am not a Jew. My father converted many years ago. We are Protestants.' But according to their rules, they say otherwise. They said I would be released on the condition that we leave Germany. When I protested, the guard struck me in the face with the back of his hand. I fell out of the chair and landed hard on my side. They forced me to sign papers that said I would leave the country within ninety days. And they said I was liable for a fine of twenty million Reichsmarks for my role in the murder of Ernst vom Rath. I don't even know who that is. It seems they are levying a fine against all German Jews. I protested again, and the guard hit me in the face with the butt of his pistol. I must have blacked out then. When I awoke, he gave me papers to sign. They are taking our paintings and our furniture as part of the fine. I am sorry, Bette. The man put the gun to my head. I signed the papers. They will be coming this evening to take inventory of our paintings."

Thus did the family learn something of the occurrences in Berlin two nights before. On November 9 and 10, during Kristallnacht, the Night of Broken Glass, two hundred synagogues were ransacked and burned to the ground, seventy-five hundred Jewish shops were vandalized, and thirty thousand Jewish males were sent to concentration camps—Dachau, Buchenwald, and Sachsenhausen.

Bette hugged Josef. "We will go someplace else. We will pack our things and leave as soon as Alfred returns."

"Where will we go? I am sure the Swiss will consider us Jews, just as the Germans do. And the Swiss have closed their borders to Jews."

Bette said reassuringly, "We will go London, or Paris, or New York. We know people in many places. I will arrange our trip right away."

Helmut spoke up at last. "Now that you are home safely, Josef, I will go back to my flat and make some calls to see if I can unearth something about Alfred."

"Thank you, Papa," Greta said.

He put on his Burberry coat and fedora, embraced his daughter, and left.

Greta turned to Josef. "I am so relieved that you are home, dear Papa Josef. When you are up to it, I will bring Hans down to see you."

Bette looked at Josef. "Let me get him cleaned up a bit and then I will call you. What will you tell Hans about what has happened?"

"The truth, Bette, the truth at least to the extent that a five-year-old can understand it."

As soon as Helmut arrived home, he opened his leather-bound planner, looked for the telephone number, and dialed it. "Hello, Frau Heydrich. This is Helmut Weber. I realize we have not spoken in quite some time, but I have a favor to ask of you. No doubt you have heard about the demonstrations against the Jewish community following the assassination of Ernst vom Rath. It seems some of the demonstrators got carried away, shall we say, and abducted my Greta's husband, Alfred Sternlicht. Could you help me get in touch with Reinhard? I am sure someone in his position, the head of the Gestapo, can help get to the bottom of this."

Elisabeth Heydrich was silent for a moment, and then her voice was flustered. "I cannot help you, Herr Weber. Please do not call here again." Before Helmut could say another word, she had hung up.

Helmut, stunned, went upstairs to his room. He put his head in his hands. What could he possibly try next?

❖ ❖ ❖

"Who was that, Mother?" asked Heinz, at present an SS officer working as a journalist and editor, producing propaganda, who was home for a few days on leave.

Elisabeth gathered herself together and said, "It was Helmut Weber, of all people, asking me for a favor from Reinhard. He's trying to find the whereabouts of Greta's Jew husband, who is missing after the demonstrations in Berlin. I hung up right away. Poor Reinhard. I hope he isn't continually bothered by such lowlifes."

Heinz was taken aback by his mother's reaction but did not betray his surprise. He was quite sure his brother hadn't given a moment's thought to Greta or the child she had borne him a decade or more before, and was too busy dealing with the "Jewish question" to assist in saving the life of one of them, no matter who he was married to. Since his father's death in 1938, his mother had lived for her pride in Reinhard. Still, they had made promises to Helmut Weber; he had overheard them himself, that day so long ago…

❖ ❖ ❖

When Greta returned upstairs, Lily was giving Hans a snack in the kitchen. Lily looked hopefully at her. "Opa Josef is home, and we can visit with him soon. But Papa is not home yet." Lily looked down at her hands to see if they were shaking.

"I miss Papa. Where is he?" Hans asked.

"We all miss Papa, Hans. You see, there are good people like your papa and, believe it or not, there are bad people like der Große Böse Wolf in the storybook. They sometimes do awful things. The bad people hurt your papa and Opa Josef because they are wicked. They are called Nazis. I do not know yet when they will send Papa home. But we hope it will be soon."

"Momma, why did the Nazis hurt Opa and Papa?" Hans asked.

"These Nazis do not like Jewish people."

"Are we Jewish?" he persisted.

Greta sighed, realizing the details were too complex to explain to such a very little boy. "Yes, Hans."

"I hate the Nazis, Momma."

"So do I."

❖ ❖ ❖

Each morning after Josef returned home, Greta walked to Gestapo headquarters, either with Lily and Hans or with Helmut, to see if they could find out anything about Alfred. Greta was convinced Lieutenant Karl and the others knew exactly where Alfred was. She thought taking little Hans along might evoke some sympathy or a sense of guilt in these men. She was clearly wrong. Their visceral hatred of Jews rendered them devoid of any such emotion.

The following week, out of the blue, Helmut's phone rang one morning. When he picked it up, the voice on the other end said, "Herr Weber, meet me at the corner of Friedrichstrasse and Mittelstrasse in precisely ten minutes. I will be driving a Mercedes staff car. Wear your hat tilted to the left. I will stop and you will get in. I have news about your son-in-law." Then the line went dead. The voice was somehow familiar, but Helmut could not place it.

He did as he was told, and precisely ten minutes later, at the corner of Friedrichstrasse and Mittelstrasse, a black Mercedes staff car flying a swastika stopped. The passenger door opened, Helmut got in, and the car pulled away from the curb.

"Herr Weber, you probably don't remember me, but I am Heinz Heydrich. I have learned from an excellent source that your daughter's husband is dead. He died of wounds to the head and his remains were cremated. Obviously, I should not be telling you this."

Helmut looked over at the driver in complete shock. "How do you know this? It can't be true."

"Herr Weber, I have gone to great lengths to ascertain this information. As you can imagine, the Heydrich name can move mountains in Germany. I am sorry to be the bearer of this news. I suggest you see to it that Sternlicht's parents leave Germany as soon as possible for their own sake. Now, I must drop you at the corner. Goodbye, Herr Weber."

Helmut exited the Mercedes and it sped off immediately.

He was in a state of utter shock and despair. He had not wanted to believe the words of Reinhard Heydrich's brother, but he had feared the worst and it did not take very long for him to accept this confirmation of the ugly truth. He wandered aimlessly, in no hurry to return home, at a loss to find a way to break the news to Greta and the Sternlichts and poor little Hans. The little blond boy with the blue eyes adored his papa. Helmut had never forgotten how devastating it was to tell Greta that her momma had died, even though she had seen her mother wither away from painful cancer and knew her passing was for the best. This boy would have no preparation for such a tremendous loss.

He stopped briefly at home, where he phoned Greta and the Sternlichts and asked to see them right away. Even at such a moment, it didn't occur to him to drop in without calling first. He arrived five minutes later and met them in the Sternlichts' flat. Helmut repeated precisely what Heinz Heydrich had told him.

Greta screamed, the most anguished, gut-wrenching scream Helmut had ever heard. The sound was like that of an animal caught in a trap. Josef and Bette cried with the agony of parents learning they had lost their only son. Helmut held Greta for what seemed a very long time as tears poured from her eyes. "We must tell poor little Hans. Come, let us do it together," Helmut said at last.

But Hans already knew. Aware that the adults were conversing downstairs, although no one had told him they were, he had stationed himself by the dumbwaiter and heard the entire conversation while Lily ironed clothes in the maid's room.

It is impossible to know how a five-year-old processes the concept of death. Yet he knew it was something permanent. There were acquaintances of his grandparents who he had been told had died, and he had never seen them again. To some adults who met him, Hans seemed an unemotional child. But his parents knew how intelligent he was, that he internalized the things he observed, and he observed everything around him with a stealthy quiet. He absorbed and analyzed. He knew even then, at the age of five, that one day he would avenge his father's murder.

Greta, Helmut, Josef, and Bette, opened the door to Greta and Alfred's flat. All of them were still weeping, and when Lily saw the expressions on their faces, she joined them in their tears. Hans grabbed his teddy bear close to his chest and stood up.

His mother ran to him, knelt down, and hugged him. Through her tears, her voice broken, she said, "Hans, your papa is dead."

"Momma," he said, not allowing himself to cry, at least not yet, "will we ever see Papa again?" even though he already knew the answer to his question.

"Someday, we will see him in heaven," she said. She held him close for what seemed to him to be a very long time.

A week later, the Sternlichts booked passage on a ship from Hamburg to Stockholm, and from there to London. It was too dangerous for Josef to trek to Switzerland to recover his hard currency and precious metals, but he had previously set up bank accounts in England for business purposes and would, perhaps, have sufficient funds to live out a comfortable life or even open a shop there.

Josef and Bette begged Greta and Hans to come with them, but she would not leave her father. "We will manage," she said firmly. "We will move in with my papa. Even now, he still holds out hope that the German people will eventually toss out Hitler and his Nazis. I hope that we will see you soon."

She stood with Hans and Lily and Helmut in front of the mantel where a Renoir once hung. The room was empty, the walls bare. The Nazis had already taken everything of value.

They embraced, and little Hans, who now allowed tears to stream down his cheeks said, "I miss you already, Oma and Opa. Must you leave me too, when I have lost my papa?" Bette was weeping too miserably to answer him.

Josef and Bette took one more look around the flat before he handed a small envelope to Greta. "This contains Alfred's numbered accounts at UBS in Zurich, should you be able to get there someday."

Bette handed Hans a small Steiff elephant that had clearly seen better days. "This was your papa's favorite toy when he was your age. Would you keep it safe for him?"

"Yes, Oma. I will," he answered earnestly.

The Sternlichts each grabbed two suitcases and handed them to the taxi driver. They got into the back seat, closed the doors, and waved goodbye.

8

THE BRONX

The Manhattan School of Music did not yet offer a college degree program, so in his last year of high school, Walter was planning to apply to Juilliard School of Music as well as Columbia University. If he was fortunate enough to be accepted by both, he would have a decision to make. He would remain in New York in the fall, but he would have to choose where he would study.

For a high school senior, Walter had a curriculum vitae that would make most college graduates envious. He had played a concerto with Pablo Casals in a packed music hall and jazz with Harry James's orchestra. He was headed toward being named salutatorian of his class and was captain of the basketball team, notwithstanding his limp, having learned to compensate for it. He stood out physically from his classmates, being quite tall, broad shouldered, blond, blue-eyed, and handsome, so he was a favorite with the girls. His parents were very proud of his accomplishments and the man he was becoming. Dora Zaslavsky was exceedingly pleased but not surprised.

Aside from his musical talents, he excelled in math and physics and enjoyed academic challenges that stretched beyond the keyboard. And therein lay his dilemma. He loved music, and perhaps a career in music was his destiny. Paula was sure of it. But Walter wasn't. Unbeknownst to his mother, Albert Einstein had become his hero, not Beethoven. At the Christmas performance at the Manhattan School of Music, sitting next to Janet Schenck was the great scientist himself. Walter could hardly contain his excitement. When he finished playing, the audience gave him a standing ovation, Einstein included. Walter was awestruck. He met the man briefly after the concert and was literally tongue-tied. Imagine, Einstein offered high praise to the pianist Walter Remer!

While he wouldn't admit it to his mother, a few words with Albert Einstein helped him make his decision. He would expand his academic horizons and, if he was accepted, attend Columbia in the fall. Paula reluctantly agreed with his decision, so long as he continued studying with Dora Zaslavsky a few times each week.

While Paula would have preferred that Walter attend Juilliard, Herbert secretly had hoped his son would select Columbia. Walter would be the first Remer to attend college, and an Ivy League school at that. Of course, while he was genuinely pleased with his son's remarkable musical prowess and the accolades bestowed upon him, Herbert hoped Walter would eventually take over his business. He didn't dare breathe a word of this to Paula, of course. She had enough trouble coming to grips with the thought that Walter might opt for a career in jazz rather than that of a classical concert pianist. *That should be our worst worry,* Herbert thought to himself.

9

EUROPE

1939-1940

Hitler hardly concealed Germany's inexorable march toward war, or his desire to eradicate the Jews, which he announced to the Reichstag on January 30, 1939: "If war erupts it will mean the extermination (*vermichtung*) of European Jews."

In March 1939, Germany occupied Czechoslovakia. The Nazis signed a nonaggression pact with the Soviet Union, a ruse to throw Stalin off guard and to allow for an unencumbered attack on Poland. Roughly a week after the agreement was signed, on September 1, 1939, Germany invaded Poland. World War II had begun.

Three weeks later, Reinhard Heydrich authorized the establishment of Jewish ghettos in German-occupied Poland. In October, the Nazis began deporting Austrian and Czech Jews to those ghettos. All Jews living in Poland were required to wear a yellow Star of David.

In April 1940, Hitler's forces occupied Denmark and southern Norway. In May, the Nazis invaded France, the Netherlands, Luxembourg, and Belgium. By the end of June, France had surrendered. Notwithstanding a nonaggression agreement signed in 1939 between Britain's Neville Chamberlain and Adolf Hitler, the

Luftwaffe attacked Britain on July 10, 1940, and the air war was on. The RAF gallantly defended itself against large-scale bombing attacks by the Nazis, delivering Hitler his first major setback. When what started as a German effort to force Britain to agree to a negotiated surrender failed, the Luftwaffe changed tactics to destroy the RAF and its strategic infrastructure. Eventually, the Nazis added terror bombing to their repertoire, attacking civilians at night in what became known as the Blitz. The German high command was certain the British would cave in.

But they did not. The RAF retaliated.

However, there were many British civilian casualties. On December 19, 1940, during one of the Luftwaffe's largest raids, three thousand British civilians were killed. Among them were Josef and Bette Sternlicht, who were unable to get to their bomb shelter in time.

❖ ❖ ❖

As the war progressed, and the Nazis claimed one relatively easy victory after another, Goring gave Heydrich full authority on July 31st, 1941 to implement a "Final Solution" for European Jews. In preparation, Reinhard tapped one of his lieutenants, Adolf Eichmann, a technocrat, to be head of the Department of Jewish Affairs of the Reich Security Main Office. Eichmann was efficient and superb at executing anything Reinhard threw his way.

Under Heydrich's orders, the Einsatzgruppen, a task force of SS quasi-military death squads, would follow the Wehrmacht (main army) into conquered territories. The Einsatzgruppen often ordered Jews, sometimes with the help of the locals, to an area just outside of town. The Jews—men, women, children, and infants—were ordered to dig a large trench and stand at its edge. Then, at point-blank range, the Einsatzgruppen shot them. The Jews tumbled into the trenches, dead or nearly so. Villagers covered the mass graves with dirt and limestone to expedite the decomposition of the bodies.

While the Einsatzgruppen killed tens of thousands of Jews, it was not as efficient as Reinhard had hoped. It required a lot of manpower. It also stretched resources, bullets, and other supplies that could have been used elsewhere. To wit, as the year progressed, the Nazis established extermination camps at Auschwitz, Chelmno, and other locations to do the job more efficiently.

Initially, some Jews were forced into vans with exhaust pipes rigged to kill the inhabitants inside via carbon monoxide poisoning. This proved inefficient, took too long, and was a waste of precious fuel. The Nazis soon arrived at a more effective solution. When cattle cars full of Jews arrived at the death camps, those deemed incapable of hard labor were murdered immediately in gas chambers, utilizing a cyanide-based pesticide, Zyklon B. Others were fed starvation rations in fetid barracks and worked literally to death. Crematoria were designed to burn the bodies with great efficiency and at lower cost.

Heinz, who had been assigned to the 697 Panzer Propaganda Kompanie as an editor for the *Die Panzerfaust*, a soldier's newspaper, had seen the Einsatzgruppen in action for himself. Indeed, Heinz was a good Nazi and a rabid anti-Semite, as was his brother and his mother, who favored the forced emigration of Jews from Germany. But this was different. Heinz closed his eyes. Now, along with mourning the death of Reinhard, as if it were a film, he saw, frame after frame, shots fired, bodies falling, convulsing, and then, for the most part, lying still. He wiped his damp forehead with a handkerchief.

It was an hour before dawn. In a few hours, Heinz would be on view, along with Hitler, Himmler, and Goebbels, at Reinhard's official funeral. But he had one section of the paperwork given to him left to read. The caffeine had been sufficient until now, but he was starting to flag. He poured one more glass of strong tea and turned to the last days of the life of his beloved brother.

Reinhard's success in dealing with the Jews of other conquered territories led to a grand reward. The new governor of the Protectorate of Bohemia and Moravia, a portion of conquered Czechoslovakia, had much work to do, bringing with him the Einsatzgruppen to deal with the Czech Jews and the Czech Resistance. Less than a year later, Reinhard's car was ambushed by two Czech soldiers. At first, it seemed Reinhard would recover from the assassination attempt; he died a few days later.

Heinz gently rubbed the bridge of his nose with his thumb and forefinger. It was almost 5:30 a.m., and he would soon have to get cleaned up and dressed for the funeral. There was one more item left in the packet, a sealed envelope. He opened it. A letter from Reinhard to him. He read the letter carefully and, as instructed, took the letter and the entire packet of papers and burned them in the fireplace in his study.

He stood, looking at the burning papers in the fireplace. He closed his eyes. It was all so useless. Then, a moment of great clarity washed over him. He knew exactly what he had to do.

10

THE BRONX

When the Germans invaded France in May 1940, Paula frantically tried to convince her parents to leave Paris immediately. She thought it would take little to convince her father, who had been shaken enough after Kristallnacht to relocate his fur business from Berlin to Paris.

But now…to think of another move at this stage of their lives was too much. Her father had reasoned that escaping Germany had been more than wise because they knew deep down that the average German had always hated the Jews and would support the madman Hitler, but surely the French were different. Besides, he was confident the French army would never let Paris fall.

Then, on June 14, the Nazis entered Paris. Communications with Paula's parents ceased shortly thereafter. She tried to contact the US State Department and the French Embassy. All her attempts to reach them were in vain. She was terrified.

News from Germany regarding Herbert's mother was no better. He had become increasingly concerned about her fate after Kristallnacht, and he had contemplated going to Germany to bring her to New York with him. Back in 1938, when Paula's parents had successfully reestablished themselves in Paris, they were still in contact with some of their friends in Berlin, and they were explicit in their warnings: Don't dare come to Berlin. It is not safe for a Jew. A Jew could be arrested on the spot and disappear without a trace. An American passport was no guarantee of safety.

Herbert sent a Western Union telegram to his mother, informing her that he had arranged her passage to Sweden. He sent her a train ticket to Hamburg. Then, he paid a king's ransom to a Gentile friend in Hamburg to have her smuggled aboard a fishing trawler to Sweden. She did not respond. She did not take the train to Hamburg. When he attempted to call her, there was no answer. His mother, it seemed, had other plans.

On July 10, 1940, after listening to a Goebbels broadcast that the Wehrmacht had launched an attack on Great Britain and that the British were on the verge of surrender, she knew precisely what to do. First, she turned off the radio. She took a lovely, relaxing bubble bath and dried herself off. She put on lipstick, rouge, and mascara. She selected her favorite dress from her closet, a pink chiffon number with lace sleeves, and put it on. It still fit, which pleased her immensely. Then, she opened a bottle of champagne she had stored in her icebox for a special occasion and poured a small glass for herself. She took the glass and sat in the large, overstuffed chair in the living room. On the coffee table next to the chair was a wedding photo. She toasted her late husband and smiled. She took a sip of the champagne. It was surprisingly good. Then she took a small glass vial containing a capsule her dear friend, Arnold Schapiro, the pharmacist, had given her at no charge. She placed the capsule between her teeth and bit down. Potassium cyanide.

It wasn't until a week later that Herbert learned of his mother's suicide. Some German neighbors had reported an awful smell emanating from her flat to the superintendent of the building. Herbert was distraught. Paula was inconsolable, envisioning a similar fate for her parents.

Herbert Remer was not a religious man. He had had a bar mitzvah in Berlin but rarely attended synagogue services. When he and Paula adopted Walter, he did insist that a mohel perform a bris, and he took Walter to synagogue occasionally over the years. He also taught Walter the blessings to be said when the Torah was read so he could receive his own bar mitzvah.

Now, however, Herbert needed to speak with God. He needed to voice his complaints directly. How could he do this? His beloved mother, who never hurt a soul in her entire life, was gone. He began to attend synagogue regularly, figuring it was best to talk to God in his office. Herbert went to the Congregation Adath Israel on the Grand Concourse and 169th Street. He went early in the morning, before work, and then later in the afternoon to say the prayer for the dead, the Kaddish. He also began attending services regularly on Saturday, when Walter would join him. The cantor, Richard Tucker, had a marvelous, operatic voice, and Walter came to enjoy the service and the liturgy. More importantly, the Remers began to get involved in New York Jewish political circles to see what they could do to help Paula's parents.

PART 2

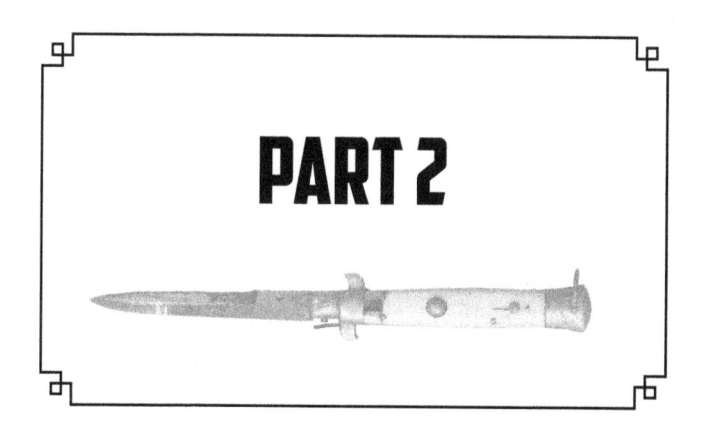

11

THE BRONX

On September 16, 1940, the United States passed the Selective Service and Training Act, conscripting men between the ages of twenty-one and forty-five. It was the first peacetime draft in US history. While the government still hoped to avoid direct involvement in the fighting overseas, Washington insiders saw the writing on the wall. Less than two weeks after the passage of the act, Germany formalized its alliance with its wartime partners, Japan and Italy, becoming the Rome-Berlin-Tokyo axis. In April of 1941, Germany invaded Yugoslavia and Greece. On June 22, 1941, Operation Barbarossa, the most audacious of Hitler's campaigns to date, the invasion of the Soviet Union, commenced. And on December 7, 1941, Japan launched a surprise attack on Pearl Harbor in Hawaii. The United States declared war on Japan the next day, and on Germany and Italy on December 11.

After the attack on Pearl Harbor, all men aged eighteen through sixty-four were required to register for the draft. Despite his parents' protestations, Walter wanted desperately to enlist. As a full-time university student, he would probably be granted a deferment, and Paula took some comfort in that. And when Walter appeared before the local draft board, he was classified as IV-F, rejected because of his limp, a physical impairment. Paula and Herbert breathed a sigh of relief.

But Walter was disappointed. So much so that he argued with the officer in charge and suggested that his skill with the German language, having learned it at home, could surely be useful. The officer humored him and it was duly noted in his file...next!

His first year at Columbia was challenging. He held his own in calculus and physics, but struggled mightily with English literature and biology. It was the first time he was not the best student, nor the best athlete, nor the best-looking, in his young life. Much to Paula's chagrin, he had to curtail the hours he normally would spend practicing the piano at home to keep up with his workload. Still, he met with Dora Zaslavsky once or twice every week to practice. He worked on classical pieces and jazz almost equally. On the weekends, he earned some money playing in nightclubs and played with some popular big bands when they needed a fill-in for their regular pianist.

MANHATTAN, December 1942

The man at the corner table at the Copacabana sat nursing his gin and tonic, chain-smoking Lucky Strikes. It wasn't the best seat from which to see the Copacabana Girls perform, but he wasn't really there for the entertainment. In fact, the proprietor, Monte Proser, was asked to seat the man in the corner. Monte's partner, and the true owner of the Copa, mob boss Frank Costello, had made the request. Costello, in turn, was taking orders from his boss, Lucky Luciano.

At the moment, Luciano, head of the organized crime Commission, was in jail but still running the syndicate from his cell, serving a sentence of thirty to fifty years for prostitution in the Clinton Correctional Facility in a remote location in upstate New York. But, in 1942, the Office of Naval Intelligence offered Luciano a deal. In exchange for commuting his sentence and relocating him to a prison closer to New York City, Luciano would use his organization to secure the docks in New York and provide contacts and intelligence in Sicily for the duration of the war. Naval Intelligence referred to it as Operation Underworld.

Frank Hinden, the man seated in the corner of the nightclub, recruited operatives—spies—for the Office of Strategic Services or OSS. A highly decorated Marine captain in the First World War, Hinden was asked to join the secretive new department by his former commanding officer in the 165th Infantry, Major William "Wild Bill" Donovan, who was the head of the OSS. Donovan trusted Hinden's instincts and selected him specifically for his uncanny knack for finding people who were especially clever and thrived under pressure.

Costello had arranged for a twenty-year-old piano player and Columbia University sophomore to fill in for the Copa's regular Saturday-night pianist. Tonight's stand-in, positioned about fifteen feet from the corner table where Hinden sat, was the reason he was there that night. He could both see and hear clearly the young man, Walter Remer, who was exactly as Costello had described him.

Just as Costello said, the pianist bore a striking resemblance to Reinhard Heydrich, the fanatical Nazi bastard and head of the Gestapo, who had been assassinated in Czechoslovakia a few months earlier. Hinden had noted in his file that Remer was the adopted son of German immigrants, spoke the language fluently, got high grades in math and physics, and was a gifted pianist. Remer had been suspended once from school for flattening two kids in a basketball game because they'd teased him. Walter Remer had a IV-F designation due to a limp, but, if he was right for the mission, perhaps that could be overcome. Hinden was looking for something specific, and it certainly wasn't a hothead who could be angered easily. He wanted someone who had grown up cool under pressure but had, if possible, an edge to him. Training could take care of everything else.

So, Hinden had arranged a small "test" with Costello's blessing. One of Frank's young toughs would try to provoke Remer to see how he reacted. Ralph DeLeo, a club bouncer, was recruited for the job on his night off. DeLeo, an amateur, light-heavyweight boxer, stood six feet tall, a couple of inches shorter than Walter, broad shouldered, and built like a refrigerator. He was told to act a bit drunk and hurl insults at the piano player. The idea was to start gradually, then become louder and more aggressive. "Just don't hit the kid. He's a great fuckin' piano player and we don't want him to get hurt."

DeLeo had a couple of drinks so there was liquor on his breath. He sidled over to the piano while Walter was playing an interlude before the next act and said rather loudly, "Hey, Kraut!" intending to insult Walter's Aryan looks. "We don't want no Krauts here, so go fuck off."

Walter continued to play as if nothing had happened. While he'd never been heckled while performing before, he had played with performers who had been subjected to verbal abuse in nightclubs. More often than not, those who managed to ignore the heckling eventually escaped anything more serious than a bruised ego.

"Hey, Kraut," DeLeo repeated. "I'm talking to you, pussy boy. I don't want no Krauts playing here. Did you hear me?"

Hinden watched carefully as Walter offered no reaction except to play on.

Now, DeLeo got up close and stood in Walter's face. "Hey, you freaking Kraut, I said, can you hear me?"

Walter looked up as he continued to play and said, "Please, sir, I'm just trying to earn a little money."

"Well, your playing sucks, you lousy Kraut. Get the hell out of my country before I beat the shit out of you."

Walter's lip quivered a bit and his fingers halted above the piano keys for a moment before continuing to play. Hinden was watching intently, as were most of the other customers.

It was obvious to Hinden that DeLeo was starting to enjoy his acting role a bit too much. "You dirty Kraut, get the fuck out of my country," he sneered, then he pushed Walter hard in the shoulder.

Walter did all he could not to fall off the piano bench. Then he sprang up and grabbed DeLeo viciously by the throat with his left hand and punched him hard in the nose with his right.

DeLeo went down like a ton of bricks. Hinden and the two Copa bouncers on duty ran over to break up the fight. DeLeo was out cold. Walter stood where he was, not sure what to do next.

One bouncer tried to help DeLeo sit up, the other bouncer standing nearby. Hinden suppressed a smile.

Monte Proser came over and said to Walter, "Are you okay? I'm so sorry about this. Boys," he turned to the bouncers, playing his role, "when the bum comes to, throw him out of here."

Walter was shaken but composed. "I'm very sorry, Mr. Proser. I tried to ignore him. But he pushed me pretty hard. I was just trying to defend myself. Honestly."

"Not your fault, Walter. Not at all. Here's $20. Why don't you go home…take the rest of the night off. I think we've all had enough entertainment, don't you?"

As if on cue, Hinden took over. "Young man, you certainly can take care of yourself. I was sitting at the table over there." He pointed. "Enjoyed your playing a lot. I got to say, you really gave it to that drunk. He had it coming. Listen, can I have a few words with you?"

They walked toward the door together, and Walter put on his wool peacoat while Hinden grabbed his coat and fedora from the coat check girl, leaving her twenty-five cents. They left together.

Inside, Proser said to DeLeo, "Are you okay, Ralphie?"

"Yeah, boss," he said, still a bit groggy. "The kid hits like a fuckin' mule. I had it coming. Maybe he should give up the piano and become a fuckin' prizefighter."

Outside, Hinden handed Walter his business card as they walked.

Walter scanned the card. It gave his name, that he was a captain in the US Army, and a phone number.

"Walter—may I call you Walter?" He didn't wait for a response.

"My car is parked on 61st. Can I give you a lift?"

"Thanks, Mr.—I mean Captain Hinden, but I live in the Bronx."

"No problem, son. Happy to do it," Hinden said.

"Okay, thanks. Do you know how to get to Yankee Stadium? I live a couple of blocks away from there."

"Sure, no problem." They reached the car and Hinden unlocked the passenger door, then walked over to the driver's side and got in after Walter did. Hinden slowly pulled away from the curb. "Walter, I gave you my card so you would have my phone number. I want to talk to you about something, and if you are interested, fine. If you aren't, you can throw the card away. I work for the OSS. Have you ever heard of it?"

"No, not really," Walter replied.

"Well, there are regular soldiers fighting the Japs and the Nazis on the battlefield, on the seas, and in the air. Army, Marines, Navy, and Air Force. You know the drill. The OSS, the Office of Strategic Services, fights them in a different way. Behind the lines. We stop the bastards before they get started."

Walter shook his head. "I'm not sure I'm following you."

"Sorry. I don't mean to be obtuse. Have you heard of the Brit's MI6? We're the US equivalent. We go behind enemy lines. We steal the Nazis' secrets, we help the resistance movements, we trick the enemy and beat them at their own game."

Walter looked at him quizzically. "Sounds exciting, but I'm a college student, not a spy. Besides, the army classified me IV-F. I'm sure I'm not the man you're looking for. Captain Hinden, if you don't mind, you can let me off at the corner. I'll take a taxi home. Thanks."

"We know you're IV-F, Walter. We know you speak German fluently, we know you're good at math and physics, and we know you're a world-class pianist; if we'd just been told about that last, that would be one thing, but I just heard you play. We've also been told you're cool under pressure, and I know, after seeing you in action tonight, you've got a great right hook. But what we're counting on is that you want to serve your country, maybe save a lot of American lives."

That hit home. Walter wanted nothing more than to serve his country. He was crestfallen when he was designated IV-F. "Okay, Captain Hinden…" he began.

"Call me Frank."

"Okay, Frank. What is it you have in mind?"

"Walter, I tell you what. Think about it overnight. Obviously, you can't mention this to your parents, or anyone else for that matter. Give me a call tomorrow if you are interested and we'll meet again. If you decide you aren't, no big deal. We'll just pretend we never met. Now, let me drop you off."

When Walter got home around midnight, Paula was waiting up, as she always did when he was out late, though she was surprised he was home early. She asked how his playing went at the Copa. She didn't love that he performed at nightclubs, but she knew she had to respect his interest in "that kind of music."

Walter mumbled a few words about things being fine and excused himself. It was late enough and he was tired, and he was grateful he'd be getting some extra sleep, thanks to the heckler and the ride home. He had lots of work to do for school. Before he went to bed, he told his mother he would probably go to the Columbia library the next day to study.

But he could not sleep. He was truly excited, energized by his conversation with the OSS captain, Hinden. What would they want him to do? Could he be a hero after all?

Sunday morning at eight, while his parents were still sleeping, he took the card out of his pocket and called the number on it.

"Hinden," the man answered.

"Hello, Captain Hinden …"

"Frank. Call me Frank. So, what's the verdict?"

"I would like to meet you," Walter said carefully.

"Great. I tell you what. Meet me in front of the library at

Columbia at 10:00, and I'll fill you in while we take a little walk."

Walter left a note for his parents, reminding them he was going to Columbia to study. He arrived ten minutes before 10:00, and Frank Hinden was waiting for him, smoking a Lucky Strike.

"Want a smoke, Walter?" he asked.

"No, thank you. I don't smoke."

"Well, if you change your mind…so, let's take a little walk over to Riverside. It's quiet there, fewer people."

It was a cold December day, the wind blowing off the Hudson keeping most people away from the park except for the heartiest dog walkers.

"I can't give you specific details of the mission we have in mind, but I can tell you it's an operation behind enemy lines. We need a fluent German speaker and, believe it or not, a piano player. It's risky. At times, your life will be in danger. But there will be an experienced team backing you up. If you're interested, we would tell your folks that, notwithstanding your IV-F status, the Army needs your skill with math and your knowledge of German. You'd become a regular Army recruit as far as they were concerned. You can finish your finals, what, in the next couple of weeks? Then we would put you through a rigorous training program, more than the basic training stuff the other recruits get. After your mission, you would be honorably discharged and you'd be able to go back to school. How's that sound?" Hinden asked.

"Count me in…Frank."

Paula was beside herself when Walter told her the news that he'd be a soldier after all. "Walter, you can't do this. You're our only child. What would happen…you can't. You have to finish your education. Herbert, say something …"

"Walter is a man, Paula. We can't stop him," Herbert said gently. "We have to be proud of him and support him. This is what free Americans do! Fight the Nazis. Fight the bastards who killed my mother."

Paula put her head in her hands, weeping. Walter put his arm around her. "Momma, I'll be fine. This is something I have to do. Besides, when I'm finished serving, I can go back to college. Don't worry."

The die was cast.

On Sunday, January 31, 1943, Walter hugged his parents goodbye. He shook hands with Sam Sonnenschein and said, "Please take care of them, huh?"

Behind his tears, Sam, trying to smile, said, "You can bet on it."

Walter jumped in a taxi with his duffel bag and waved goodbye. He told the driver to take him to Penn Station. Hinden met him there, at the bottom of the steps near the entrance at 34th Street and Seventh Avenue. He handed Walter his ticket and a small stack of stationery and envelopes, already stamped. "This is your ticket to Toronto. Yes, Toronto. It's a long train ride, so you'll have plenty of time to write some short letters to your parents for while you're supposed to be in basic training. Ten of them should do it; training is about ten weeks. Write something in each one about how boring it is, that the food is terrible, but you played the piano every weekend and the soldiers seemed to enjoy it.

"When you get to the Toronto train station, a young woman—about five-foot-six with long, dark hair wearing a red beret, with a smile from here to there—will greet you like she's your long-lost girlfriend. She'll tell you her name is Gloria. She'll drive you to the facility. Takes about forty-five minutes. She'll fill you in on some details.

"Good luck, Walter! Thank you on behalf of the United States of America. I look forward to catching up with you when you get back."

Before Walter could even say goodbye, Hinden turned and marched up the steps to Seventh Avenue.

Walter had never been on a train other than the subway. The only time he had been out of New York at all was when he was an infant, sailing from Germany. At first it was fascinating to watch the beauty of the New York countryside roll by; after a few hours, the novelty wore off. The monotony of the scenery and movement of the train eventually lulled him into a fitful sleep. When he woke, he managed to finish writing the letters and put them in the envelopes, addressing them to his parents. Hinden had told him not to seal them; the instructors would mail them for him. He figured he wouldn't have time to write letters once training commenced.

12

TORONTO, ONTARIO

The conductor walked through the train, announcing, "Toronto, last stop."

The fourteen-hour train ride was at its end. Walter's excitement had begun to build. He slung his duffel bag over his shoulder, ready to disembark.

He stood on the platform, looking around, not sure in which direction to go. Suddenly, a girl loosely fitting the description Frank Hinden had given him ran over to him with a huge smile on her face, threw her arms around him, and gave him a big kiss on the lips. He looked at her tentatively and asked, "Gloria?"

She looked at him sternly and whispered, "That's your first mistake. You don't identify me, I identify me. Listening to instructions carefully and executing them accordingly might just save your life one day. For what it's worth, hi, I'm Gloria."

Gloria put her arm through his and held him close, as if they were lovers reuniting after a long absence. When she approached an old, battered black Buick in the parking area, she smiled the lustrous smile Frank Hinden had described and said, "C'mon, honey, get in."

The car pulled out of the parking lot and proceeded to drive in a westerly direction. "Nice to meet you, Walter. You'll notice we don't use last names, for obvious reasons. That way the bad guys truly can't identify our peers if we're captured…even under torture. So, your first question is probably, why are we in Canada? Doesn't the OSS have a training camp in the States? The answer is no. Until a couple of years ago, there was no OSS at all; probably, I guess, because there was no need for it. But now, with the war on, the powers-that-be established this camp to train people like you. The big boss, who is from Winnipeg originally, is friends with Roosevelt and Churchill. Most of your instructors and the people who work here are either Brits or Canadians. The instructors for each course are very experienced in real-life situations.

"We're basically operated by British Security Coordination in cahoots with the Canadian government. As you can see, we're located in farmland, far from snooping eyes. It's a nice, bucolic place. But don't let that fool you. You'll learn an awful lot here during the next ten weeks: Morse code, map reading, demolition, how to assist members in the resistance, sabotage, and silent killing. After that, the brains here or in England will deploy you someplace interesting. Just keep your eye out for Dangerous Dan. Not his real name, of course. He teaches the course on silent killing. Pay close attention, and don't let your guard down."

Walter would soon learn that Dangerous Dan, the close combat instructor, believed there was no such thing as fighting fair: "Get tough, get down in the gutter, win at all costs. There's no fair play, no rules except kill or be killed."

"Oh," Gloria added, "do you have the letters for your parents? I'll mail them for you at the appropriate times."

As soon as they arrived at Camp X in Whitby, near Lake Ontario, she smiled and showed him to his barracks.

For someone who on the surface might appear a bit of a spoiled, soft American, Walter showed immediately that he was down-to-earth and as tough as any prizefighter. Like the other recruits, he had much to learn—but he learned quickly. Spy school activities took place day and night, with nothing you could call free time.

He learned to make bombs, clean a pistol, and shoot it accurately with either hand. He learned knife-fighting techniques, Dangerous Dan's specialty, and a form of martial arts Dan called Defendu. Walter, it turned out, became quite good at the latter.

The more he excelled, the more difficult Dan made it for him. Toward the end of his training, Dan admitted he was impressed with the lad with the limp. Walter may have had a physical impairment according to US Army classification, but he was anything but disabled. He was a powerful, coiled spring. By the end of the ten weeks, he was an apex spy.

One day in April after his training was finished, Frank Hinden arrived.

"Good to see you, Walter," he said. "It looks like Camp has treated you well. You look good. My old friend, Dangerous Dan, says you're a beast. Trust me, that's high praise. Listen, go get your bag. We're ready to go for the next part of your training."

Hinden explained that he'd be permitted to go back to New York to visit his parents and have a couple of weeks off to relax. Then he would board a troop ship across the Atlantic to Scotland for finishing school.

"Finishing school?" he asked quizzically.

Hinden turned the key in the ignition of his car. "That's where the Special Ops Exec and the OSS folks train you for your mission. Your troop ship is the *Queen Mary*, the ocean liner. It's been refitted for the war. There will be more than fifteen thousand soldiers aboard, and there aren't enough berths for everyone, so you'll be sleeping in three shifts. Make sure you get some sleep on your shift because once you land, you'll be running at a hundred miles per hour. The trip should take about a week."

After ten hours of driving, a good portion of which Walter slept, Hinden dropped him off at his parents' building on the Grand Concourse. "Have a good stay with your folks. You're scheduled to leave New York on April 23. Good luck."

13

THE BRONX

Walter enjoyed his time off back in New York. He had arranged a deferment of his studies at Columbia before he left for basic training, of course, so now he took the opportunity to see some friends, play some jazz at a few clubs, and practice with Dora Zaslavsky. Mostly, though, he spent time with his parents and Sam Sonnenschein. A couple of days each week, he went to work with his dad and Sam. Herbert was always beaming with pride. When Paula saw him, she invariably burst into tears; little wonder Walter chose to go with his father.

When it was time to board the *Queen Mary*, Herbert, Paula, and Sam were all a mess. Paula, of course, couldn't stop weeping. Herbert had taken Walter aside and told him to forgive her for her emotional outbursts. Aside from the fact that her only son was being shipped off to fight in Europe, they were hearing more and more news reports that the Nazis were exterminating Jews. It was impossible to grasp. How could the cultured country of their birth intentionally massacre people as if they were killing mosquitoes? On top of the rumors, Paula still hadn't heard anything about or from her parents in Paris. She feared the worst but hoped for the best. After many tears, Walter hugged them goodbye and boarded the ship.

GOUROCK, Scotland

When Walter disembarked, he and another dozen or so Camp X graduates were sent to Arisaig House, the finishing school in the Scottish Highlands.

On the grounds, he honed many of the skills he had learned at Camp X, practicing hand-to-hand combat, knife fighting, pistol shooting, sabotage, and parachuting over and over again. A week and a half was devoted specifically to language skills, including speaking, writing, and reading German and Italian. It reminded Walter of the mind-numbing preparation for his bar mitzvah. There was also a painfully protracted series of lessons devoted to listening to nuanced regional German accents and dialects. Fortunately, he had a good ear.

After nearly ten weeks of training with only a bit of intermittent time off, Walter was called into the commander's office. Colonel Turner, assuredly not his real name, introduced himself and closed the door. Waiting inside was a large man wearing a major's uniform.

"This is Major Morris. He is going to be your contact going forward and will give you the details of your mission. As you've probably heard, we undertook an invasion of Sicily last summer, and we've pretty much secured it. We have some friends and contacts there, which made things a bit easier. We now have a legitimate foothold for staging operations in Europe. You will be deployed from Sicily and parachuted behind enemy lines into Austria, the Tyrol, to be exact. The major will take you to a secure area now and provide you with everything you need. Good luck, son."

Major Morris was a bull of a man, with thick shoulders, massive hands, and dark hair cut close to his scalp. He had a number of savage scars on his right cheek and on his hands, Walter guessed from knife fighting. The major said nothing until they arrived at a nondescript, gray building. They entered, and Walter followed him directly down the stairs to a small room with an open door and no windows. Morris closed the door and invited Walter to take a wooden chair with a high back while he sat behind a battered steel desk with a leather case perched on it.

For a war-hardened, huge soldier, Major Morris had a surprisingly high voice. "I'm going to lay out the details of your mission. Obviously, this is highly classified, and most of the people you will engage with will be using code names, though there will be certain exceptions. The idea, of course, is that if you are captured and tortured, you won't be able to divulge anyone's actual identity." He seemed to speak with the certainty of someone who had experienced both capture and torture and lived to talk about them.

Morris began to take out the contents of the leather bag and place them on the table. Walter was familiar with most of the items, but the major elected to describe each one. "This matchbox is a miniature camera. This little cylinder that looks like a firecracker is called a Hedy; when you activate it, it will make a shrieking noise followed by a deafening boom that will scare the shit out of anyone—and I mean anyone—and scatter a room should you need to make a quick exit from a dangerous situation. Ration cards, Swiss francs, marks, and your papers.

"While you are in Austria, you will be posing as Gestapo Major Walter Schneider. You'll have a different identity while traveling in Switzerland and occasionally while you're in Austria. I'll explain that shortly. When you are operating in Austria, you'll be working closely with 'SS Lieutenant Ernst Fischer' and 'Sergeant Frederick Schmitz,' both experienced operatives who also trained at camp and finishing school. Both have already completed missions in Austria. Fischer is the tactical officer; Schmitz, communications. If you need to arrange train tickets, hotel stays, weapons, Fischer. To contact HQ, Schmitz.

"After you parachute in, you will be met by Fischer and Schmitz, who will furnish you with a uniform, a Luger, the works.

This, here, is obviously a cane or walking stick. It's a cover for your limp. If anyone presses you, you damaged your tendon on the Eastern Front. Of course, it isn't just an ordinary walking stick. If you depress the button under the handle, a stiletto will deploy like a switchblade." Morris paused to demonstrate the use of the cane, as well as the other items he described. "And the components in this little box make up your Morse code kit. I am sure you are well practiced in how to assemble it. Use it discreetly, never more than sixty seconds at a pop, and only in emergencies. Finally, this nice gent's ring contains potassium cyanide should you have no other choice. Any questions so far?"

"Not yet, other than what I'll be doing and where I'll be doing it," Walter responded.

"Just some background first. We have been working closely with members of the Austrian resistance in Tyrol. The same group is affiliated with the Italian resistance. A year or so ago, they made contact with a Swiss attorney, Kurt Grimm, originally from Austria, who in turn, contacted Allen Dulles, our man in Bern. The operatives have visited Grimm and Dulles a number of times in Switzerland. They have passed along a treasure trove of important and useful information to us, from the location of armaments factories from the secret V-rocket factory in Peenemunde to the Messerschmitt aircraft factory and the Raxwerke plant in Wiener Neustadt, near Vienna. Suffice it to say, very helpful for American and British bombing planners. One of the operatives is actually a high-ranking executive in a plant that is making a synthetic rubber and has connections with a variety of Nazi industries. One is a Catholic priest, another a concert pianist. Obviously, we can't afford to have these contacts fall into the hands of the Gestapo or meet with any unfortunate accidents.

"That said, we have grown increasingly concerned that they've either been spotted in Switzerland by Kraut spies or worse, that the group has been penetrated by a double agent. Why are we suspicious? No, the Gestapo has not arrested anyone…yet. But there are some disturbing signs. Recently, several of our long-range bombing raids have hit decoys when the group's information had previously substantiated a target with certainty. In another case, a target we had pinpointed in aerial photos taken by a surveillance run one week somehow disappeared the next, when the actual bombing raid was scheduled. The majority of our bombers came under very heavy fire and had to abort. One bomber made it through only to find the target was completely gone. Vanished.

"So, if the Krauts are on to them, it's only a matter of time before the Gestapo will lower the boom. Our guess is that they want to identify as many members of the resistance group as possible and arrest them all. HQ thinks we are short on time—we might have a couple of months, weeks, or days—we can't be sure. Bottom line is, we cannot afford to lose this source, nor can we have the Gestapo get ahold of them. It puts everyone in the entire chain at great risk."

Walter nodded his understanding.

"That's where you come in. If our friends are being watched in Switzerland and their movements are being followed by Gestapo agents, we need to identify the watchers as soon as possible. If our assets have been compromised in Switzerland, we will have to abort all intel gathering and move them out of danger immediately. So, the first part of your mission is to see if any enemies are surveilling our people when they are on their way to meet Dulles in Bern. Bear in mind that the Gestapo operates incognito, just as you will. The Swiss don't take kindly to foreign uniforms in their country. We are certain that if there are Gestapo tails on our assets in Bern, you'll spot them, and there's even a possibility they'll think you're one of them and make contact with you.

"However, if our friends are being turned inside Austria, we'll need you to sniff out the mole and eliminate him. Your role as Major Schneider in Austria is that of a top Gestapo operative looking for collaborators. Our guess is that when the mole thinks it's safe, he or she will try to engage you, not realizing you are one of us. You follow me so far?"

"Yes, sir, I think so," Walter said.

"I know it's a bit complicated. But to summarize, we're thinking either a Gestapo creep is tailing our assets on Swiss soil and/or there is a traitor in the organization on the Austrian side. You will parachute into Austria two weeks from now. There will be zero moonlight: hard to spot a parachute even if someone is looking for one. The drop site is near Kramsach. We've conducted a number of drops there. Mountains, lakes, rolling hills, farms. Lots of friendly Austrians nearby, and you aren't likely to see any Krauts. Certainly not at night. Fischer and Schmitz will meet you and take you to a safe house and give you a Gestapo uniform for your work in Austria and your civilian street duds for your work in Switzerland. You'll make your trips to Switzerland alone."

From that point, the major began explaining what he would be doing behind enemy lines. Walter's head began to swim, and he only hoped he'd be able to remember everything he was told.

"Okay, kid," Morris said, "let's go over it again from Genesis," and Morris went over the mission in detail again. Walter swallowed, then indicated he was good to go. He'd already memorized the photos, the train schedules, and the rendezvous instructions with which he'd been provided.

"Before you go, here's my phone number. Call me if you have any questions."

That, too, Walter committed to memory.

Morris's eyes ran over his face. "You've been selected for this mission by the top brass. You've got the look, like one of those big-time Aryan bastards, you've got the smarts, the talent and physical capabilities, and, unlike me, you know who Chopin is. We're counting on you, son. Good luck."

Walter took a moment, then said, "Can I ask you a personal question, Major?"

"Sure, why not?"

"Were you on a mission behind enemy lines? I mean, did you get caught?" Walter looked down at the scars on Morris's hands.

"Let's just say I'm here and glad to be and leave it at that. After your time here and in Canada, your training and survival instincts should be second nature to you. If you get into shit, you'll figure your way out. Don't worry. Just do what you've been trained to do and you'll be fine."

14

TYROL, AUSTRIA

SS Officer Walter Remer successfully landed in Austria, quickly buried his parachute in nearby woods, and hid in the darkness. He could see the lights from a farmhouse not far away but stayed hidden, in accord with his instructions. Within minutes, a German staff car, lights blackened, rumbled slowly up a dirt path from the direction of the farmhouse and came to a halt. The driver and his passenger got out, and one of them quickly waved a flashlight twice toward the woods, once for two seconds and then three times quickly. That was the signal the major had given him.

Walter emerged from the woods, his hands behind his head as he'd been told, and approached the car.

The uniformed Gestapo officer holding the flashlight pointed it at Walter's face and recognized him from a photo he'd been shown, then said in perfect German, "Welcome, Major Schneider. My name is Lieutenant Ernst Fischer and this is Sergeant Schmitz. You can put your hands down. Where did you leave your chute? We'd best dispose of it on the outside chance a patrol heard your plane or some local Nazi supporters called it in."

They unearthed the parachute, dropped it into a hastily dug hole, refilled it, and covered it with some branches and high grass. Then they threw some oats, carrots, and a little cow manure on it for good measure. That way the local fauna would have some dinner and leave their scent, covering Walter's in case some overzealous patrol dogs were called in to sniff around. Silently, they drove to the safe house, which turned out to be a small building behind the farmhouse.

Fischer said, "You'll stay here tonight. Tomorrow morning, early, you'll get freshened up, put on these clothes, and we'll take you to Innsbruck for the train to Zurich. Your uniform is under the false bottom of the suitcase. It's a little heavy…the Luger is loaded. Take your other stuff with you as well. When you come back from Switzerland, we'll pick you up at the train station and take you to your official residence in Innsbruck. Nice digs; once belonged to some Jewish family."

Early on Monday morning, Walter cleaned up in the washbasin, then secured the false bottom of his suitcase, which held a set of papers for his primary persona, Major Walter Schneider, as well as the goodies Morris had given him in Scotland. He packed clean underwear, socks, a button-down shirt, a shaving kit, and a hair brush. The materials were an important element of his disguise, and a newspaper went on top of them. The charcoal-gray suit, starched white shirt, and dark tie Fischer and Schmitz had left for him fit perfectly.

At that moment, Walter became underground Gestapo posing as a civilian, Horst Reinhardt, Schweinfurt Ball Bearings executive and troubleshooter. Schweinfurt was located in the middle of Germany, but this civilian cover had him spending much of his time on the road, near Vienna, at the Wiener Neustadt Messerschmitt plant and Raxwerke's V-2 rocket assembly plant. Morris had assured him he knew enough about physics and aerodynamics as they applied to the use of ball bearings to be convincing to prying eyes and ears. Walter had been given some early drawings of the advanced Messerschmitt and V-2 that "friends" had been able to smuggle out and had familiarized himself with them just in case some smart aleck asked him how many ball bearings went into them.

If some Gestapo wise guys checked him out and didn't find a Horst Reinhardt on the payroll at Schweinfurt, Walter had to be prepared to be pressed to tell them who he really was. A quick glance at Major Walter Schneider's papers should convince them he was undercover Gestapo, just like them, and, according to Morris, they'd likely want to steer clear of him.

"You'll just be another Kraut spook trying to catch a break to make yourself look good to your higher-ups," Morris said. "The key resistance contacts will know of your dual identity."

He rode to the Innsbruck train station in the back of the staff car with the uniformed Fischer and Schmitz in the front.

At the station, Schmitz got out, opened Walter's door with deference to his rank, notwithstanding he was in civilian clothes, and then took the suitcase from the trunk. Schmitz saluted Walter. "Sir, may I?" motioning to the westbound train track, suggesting that it would be his honor to carry Walter's bag, as any good underling would.

"Certainly, Schmitz," Walter responded in his most arrogant German. "Heil Hitler," he saluted.

Schmitz and Fischer drove off, and the train arrived at 7:44 a.m. Walter boarded and the train left Innsbruck for Zurich at 7:48 a.m. sharp.

Shortly after the train departed, a conductor came by examining tickets and papers. "Thank you, Herr Reinhardt. Everything looks to be in order here," and he continued on to the next passenger.

Walter studied the Schweinfurt materials but spent most of the long train ride to Zurich mesmerized by the beauty surrounding him. It was hard to imagine the beautiful, rolling green hills and magnificent snow-capped Alps could stand so serenely in the middle of a vortex of death and destruction, like the eye of a hurricane.

At the Swiss border, several uniformed German officers

disembarked. The conductor once again checked tickets and papers.

At 12:55 p.m., in Zurich, Walter switched to a train to Bern, arriving ninety minutes later. Walter exited the train, and if not for the weight of his suitcase, he would have walked the ten minutes to the Hotel Bellevue Palace, where he would be staying. Instead, he took the short taxi ride there. His room was ready, so he was able to freshen up as soon as he checked in.

"It's like a spying playground," Morris had said of the hotel. "The fucking place is crawling with Gestapo, MI6, and OSS. Spies, politicians, and prostitutes, all indistinguishable, if you ask me. They hang out there like it's a fucking country club. Try to memorize faces. You're there to see if anyone is following our assets. You are scheduled to meet with several of our resistance leaders. You have a reservation for lunch at the hotel's La Terrasse Restaurant at 4:30 p.m. under the name 'Messner.' Franz Josef Messner, chairman of Semperit, a company that developed a synthetic rubber called Buna; Ernst Kraus, a director at Siemens; and Josef Joham, chairman of Creditanstalt-Bankerverein, an Austrian bank that was once owned by the Rothschilds and was taken over by the Deutsche Bank, thanks to the Nazis, will be your lunchmates. All are heavy hitters in Vienna business circles and well known, well liked, and a dependable part of the Krauts' well-oiled industrial complex." Morris had shown him some photos of them. "Your lunch should be sufficiently audible to be heard by any nearby spy and contain nothing more secret than the weather. The subject matter will revolve around financing the war effort, and someone might mumble something about the recent Allied invasion of Italy just to make the conversation believable."

At precisely 4:30 p.m., the maître d' showed Walter to the table where Messner, Joham, and Kraus were already seated. They stood when he joined them. He smiled and said, "Please," gesturing to everyone to be seated.

Messner introduced himself and the others to Walter. The waiter immediately came to the table. "Gentlemen, would you like a cocktail before lunch?"

Each ordered his preferred drink, followed by several delicious courses of lunch, followed by coffee and dessert.

Walter had never before attended a business lunch, no less one with such important men. The conversation was as bland as he thought it might be. The only surprise was a brisk conversation about the consistency of the foie gras. If there were any spies listening who had trouble sleeping, they were sure to be cured of their insomnia. Messner paid the bill, left a generous tip, and everyone rose, shook hands, passed a bit more small talk, and dispersed.

Walter, as instructed, had repaired to his room, and then, a few minutes after nine, entered the hotel bar and ordered a vodka and tonic. He feigned enjoying the cabaret singer and pianist, the former being somewhat off-key and the latter as skilled as a tone-deaf child playing "Chopsticks" for the first time. At 9:30, right on time, Messner walked in, and Walter waved to him as if greeting a long-lost friend. He offered to buy Messner a drink, and they sat at the bar together, having an animated conversation about ration cards and public sanitation. At 10:00 p.m., Messner excused himself and walked out of the hotel. He was headed to Allen Dulles's place, a few blocks away at Herrengasse 23.

"After he leaves the hotel grounds," Morris had instructed Walter, "say a minute or two later, you'll walk outside, ostensibly for a smoke. I take it they taught you how to smoke and drink in camp?"

Walter waited a minute or so, then paid his tab. He went out the entrance of the hotel and lit a cigarette, confident he looked like an executive after a hard day of negotiations, enjoying a satisfying smoke and the balmy evening. He finished his cigarette, noticed no one following Messner, and returned to the bar, this time placing himself in the corner so he had a view of the entire room.

The singer had finished her set and the pianist was playing something Walter assumed was an interlude. The bar was crowded now. There were any number of men and women, as Morris had joked, all largely indistinguishable from one another. At any rate, Walter didn't think he was experienced enough to tell the prostitutes, diplomats, and spies apart.

At 10:50 p.m. Messner entered the bar, and Walter assumed he must have just returned to the hotel—right on time, according to Morris. He made his way to the end farthest from the pianist. Walter didn't expect the man to engage him in chatter at this point; his responsibility was to see whether anyone had followed him back and memorize the faces if they had, enjoy the music a little longer, then go upstairs to his room and hit the hay.

Shortly thereafter, a tall woman with dark, shoulder-length hair tapped Messner on the shoulder. She threw her arms around him and his arms encircled her waist. Their lips met as if they were lovers who had not seen each other in a long time. Walter could see that she was absolutely stunning. She had high cheekbones, sultry eyes, long legs supported by stiletto heels, and a low-cut dress that left little to the imagination.

The bartender poured their drinks, and they engaged in animated conversation, though Walter was too far away to hear what they were saying. They quickly finished their drinks and, smiling like lovers, left the bar holding hands.

Walter left money on the bar, far exceeding his tab, and stealthily followed Messner and the woman in the direction of the elevator bank, being careful not to be seen.

Major Morris had not mentioned anything about girlfriends, mistresses, or wives meeting any of the assets in Bern. That, of course, left the possibility of this woman being a diplomat, a prostitute, or a spy. Without giving it much thought, Walter ruled out diplomat. Now what? He had no idea whether Messner's room was anywhere near his own, and even if they were close to each other, it would likely be impossible to eavesdrop on their conversation or observe anything more. There was nothing he could do now except make certain he was on the 8:04 a.m. train to Zurich, and the 10:01 from there to Innsbruck, as planned, and see if this woman or anyone else he had seen at the hotel was following Messner onto it.

He thought briefly about using his Morse code communications kit to contact Fischer and Schmitt to ask them to check with HQ for further instructions, but the place was crawling with spies, so there was a high probability that listening devices would pick up anything he sent.

In the morning, Walter took a taxi to the train station and boarded the 8:04 a.m. train to Zurich nine minutes early. At 8:01, Messner walked into Walter's car and proceeded past him toward his own. Walter studiously kept his head buried in his ball bearing information, so it was easy for them to ignore each other. Walter had memorized the faces he had seen in the hotel and did not recognize any as he waited for the train to leave Bern. He certainly did not see the woman.

When he changed trains at Zurich for Innsbruck, Messner walked through the train past him. Again, Walter didn't observe anyone following the Semperit executive, who was continuing on to Vienna. Morris had indicated that the other two lunch companions would be returning on other days; they were clearly less important to the OSS.

When Walter disembarked at Innsbruck, Fischer and Schmitz were there to meet him in the staff car. If there were any suspicious Gestapo following him, Morris had said, this would confirm to them that he really was one of the boys, most likely that he was also out to catch Messner himself.

On the short drive to their "office," the home once belonging to a Jewish family, Fischer and Schmitz asked about his experiences at the hotel. They discussed the woman and decided it was best to send a coded message to HQ, asking for advice on how to proceed.

The next morning, Schmitz decoded the reply, which suggested there wasn't much that could be done now, but on Walter's next trip to Bern, he was to keep his eye out for the woman and get a photograph of her if possible. There was one thing of which HQ was certain: She was neither OSS nor MI6.

On Wednesday, Walter donned his full Gestapo uniform for the first time, and he could see why the higher-ups thought he looked the part. He joined Fischer and Schmitz at a local café for breakfast. Later, they gave him a brief tour of Innsbruck so he could get his bearings, and in the afternoon they took the six-hour drive to Vienna, stopping for lunch in Salzburg along the way. Vienna was a magnificent city. For Walter, it was more than just the remarkable architecture and cleanliness. It meant Mozart, Haydn, Schubert, Strauss, and Mahler.

They stayed overnight in a stately home Fischer had rented as their Vienna base of operations. Like the house in Innsbruck, it once belonged to a wealthy Jewish family. Walter looked forward to returning someday to spend more time exploring Vienna. They drove south to see the industrial complex in Wiener Neustadt to give Walter some perspective. Then they drove back to Innsbruck so Walter could get some rest and prepare to leave for Bern the next morning for his rendezvous with the next asset, concert pianist Barbara Issakides.

15

On Friday morning, Walter dressed for his second trip to Bern, following the same travel routines as he had on his earlier "business trip" to Switzerland, as if he were adhering to some business protocol.

While focused on the mission at hand, he wondered whether he would see Franz Josef Messner's female friend again. He tried to think through probable scenarios. Was she his girlfriend or mistress? A gold digger? A prostitute? Or, perhaps, a German spy? He could not let down his guard for a moment. Meanwhile, he would scour the train for any faces that might look familiar from his previous trip. He had been taught that in the world of espionage, one must always expect the unexpected. He felt he was prepared.

Between Innsbruck and the Hotel Bellevue Palace, he noticed nothing out of the ordinary. He checked into his room and, as he did the first time, examined the telephone, lamps, and appliances for listening devices. He checked the closets, the bathroom, and the ceiling for any small holes or cameras that could be used to watch or photograph him. As far as he could tell, the room was clean.

He had a quick lunch for one at La Terrasse at 4:30 p.m., eating while pretending to read an industry paper, but also carefully scouring the restaurant for memorable faces. He paid for his meal, then returned to his room to prepare for the encounter with the pianist, who, Morris said, was "well known in Austria, Hungary, Germany, and Switzerland—she studied at the University of Music and Performing Arts in Vienna before the war. Last October she performed Chopin in the Great Hall at the Musikverein. Rave reviews. You'll see her in the bar at the hotel, where she's also staying."

Morris had passed a photograph to Walter, who'd studied it for a moment. "She's very attractive."

"Keep it in your pants, Walter." Morris had shaken his head. "Dames can only get you in trouble in this business. Strictly professional relationship, capisce? She'll be the entertainer at the hotel on Friday night. She's scheduled to perform at 8:30; the Swiss, like the Krauts, start on time. Get to the bar a bit earlier, say 8:10, so you can have a couple of drinks in you before the entertainment starts. She usually draws a crowd. She'll start to play her second piece, Chopin's Fantaisie-Impromptu, at roughly 8:45. Do you know how to play it?"

Walter had nodded.

Now he reviewed the inebriated repartee in which he would indulge with Barbara Issakides, hoping it would be convincing, his rendition of Chopin's Fantaisie-Impromptu adequate.

Walter slid up to the bar at a few minutes after 8:00. He ordered a couple of drinks so there would be liquor on his breath. Tonight he was ball-bearing businessman Horst Reinhardt, more than a little bit tipsy, with cocktail in hand.

At 8:25, Barbara entered the room, sat down on the bench, and tested the piano's tune with a few short combinations. It wasn't perfect, but close enough. The maître d' announced the evening's special guest, and there was a smattering of applause. Barbara began to play at precisely 8:30. Her first selection was Chopin's Nocturne op. 9 no.1. She was truly marvelous; the applause for her was well deserved. She was an extraordinary talent.

Walter scanned the room and was surprised not to see any of the same faces he had memorized just a few days before on his first trip to Bern.

At roughly 8:45 p.m., Barbara began to play Fantaisie Impromptu…brilliantly.

He was ready. With cocktail in hand, Walter sauntered over to the piano and sat down on the bench. In the well-practiced, slurred speech he hoped would make any drunk proud, he said, "Would you mind? I love Chopin."

Barbara stopped abruptly. She looked at him, aghast, but he was sure he could see some recognition in her eyes.

The maître d' moved to approach the piano from the other end of the room and the murmuring from a shocked audience was more than audible. Then Walter started to play where Barbara had stopped when he appeared.

"Some people will be pissed off at you. Others will be amused that some half-drunken knucklehead executive has such a large set of balls to interfere with the show. They'll be even more astonished that you're actually talented…neither here nor there, but that's how she will identify you," Morris had explained.

The crowd no doubt did find him magnificent; this was clearly no bum off the street. The maître d' slowed his approach and then stopped just short of the piano, folding his arms as if he were about to scold a child for a minor transgression. But he let Walter complete the piece. And before the maître d' could chastise him, the audience stood, giving him a round of applause.

Walter smiled as if he had won the Nobel Prize and turned to Barbara. Then, in his best inebriated voice, he said, "May I buy you a drink?"

She tried to look at him with disdain, but he could see she was having difficulty suppressing the slight smile at the corner of her mouth and said, "No, thank you, sir. Perhaps another time. Now, please go. I am performing."

Walter looked embarrassed, muttered an apology, and went sulkily back to the bar, followed by the maître d'.

Barbara quickly began to play another piece. The audience's reaction died down, and their attention returned to her.

At the bar, the maître d' was explaining, "Sir, you are not permitted to play while Miss Issakides is performing. Is that understood?"

"Yes, sir. I am terribly sorry. I did not mean to cause a stir. Please accept my apologies. I don't know what came over me," Walter replied.

"Well, don't let it happen again. By the way, you are quite good. Perhaps next time we can arrange for you to play...officially. I think the crowd was very impressed to hear such a talented guest. But not tonight, yes?"

Walter nodded and smiled sheepishly. Morris had prepared him for being tossed out of the bar; now all he needed to do was order another drink, act quietly embarrassed, and hide behind his drink to see if anyone followed Barbara when she left the bar.

"If anyone starts talking to you," Morris had said, "keep your antennae up. Memorize the face; you'll probably see it again, if you haven't already. Whoever it is, he or she is probably a spy. Listen carefully for an accent, nuanced speech, or a mistake that gives them away. But offer nothing other than how fascinating you find ball bearings. You'll bore the shit out of them, and they'll probably leave. The only thing you want people to think is that you are Horst Reinhardt, a somewhat drunk but truly embarrassed executive from Schweinfurt Ball Bearings."

Walter was truly enjoying the pianist's skill as his eyes surveyed the room, memorizing faces, when he felt a tap on his shoulder from behind and a woman said, "May I?" taking the place next to his.

It was the woman. Messner's woman.

Without hesitation, she raised her hand to the bartender, signaling for a drink. He seemed to know her preference. She was no stranger to the bar.

She was leaning very close to Walter now. Her dark brown eyes penetrated his blue ones, her lustrous black hair curled in waves about her slim neck, and her ample breasts strained at her tight, low-cut dress. There was the scent of jasmine about her. She took his hands softly in hers and said, "I heard you play Chopin. You are magnificent. These hands. They are exquisite. I am Nina." She did not release his hands.

"I am Horst," he replied.

"Well, Horst, it is a great pleasure to make your acquaintance," she said, moving even closer. "You are very gifted and very handsome. Are you staying at the hotel?"

"I am here on business," he said.

She laid her hands between her thighs. Maintaining eye contact, she said, "Ah, wonderful. I am here on business as well." She winked. "I work for a cosmetics manufacturer in Geneva. What do you do, Horst? You are a professional pianist, no doubt?"

He tried to place her accent. Walter depended on the accents and dialect nuances he'd been taught at finishing school. German, with a hint of French. Could she be from Alsace-Lorraine? Nina was almost certainly not her real name, nor was she likely the employee of any cosmetics manufacturer. In his mind, he replayed the scene he'd witnessed between her and Messner. It was fair to assume, now, that she was not Messner's lover—or at least not his alone. Walter would have to play along to see if he could determine who she really might be, prostitute or spy.

"Well, during the day, I work for a ball-bearings manufacturer, and in the evening, I play piano, hoping one day to be as good as the woman playing now."

She moved his hands between her legs so he could feel her. "You may have even greater talents. Perhaps you could show me."

Walter stammered, "Well, I–I..." having no doubt now where this was leading.

"Why don't we take our drinks up to your room, Horst?"

Walter put a few Swiss francs down on the bar and, with her hand in his and no space between them, they made their way to the elevator bank. The agenda of watching to see whether Barbara Issakides was followed on her way to and from Dulles's place at Herrengasse 23 would have to change. He would have to improvise.

Was Nina a prostitute or a spy? If she were the latter, she clearly had a lock on Messner, possibly others as well. Perhaps she had surveilled Walter as well. He didn't recall seeing her that afternoon at lunch with Messner, and he prided himself on being exceptionally good at memorizing faces.

Walter unlocked the door to his room and she followed, almost glued to him. Every nerve in his body was on high alert. They walked to the bed and sat down on the edge. She finished her drink and put both her glass and his on the nighttable. She put his hands between her legs again and kissed him on the mouth. She moved away from him for a moment, staring deeply into his eyes, then ran one hand through his blond hair. The other she placed confidently on his trousers.

He gasped as she unbuttoned them, pulled them down, and discarded them, then slid between his thighs.

She rose slowly and proceeded to remove his shirt, kissing him again. Expertly, she took off her dress and her brassiere, dropping them to the floor. Her body was exquisite. She touched him in ways he had never been touched before. She was remarkable, teaching him things no instructor had felt it necessary to discuss at the finishing school. Certainly nothing he had experienced with the girls he dated at home.

Afterward, they fell back on the bed, exhausted. He removed a cigarette from his nighttable and offered her one. They both smoked, their bodies relaxing in unison. Their heavy breathing slowly returned to normal. Nina cuddled against him until Walter fell asleep.

He had not really fallen asleep, but he appeared to be. She tested him by squeezing his genitals. Somehow, he managed not to react. She left the bed and carefully rummaged through his suitcase. If she was a prostitute looking for money, she would have gone through his jacket or pants pockets first. He could see that she'd discovered the false bottom and watched silently as she struggled to open it. It had a tiny, cleverly hidden combination lock, and she wasn't able to locate it. In the dark, he could see her naked silhouette tugging at the false bottom for a few minutes more but must have determined it would be too noisy and abandoned the effort so as not to wake him.

Then, oddly, she bent over to grab one of her high heels. She seemed to be unscrewing the stiletto heel from the shoe. She tiptoed around to her side of the bed and carefully lay down next to him. Then, in an instant, she rose up above him, raising her arm, obviously intending to drive the stiletto into his chest.

But he was too quick for her. In one powerful move, he grabbed her wrist, rolled over on top of her, and straddled her legs with his, pinning her down and closing his other hand over her neck just under her chin and smashing her head hard against the headboard. The stiletto dropped harmlessly from her hand. He quickly closed his other hand around her throat and twisted violently, as he was trained. He heard the horrendous snap of her neck being broken. She lay still, her eyes wide open. He felt her throat. No pulse.

He exhaled and tried to catch his breath. *Think.* What to do now?

He had to dispose of her body and her clothing. Fortunately, there was no blood on the bed. Thank goodness.

His mind raced. Three choices, none of them especially good.

He could call the front desk and ask for a doctor. He could say she seemed to have stopped breathing during passionate sex. Maybe it was a heart attack. Unfortunately, almost anyone could see her neck was broken, her head badly bruised. He would be held for questioning at the very least, and an autopsy would reveal that her neck wasn't broken by accident.

Scratch that.

He could dress her, carry her body to the roof of the building, make sure he wasn't observed, and throw it to the sidewalk below…hoping the police would consider it a suicide. Again, an autopsy would reveal bruises on her head, her throat, and a broken neck. Even an amateur pathologist would see her neck was not broken by the fall, not to mention the finger marks on her neck and wrist. And a cursory investigation of people who last saw her, like the bartender, would make Walter the number one suspect.

That left only one alternative. He needed a large bag. A hotel laundry bag.

He washed and dressed quickly, then closed her eyelids and placed the sheet over her body. He went down the hall to what he assumed was the maid's closet. It was locked. He looked around and listened for anyone roaming the halls or exiting the elevator. He deftly turned the lock's tumbler with a pick inserted in the heel of his shoe. Another useful gift from finishing school. He found a stack of extra-large, heavy-duty laundry bags and took one. Then, he noticed a dozen or so irons lined up on a shelf, just like the one in his room's closet. Added weight; excellent. He took several of the heavy irons and stuffed them in the bag and returned to his room. He stuffed Nina's remains, her clothes, and her shoes in the laundry bag. He would have to carry the body down the service staircase, which he had noticed on his first stay at the hotel. It seemed it was rarely used, and then only during the day.

Walter would have to cross the Münzrain, the quiet street behind the hotel, and make his way through the trees that abutted the street. Then he would have to cross the Aarestrasse, making certain not to be seen. He would have to drop the bag in the Aare as close to the riverbank as possible; an object of that size would more likely be noticed farther out in the clear water. The process would be much like laying explosives to sabotage a bridge, an activity in which he had excelled at both Camp X and finishing school.

A few minutes before 3:00 a.m., before morning traffic began, when he still had the benefit of complete darkness, Walter slowly descended the service staircase. The bag was heavy. His adrenaline was pumping and his heart racing.

Outside, he crossed the Münzrain and ducked into the patch of trees that led down to the Aarestrasse. He saw lights approaching from an oncoming car and kneeled down among the trees. As soon as it passed, he hurried across the Aarestrasse, sliding the bag carefully down the embankment into the river. He could only hope the mild current would not dislodge the body from the bag and pray the weight would keep it submerged.

He looked around in every direction and saw no one. Quickly retracing his steps, he found himself praying again that he hadn't been seen. Before he reached the hotel, he brushed off his shoes with his handkerchief so he would not track any dirt inside.

He recrossed the Münzrain, entered the hotel close to the service staircase, climbed the steps to his floor, and was back in his room by 3:25 a.m. He took off his shoes, then checked the bed to make sure there were no blood or lipstick stains he might have missed earlier. He even checked his suitcase to make certain Nina had not dropped a listening or tracking device in it. Then he lay down in the bed, and somehow sleep overcame him.

Walter managed to force himself awake at 6:30 a.m. He took an ice-cold shower, shaved, and dressed, then checked one last time to see if there were any traces of the woman. Nothing.

Nina must have someone who controlled her, and if that person did not hear from her in a few days, he would come looking for her. Perhaps that would be all Walter would need to return to Innsbruck and notify HQ that he had been unmasked but had neutralized the Gestapo spy. Which would be followed by his immediate exfiltration. It would be far too risky for him to remain in Europe. The resistance group would also have to be disbanded and quickly removed from Austria to safer ground, but that would be up to

HQ to handle. Still, he acknowledged this was all his fault. If he had brushed Nina off the night before and just done exactly what he was there to do—watch the assets—instead of trying to play the hero—and "kept it in his pants," as Morris had joked—he wouldn't be in this embarrassing and dangerous situation. He wouldn't have been forced to kill anyone, even if she *was* the enemy; he wouldn't have endangered himself and others.

At 7:40 a.m. the next morning, Walter checked out of the hotel and caught a taxi to the train station. He had bought a newspaper and lit a cigarette before he remembered the pianist also would be taking the 8:04 a.m. train. He obviously could not communicate with her, could do no more than watch her pass him on the way to her seat. Still, he was obliged to be vigilant. After all, it would not be surprising for the Gestapo to have more than one agent following members of a resistance group they were tailing. He boarded the train at 7:59 a.m. and two minutes later she passed him on the way to her car. When he changed trains in Zurich, Barbara also passed him on the way to her car. As far as he could tell, she was not being followed.

On the long ride from Zurich to Innsbruck, Walter replayed the entire week in his mind. If the Gestapo had discovered the group and its leadership, why would they risk one of their agents to kill just him and not Messner or one of the others? She was a professional. She could easily have killed Messner. Perhaps, as Major Morris had suggested, the Gestapo would want to identify all the leaders of the resistance, to arrest them all. So why just kill Walter? The only way that made sense was if the Gestapo knew in advance who Walter was and why he was in Bern. The traitor had already identified Walter and the Gestapo had to kill him before he uncovered the mole. He was still in grave danger, and so was everyone else.

His train arrived in Innsbruck at 2:55 p.m. Fischer and Schmitz met him and drove him back to the Innsbruck house. Walter directed them to join him in the secure room in the basement. Then he relayed everything that had transpired.

"The woman's controller will definitely go looking for her when she doesn't report in. When they can't find her, they will come looking for me. They'll speak to the maître d', the bartender, the desk clerk, the bellhops…anyone and everyone who may have seen us together. There is no way I can go back to Bern. My rendezvous with the priest next week will have to be canceled.

"I suspect that even if the Gestapo don't find the body in a day or so, they will presume I killed her and got rid of it. They'll contact the mole and then come after me. My guess is we won't be safe here either, assuming the informant has been keeping tabs on me. Schmitz, should you get in touch with HQ?"

Schmitz said, "Roger that. We'll wait here for their instructions."

Walter and Fischer went upstairs to begin packing things up, while Schmitz took care of sending the coded message. HQ would probably have them close up shop immediately, not leaving a trace behind. Schmitz joined them upstairs as soon as he received and decoded the reply from HQ.

"Send coded message to Maier, Messner, and Caldonazzi Now. READ: Now. M, M, C, take train today to Bern. Instruct all operatives to scatter and seek neutral locations. Await further instructions from Dulles. REPEAT. M, M, C, take train TODAY to Bern. Now. STOP.

Instructions for Schneider, Fischer, Schmitz. READ: Take staff car to safe house 110 Borgo Pieve, Castelfranco Veneto, near Padua. Schmitz has map and directions. Await further exfiltration instructions upon arrival. STOP."

The implications were obvious. As Walter had surmised, the Gestapo knew he was there to find the infiltrator. The mole somehow had ferreted him out quickly and informed them of his identity. The Gestapo, concerned that this might upset their chances of closing in on the entire spy network, had chosen to eliminate

Walter before he could identify the informer. So, the Gestapo had sent their agent, the woman who had already marked Messner, to dispose of Walter before he could finger the mole.

HQ had decided to send the network's leadership to the relative safety of Bern. They would remove Walter, Fischer, and Schmitz as soon as possible, but in the meantime they were being sent to a safe house not far from Venice, according to the map. That made perfect sense. With their Gestapo uniforms, identification, and staff car, they could easily drive through Mussolini's Italy to get to the exfiltration site. Venice was a port. Exfiltration would likely be accomplished via fishing or cargo boat, or even submarine. This site would also put distance between them and Austrian Tyrol. Local Tyrolean informants would be happy to point out members of the resistance for a few marks. Any resistance members turned in would be tortured and probably killed.

Walter, Fischer, and Schmitz cleared out their belongings and put them in the trunk of the staff car. They stripped the place clean, burned any paper, and left the Innsbruck house behind, preparing to leave just before 3:30 p.m. on Sunday. Schmitz estimated the drive time from Innsbruck to Castelfranco Veneto was five and a half hours without stopping.

16

VENETO, Italy

The magnificent Parrocchia di Santa Maria della Pieve Church stood across from 110 Borgo Pieve. Upstairs, in the rectory kitchen, Father Pietro Salerno was preparing his locally famous pasta sauce. Crushed tomatoes, onions, garlic, olive oil, salt, oregano, black pepper, lard, and some sugar. If anyone asked him the specific proportions of each, he hadn't a clue, but his sauce was without rival. From the kitchen window, he could see into the courtyard of the small building across the street. Just before 8:30 p.m., he watched as three uniformed Gestapo officers emerged from their staff car. The driver was a sergeant, his front seat companion a lieutenant, and from the rear seat, a major who had a distinct limp and carried a cane. This last one was vaguely familiar. Within a few seconds, another car pulled up behind the first one, which would block the view from the street.

Four large Gestapo men rolled out of the second car and five additional uniformed Gestapo, led by a colonel, a captain, two lieutenants, and a sergeant came out of the house to greet the newcomers. Something didn't look right. Two of the larger Gestapo gorillas grabbed the major with the limp from behind. One slapped handcuffs on him and, together, they lifted him off his feet.

❖ ❖ ❖

Fischer knew instantly they had been set up. He reached for his firearm, but the Gestapo colonel was much faster. In one swift motion, he raised his silenced Luger and shot Fischer between the eyes. His lifeless body crumpled to the ground. The colonel motioned for two Gestapo officers to drag Walter inside, then dispose of Fischer's body.

The colonel smiled and nodded at Schmitz, who got in the staff car, and drove away. Schmitz was Walter's last thought before something came crashing down on his head, knocking him unconscious.

❖ ❖ ❖

Father Salerno, known to his parishioners as a kind and caring priest as well as the maker of the best red sauce west of Venice, was also a member of the Italian resistance. He sat near the window of his kitchen, trying to process what he had just seen.

He knew the Gestapo had moved into 110 Borgo Pieve four months earlier. He had seen all of the members of the Gestapo team that had commandeered the house more frequently than he cared to. They were often visited by pro-Mussolini carabinieri, dragging some poor soul, conscious or not, into their devil's den. It didn't take a genius to know it was a Gestapo safe house, used for torturing captured soldiers or resistance fighters. He never saw them again, may God have mercy on their souls. But as much as he prayed for them, there was nothing he could do to help them. He knew he could do more good by helping the Allies win the war. His job in the resistance was to report unusual troop movements, railcar shipments of heavy equipment, and the erecting of new industrial complexes in northern Italy. The collar he wore allowed him to travel with relative impunity.

Then it occurred to him: He recalled where he had seen the major before. A week ago, the tall, young blond fellow, in civilian clothes, was having lunch in Bern, at the Hotel Bellevue Palace with a member of the Austrian resistance. The father had gone into the hotel to purchase a newspaper and get a quick bite of lunch. He had recognized Messner and Joham but wasn't sure about the third man. Earlier in the day, he had met with his friend, Father Heinrich Maier, a member of the Austrian resistance, at the Pfarramt Dreifaltigkeit Church. Maier had expressed his concerns that the Gestapo was on to their network, and that the blond man was brought in by the OSS to ascertain whether the group, in fact, had been discovered.

What Father Salerno had just seen was perplexing. Why would the Gestapo colonel kill the lieutenant and let the sergeant go on his way? Perhaps the sergeant was a traitor and Father Maier's fears were justified. While he was not sure what was going on, it seemed to be as important as any troop or equipment movement, so he descended to the bowels of the church, where there was a small wine cellar. Hidden behind the casks was a false wall panel that led to a crypt that held a chair and a small table where he kept the transmitter. At 9:43 p.m. he began transmitting coded messages to his contact in the underground, detailing what he had seen, each no more than sixty seconds long.

The priest did not know the identity of his communications partner, though rumor had it his base of operations was in Sicily, and he was perhaps a much-feared Mafia don from Palermo, who hated the Nazis and Mussolini. Whoever he was, he seemed to have connections with powerful people throughout Italy and the United States. Father Salerno described everything he had seen in as much detail as possible.

❖ ❖ ❖

Salvatore Giordano, small, slim, and pale in contrast to his father, large, olive-skinned, and florid-faced, decoded the urgent message. Don Pasquale read the communication carefully, then dictated an equally urgent message to his two key contacts: Frank Hinden, his OSS man in New York City, and his boss, Charles Luciano, in a New York State prison.

Hinden's aide immediately got the message to his boss. "Damn it to hell," Hinden exclaimed. He swore a few more times and then said, "We've got to get Walter the fuck out of there, if he's still alive. Get me Donovan on the line."

"Wild" Bill Donovan was about to leave on a ship to Italy. "What's up, Frank?"

Hinden told him.

Donovan barked, "Whatever resources you need, use 'em. You have my blessing." With the invasion of Italy still in its early stages, there was no way to land Special Forces or a rescue crew behind enemy lines in German-occupied Italy. It simply was not possible. Hinden would have to come up with something unorthodox.

At virtually the same time, a guard at the Great Meadow Correctional Facility in Comstock, New York, handed Don Pasquale's message to inmate Charles "Lucky" Luciano. As he began to walk away, the telephone in the corridor rang. The guard answered it. "Mr. Luciano, it's for you. Your buddy, Costello."

"I just got a call from your friend, Frank Hinden," Frank Costello said. "He's hoping you can help him."

Costello explained the plan to Luciano, who had already digested the message from Don Pasquale. "Is it the blond kid with the limp? You know, the piano player from the Bronx?"

"Yes."

Luciano sighed. "I give my blessing. I hope the poor son of a bitch is still alive. Have Hinden send a coded message to Don Pasquale signed by me."

❖ ❖ ❖

Walter had no idea what time it was when he woke. He could only tell that it was dark and the room smelled of mildew and urine. His arms and legs were strapped to a wooden chair and all he wore was his underwear. A rag was in his mouth, tied tightly around his head.

"Ah! You are finally awake, Herr Reinhardt, or is it Major Schneider…whoever you are. I am Colonel Hoffmann. There is much I need to know and you will tell me everything." Hoffmann motioned for a sergeant to remove the rag from Walter's mouth. "Who do you work for?"

Walter remained silent.

Hoffmann struck Walter across the face, hard, with a gloved hand, drawing blood. "I know you are not deaf or mute. Who do you work for?"

Walter said nothing.

A gloved hand smashed him twice across the face, even harder this time. "Herr Reinhardt, we can make this as pleasant or as difficult as you would like. I am generally a patient man, but I would not try my patience if I were you. I will make it easy for you. You are with the OSS? I am good, yes? So, I will ask you something more pressing. I want names. I want you to give me the names of your friends in the Austrian resistance."

Walter spoke for the first time. "I am sure your friend Schmitz has all the information you need."

"Ah. So you do speak. Good. Our mutual friend Schmitz has been kind enough to provide us with some names. However, sadly, he is not privy to them all. But I know you are. So, please tell me."

"Fuck you!"

Hoffmann punched Walter in the face with a closed fist, then slammed his fist down on Walter's testicles. He screamed, writhing in pain. Hoffmann punched him again on the side of his head and

Walter blacked out. Hoffmann took a bucket of ice-cold water and dumped it on his head. Walter's body jerked, but he did not waken.

When Walter next started to come to, Colonel Hoffmann slapped him lightly on both cheeks with the back of his hand. "Wake up, Herr Reinhardt! Now would be a good time to tell me all the names you know in the Austrian resistance. You see, I am in a good mood."

Walter glared at Hoffmann and said nothing.

"All right, have it your way." Hoffmann motioned to someone standing behind Walter, who could not tell if it was one or two men who pulled a hood over his head, tied it tightly, and violently tipped his back into a tub of water.

They held his head in the water for what seemed an eternity. He was drowning. Just before he blacked out, they pulled him back and sat him upright. Walter gasped for air.

"Herr Reinhardt, the names," Hoffmann shouted.

Walter remained silent.

Hoffmann motioned to his men to repeat the procedure.

He was certain he was drowning this time. He lost consciousness. Hoffmann was furious. "Is he still alive?"

An assistant felt for a pulse and nodded in the affirmative.

"Pour ice water over his head every fifteen minutes when he comes to. Keep doing it all night. Keep him awake. I will be back in the morning."

❖ ❖ ❖

Walter was alternatively freezing and burning up. He soiled his underwear.

"Ah, Herr Reinhardt. I have warned you not to try my patience. Give me the names of the Austrian resistance. Now. This is your last chance."

His voice was barely audible when he said, "I will give you their names."

Hoffmann signaled to his sergeant to be ready to write.

Walter whispered, "Josef Haydn, Franz Schubert, Gustav Mahler, Johann Strauss, Wolfgang Amadeus Mozart..."

Hoffmann was enraged. "Enough!" He took a hammer and smashed it down on Walter's left index finger, his middle finger, his thumb, and his ring finger. One at a time. Walter screamed in agony. His bones must be in pieces. "Names! Now!" Hoffmann shouted.

Walter continued to scream uncontrollably.

Hoffmann now slammed the hammer down on Walter's right hand, destroying all his fingers except the thumb, one at a time. "Speak! Names!"

Walter could not speak. He could only scream. The pain was indescribable.

Hoffmann took the hammer and flung it to the floor in disgust. He left the room, closing the door behind him.

❖ ❖ ❖

The night lights on the fishing boat that arrived roughly a mile south of Venice at 2:00 a.m. were turned off. The captain had fished in these waters at night all his life, but he had no catch in the hold this evening. The boat docked silently and sixteen well-armed men, concealed below, emerged without a sound. Three small delivery trucks were waiting on the dock and quickly loaded their human cargo under false bottoms.

In less than an hour, the three trucks had released their passengers two blocks away from 110 Borgo Pieve. They were Sicilians, Mafia-trained, silent killing their specialty. While expert at their craft, tonight their assignment was more nuanced than usual. Their orders were not to kill. Obviously, they would if they had to, but their charge was to kidnap and neutralize the five Gestapo officers inside and anyone else who might happen by and rescue one hostage if he were still alive, then all were to return to Palermo in the fishing vessel immediately. Don Pasquale was well aware that for every Gestapo killed in an attack by partisans, the Nazis would arrest and murder ten times as many civilians. So, no killing tonight. The Gestapo would simply vanish. With the invasion of Italy at full tilt, it was unlikely the Nazis would be paying much attention to a small operation such as this, especially close to where Allied bombs were falling.

The Sicilians surrounded 110 Borgo Pieve. Silently, they entered the building. Having a detailed description of each floor, including the basement, courtesy of Father Pietro Salerno, they advanced quickly. Three teams of five for each floor, with one man remaining just inside the front door as a lookout.

Upstairs, on the second floor, Colonel Hoffmann slept peacefully. In the living room, the lieutenant and the captain were passed out in comfortable, overstuffed chairs. In the basement, the second lieutenant and the sergeant were fast asleep. Only the prisoner was still awake. The lieutenant and the captain were bound and gagged without a sound. The door to the basement squeaked slightly, but the Mafia soldiers were quick to disarm, bind, and gag the sleeping Gestapo officers guarding the prisoner.

Walter was in poor condition yet raised his head as if to speak. One of the Italians raised his index finger to his lips in the universal sign for "stay quiet." The stairs to the bedroom creaked. Hoffmann, a light sleeper, rose to a sitting position and grabbed his Luger. "Schultz, is that you?"

The door opened and several men rushed in.

Hoffmann fired the Luger twice. One man groaned and fell to the floor. Before Hoffmann could fire again, he felt a sharp, searing pain in his arm, forcing him to drop the gun. An expertly thrown knife had hit its mark. Next, the butt of an old carbine came crashing down on his skull, knocking him unconscious.

In Italian-accented German, the two Gestapo officers in the basement were ordered upstairs and into the back of one of the trucks. Four hardened men pointing carbines at them assured their hasty exit. The two Gestapo in the living room also offered no resistance.

Two men bound and gagged Hoffmann and stuffed him unceremoniously in a large burlap sack.

The fallen assassin slowly got to his feet and said, "I'm all right—shoulder." The other bullet, fortunately, had lodged in one of the pieces of steel he had inserted in each of his vest pockets.

Two other assassins quickly removed the bedding stained with Hoffmann's blood and replaced it with a sheet taken from a linen closet. They shone flashlights, looking for any other bloodstains. There were none they could see. The bag containing Hoffmann was loaded into the third truck, with two of the men guarding him. The wounded assassin also sat in the third truck.

Two Mafiosi returned to the basement and cut Walter loose. He was shivering, sitting in his own waste. It took those two men to hold him upright while a third attempted to clean him up with a couple of towels from the bathroom. They put a large blanket around him and gingerly guided him up the stairs into a truck where the two assassins sat guarding the sack containing Hoffmann. At precisely 3:35 a.m., the trucks returned to the docked fishing boat.

When the fishing boat was roughly three miles offshore at a predetermined coordinate, an American Gato-class submarine emerged from the water. Two of the assassins helped Walter board a dinghy. Four men already in the small boat paddled quickly to the submarine. Several sailors helped Walter board the sub and took him immediately to the sick bay. The assassins returned to the fishing boat for their return trip to Palermo. They had no doubt that Don Pasquale would offer the Gestapo his own version of justice. Hoffmann would receive special attention.

The submarine's cook helped feed Walter some soup, seeing his hands were of no use, mitts of bloody pulp, bones broken beneath the skin into useless shards. Only his left pinkie and right thumb remained unbroken. The doctor aboard the submarine administered morphine for his pain, allowing him to sleep. He had never seen anything like it before. It was as if someone had taken a hammer and deliberately smashed the man's fingers to bits. The doctor thought much of the damage was irreversible, and that a couple of the fingers likely would need to be amputated. The unsanitary conditions in the Gestapo lair and the time that would elapse since the torture would be problematic; the damage to the bones, tendons, joints, and nerves catastrophic.

❖ ❖ ❖

When the sun rose, Father Salerno began his walk toward the local market to secure fresh ingredients for the day's sauce. When he crossed Borgo Pieve, he noticed a slim object shining in the gutter. It was a walking stick. It must have fallen out of the car from which the man with the limp had emerged. The priest picked it up, and instead of going to the market, returned to the church. He examined the cane and noticed a button under the handle. Not sure if it was some newfangled communications device or a weapon from the British MI6, he decided it was best not to find out the hard way. He took it inside and went down to the crypt below the church. He depressed the button, bracing for a bullet or some loud sound. Instead, a stiletto popped out like a switchblade. Too late for it to help now. He said a prayer for the major.

17

BLANDFORD, ENGLAND

Walter was transported to the 22nd General Hospital on 802nd Hospital Centre in Blandford. Several orthopedic surgeons, including Major Marshall R. Urist and Captain Lincoln Ries, who had trained in the United States, evaluated him. They performed the first of several surgeries Walter would endure in Europe.

Unfortunately, the middle and index fingers on his left hand had to be amputated just below the knuckle. He also lost part of the pinkie and forefinger on his right hand and the tip of that index finger. He continued to suffer severe pain, and the doctors told him he would probably experience phantom pain consistent with amputations for the rest of his life.

Major Morris arrived in Blandford to debrief Walter. The young soldier was in a morphine-induced sleep when Morris first saw him. Blood stained the white bandages covering what was left of both of his hands. Notwithstanding the fact he had been told the extent of Walter's injuries, the battle-hardened Morris had to leave the room. He broke down and cried like a child who had lost his most prized possession. *The kid wanted to be a piano player... fucking Gestapo.* He pulled himself together and told the nurse and doctor on the floor that he was ready to speak to Walter, and they would have to lighten the morphine so he could come to. They did so reluctantly.

Walter was able to recall the specifics of Schmitz's betrayal. Morris confirmed that Schmitz had never requested orders from HQ, nor had he sent a cable to the Austrian resistance team alerting them that they had been discovered. He did not provide them instructions to seek the safety of Italy. The only coded cable he did send was to inform his Gestapo handlers that he and the two men were clearing out of the Innsbruck house and would arrive at 110 Borgo Pieve after dark. He included the information that the tall, blond OSS operative had murdered Nina, the Gestapo spy.

As fortune would have it, Schmitz was killed when the Allies bombed the Wiener Neustadt aircraft factory, in large part due to the information provided by the Austrian team. Major Morris seemed terribly disappointed to learn of Schmitz's untimely death. He had sworn to himself that he would kill the traitor with his bare hands.

Walter spent several weeks recuperating in England. He spent many hours speaking with a psychiatrist but still could not process the fact that his piano playing days were over. On September 5, 1943, he boarded the *Queen Mary*, arriving in New York less than a week later.

Hinden, the Remers, and Sam Sonnenschein met Walter when he disembarked. Paula promised herself she would be strong and maintain her composure for Walter's sake. But when she saw his bruised face and looked down at his gauze-mitted hands, she was unable to contain herself. Herbert and Sam hugged him gingerly but also could not help but cry.

Hinden saluted Walter. "I am so sorry, son. I know these words will seem hollow, but your country thanks you. You are a great hero and we are forever indebted to you. Spend a few days with your family. Next week, we'll take the train to Washington, DC. We have an appointment with Dr. Sterling Bunnell at Walter Reed General Hospital. He's the best hand surgeon on the planet."

Walter endured three additional surgeries between October 1943 and the fall of 1944. Bunnell was able to restore some of his hand and finger function. Yet his grip and hand strength would always be limited by the amputations and the sheer degree of damage to the bones, nerves, and tendons. During the long postoperative periods of convalescence at Walter Reed, Walter actually enjoyed the visits from his mother, who could now see him without crying, and Sam Sonnenschein and, occasionally, his father, who was working harder than ever.

He experienced periods of depression, knowing he would never be a concert or jazz pianist. He maintained a regular schedule of visits with a psychiatrist. But when he considered the brave men and women he met in Austria and Switzerland, risking their lives for freedom, and the Nazis' annihilation of European Jewry, he had difficulty feeling sorry for himself. He could certainly return to Columbia and complete his degree or work in the family business. Herbert and Sam would have liked nothing better. And Frank Hinden had offered him a job in the OSS.

"Give it some thought, Walter. We could use your skills and we would be proud to have you. Call me anytime. I mean that. Anytime."

Of course, he was largely dependent on nurses and hospital aides, given his lack of strength and dexterity. Over time, his embarrassment with regard to needing help bathing, or with his bodily functions, or eating and even reading, diminished. Several of the nurses vied for the opportunity to "work on him." He was, after all, blond, blue-eyed, tall, and a handsome war hero who came from an affluent family in New York City.

Janet Silverstein, the twenty-three-year-old head nurse for postoperative patients on Walter's floor, had seniority. She made certain to pull rank frequently and often tended to him. Janet was about five-foot-five without heels, had short, dark hair, brown eyes, an easy manner, and a broad smile. She would read to him often, even on her off-hours. They became something of an item. Almost inseparable.

When Dr. Bunnell informed Walter that there would be no

additional surgeries and it was time for him to go home, his parents came to pick him up for the train ride back to New York. He made certain to offer his profound thanks to all the nurses, doctors, and staff who had seen him through the painful days and dreadful post-op nights. But he had great difficulty conjuring up the words to say farewell to Janet.

She came into his room just as his parents were on the way up to get him. She threw her arms around him and gave him a big hug and kiss on the lips. He gently pulled away, sullen, and said, "Janet, I…I am going home now. Back to New York with my folks. Dr. Bunnell said I wouldn't be having additional surgery. So, I…well, I—"

Janet interrupted him. "Why the sad face? That's good news. It means you're on the road to recovery. And I have some more good news. I am transferring to New York City. I start my new job, head nurse of orthopedic surgery at Columbia Presbyterian Medical Center in two weeks!"

Now Walter beamed. "That's great news, Janet…I thought I might never see you again."

She smiled. "Not on your life, soldier."

PART 3

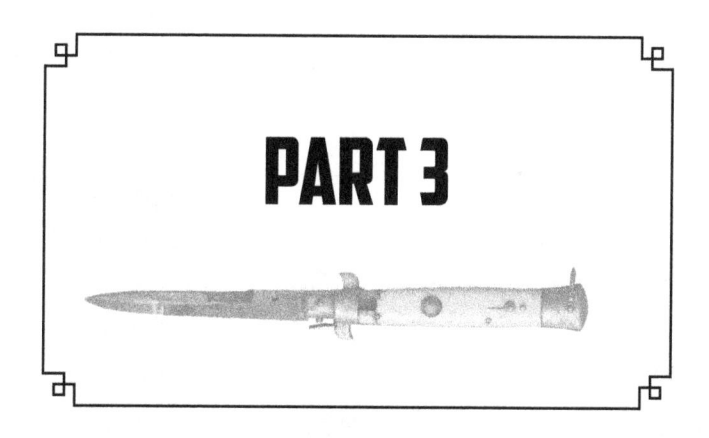

18

BERLIN

June 1943

Just as he was about to go out to purchase some rations, Helmut Weber's phone rang. He immediately recognized the voice on the other end of the line. Completely out of the blue, Heinz Heydrich instructed Helmut to meet him, as he had almost five years before, at Friedrichstrasse and Mittelstrasse in ten minutes. Helmut told Greta and Lily that he had some errands to run and would be back shortly.

As he walked to his rendezvous, Helmut wondered why Heinz Heydrich would contact him now. Was he going to provide the whereabouts of Alfred's ashes for a proper burial? Or was he calling to warn Helmut that the Webers were on the list to be sent east? His mind was racing. He reached the corner just as a large Mercedes came to a stop. "Get in," Heydrich said.

As soon as Helmut was inside the car, Heydrich handed Helmut a buff-colored manila envelope. "Take this, please," he said as he pulled away from the curb. "Open it."

Helmut did as Heydrich said. The envelope contained a set of perfectly forged identity papers bearing Greta's photograph. Monica Huber. Birthdate: November 25, 1907. Hair: Blond. Eyes: Blue. Height: Five-foot-six inches. There was also a Grosser

Ariemachweis, the official Aryan certificate, and a ration card for Monica Huber.

"I don't understand," Helmut said.

Heydrich spoke in a condescending tone. "Herr Weber, your daughter is a Jew. I imagine you have heard Propaganda Minister Goebbels on the radio announce that Berlin has been cleansed of Jews. All Jewish organizations in Berlin have been closed down, and all remaining Jews have been deported to Auschwitz. Any and all Jews who are found will be deported to the East at once. Berlin is *Judenrein*," he repeated. "Your daughter is now Monica Huber. A true German. The real Monica Huber was killed in a car accident. She had no immediate family. The body was cremated."

"Why do you do this, Herr Heydrich?"

"Herr Weber, for your sake there are certain questions that should remain unanswered. I will drop you back at the corner."

"May I be so bold as to ask, what of Greta's son? My grandson? And my housekeeper?"

"I suggest you keep them hidden somewhere where the Gestapo will never find them." The car stopped abruptly. "Good day, Herr Weber."

The Mercedes sped off and Helmut stood at the corner, holding the envelope in his hand. He remained there for what seemed a long time, contemplating what had just occurred. Then he took a detour on the way home and stood silently for a few moments in front of Pariser Platz 7, the home where his dear friends, Max and Martha Liebermann, once lived.

In retrospect, he thought Max was fortunate to have died in 1935, at age eighty-seven, before Kristallnacht. There was no doubt in Helmut's mind that Max had died of a broken heart, with the rise of Hitler. Their daughter, son-in-law, and granddaughter had emigrated to the United States, soon after Kristallnacht. Yet Martha refused to leave her husband's grave. Meanwhile, the Nazis confiscated virtually all her wealth and valuable belongings. On March 5, 1943, the Gestapo had come to arrest her and deport her to Thereseinstadt. Instead, Martha, then eighty-five, took an overdose of veronal, dying five days later in the Jüdisches Krankenhaus, the Jewish Hospital of Berlin. A tear rolled down Helmut's cheek. He gathered himself together and walked home.

In a way, Helmut considered them lucky that the Gestapo hadn't come for Greta, Hans, or Lily yet. He assumed that his being of Aryan stock afforded the family protection. But now, according to Goebbels, Berlin was *Judenrein*. It was clear from Heinz Heydrich's gift that any such advantage would soon disappear.

Helmut entered the flat, and Lily teased him, "So, Helmut, where are the rations? You expect me to make a leg of lamb out of an envelope?"

He couldn't help but smile. "Lily, you are a wonderful cook. If anyone can do it, you can." He looked around. "Where are Greta and Hans?"

"In the dining room. Greta is teaching him mathematics. Papers spread out all over," she replied. Because Jews were not permitted in schools, Greta was teaching her son at home. Fortunately, she had saved her textbooks from her own years at school, so she was able to prepare simple lessons in a variety of subjects: science, geography, literature, mathematics, and a bit of English. Normally, they would work together in the quiet of Helmut's study, but math seemed to require an abundance of space. "It is almost time for lunch. I'll prepare a little something…and I mean just a little, given the meager rations we are allocated. For an appetizer, we can have some bread, potatoes, and jam. Then, for the main course, perhaps some bread, potatoes, and jam," she quipped.

"Well, Lily, lots of people have lost everything," Helmut said, thinking of the Jews who had disappeared from Berlin. "I would imagine the Jews who have been sent to the camps have far less than we do. We should be thankful." Lily looked down at her folded hands, sullen. He touched her shoulder. "I am sorry, Lily. I know you know."

She went to the kitchen to prepare lunch while Helmut walked into the dining room. "Knock, knock," he said. "How is the studying going?" he asked.

"Very well, Papa," Greta replied. "Hans is a mathematical wiz!"

"Oh, Momma, that isn't true," Hans said.

"Hans is too modest."

"I agree," Helmut added. "Let's take some lunch in the kitchen. There is something I have to discuss with you."

They sat down for the expected lunch of bread and jam. Helmut removed the contents of the envelope and handed it to Greta.

"Who is Monica Huber?" She frowned, confused.

"You are, my dear." Helmut described his meeting with Heinz Heydrich. "These papers will entitle you to a ration card. Between mine and yours, we should have sufficient food to eat and fuel to keep warm. It is like a miracle."

"Helmut, the Gestapo has been rounding up Jews. All Jews. They know we live here," Lily interrupted.

"Yes, I know. But this should afford Greta—*Monica*—protection from the Gestapo. Not to mention the extra rations. One hundred percent Aryan she is. Heydrich said we need to find a hiding place for you and Hans should the Gestapo make an appearance, and I have thought of the perfect place. Behind the butler's pantry, there is a panel that leads to the dumbwaiter. I will show you. First, we'll need to take the pots and pans off the shelves, then remove the shelves themselves."

Helmut led them to the butler's pantry. "You see, it slides like a pocket door. When you remove these floorboards—please hold this flashlight, Hans—you can see this ladder that descends to the flat below. At one time the two flats must have been owned by the same people. But later, the residents downstairs closed off the connection with plaster and boards on the other end. There is more than enough room for a few people to sit in here should the Gestapo come calling," he said confidently.

Lily said skeptically, "Helmut, if you haven't noticed, I am not

Marty Glickman or Jesse Owens. If the Gestapo come barging through the door, I doubt we will have enough time to sprint over to the butler's pantry, remove the pots and pans on the shelves in front of the sliding panel, remove the floorboards, and fly down the ladder while you and 'Monica' put everything neatly back in place to fool them."

Helmut sighed. "It is not a perfect plan, Lily, but it is the best I can think of. We should rehearse it a few times to see how long it takes. Just like an air raid. We will practice."

19

SEPTEMBER 25, 1943

"Happy Birthday, Hans!"

Lily placed her best attempt at a cake on the table. She'd used two weeks' worth of sugar rations and a week's worth of butter, plus some cocoa, and whipped up a chocolate cake almost worthy of the occasion. "I couldn't find ten candles, so we will use just one," she said. She lit the candle. "Make a wish, Hans, and blow out the candle."

He closed his eyes and furrowed his brow, deep in thought, then blew.

"I hope all your wishes come true," Greta said, beaming.

"Hear, hear," exclaimed Helmut. "To the man of the hour!"

"Hans, Opa Helmut, Lily, and I got you this…open it," Greta said excitedly.

It was the size of a large shoebox and covered in newspaper.

Hans tore away the paper to reveal a radio. For a boy who smiled little and, frankly, had little to smile about, it was wonderful to see him grinning from ear to ear. "Thank you so much!" He hugged his momma, his opa, and Lily as if they had presented him with a brand-new Maserati 8CL race car.

The radio was a Volksempfänger VE301 Helmut had bought secondhand, likely having previously belonged to a Jewish owner.

To Hans, it meant the world.

Lily said, "Would everyone like some weak tea to wash down the weak cake?" partly in jest.

"No, thank you, Lily. But could I be excused to turn on the radio?" Hans asked.

"By all means," Helmut replied.

"Thank you so much," Hans said and dashed off to his room with his precious gift.

"I have never seen Hans smile so," Lily said. "I could not be happier. No ten-year-old boy should have to live like this."

"You are so right, dear Lily," Helmut said. "Excuse me, I am going to go to see how Hans is doing with the radio. Enjoy your cake and tea. And the birthday cake was very good."

"Opa, this is terrific. I love it. Thank you," Hans said when his grandfather joined him in his room.

"You are very welcome. I have another gift, Hans, but you must promise me that you won't show it to your momma."

"All right, Opa. I promise."

Helmut took a shiny steel instrument from his pocket. "This is a Solingen switchblade." Before handing it to the young boy, he added, "This is a marvelous tool for cutting things and for peeling fruits or vegetables. Perhaps, more importantly, though, it is also a weapon, and heaven forbid you should ever need to use it for that purpose."

Now he handed it to his grandson. "I think you are now old enough to understand how to use it, when it should be used, and why. Of course, it is something you have to be careful with at all times and treat with the utmost respect. Let me show you how it works."

Helmut reached out to depress a small button, and with an almost imperceptible click, the blade deployed, locking instantly into place. "It is very sharp and takes much practice to use properly." He showed Hans the correct way to close the knife. "Here,

Hans. It is yours. My father gave me my first knife when I was ten. I often used it to whittle wood branches or to cut an apple into slices. But my father also taught me how to use it as a weapon of last resort. If you thrust it upward toward an enemy's midsection," he demonstrated with his index finger, "it is easier for him to block than if you thrust it down into his neck or torso. If you must thrust it upward," he pointed with his finger to Hans's own midsection, "you must do so in the belly just below the ribs on his left side, which is the right side you are facing. That will pierce his heart. If you can only do so from the back, jab upward into the left side, again upward into his heart. Or through the kidney. In a life-or-death situation, this is an important thing to know. It requires speed, agility, dexterity, and quite a bit of practice."

"When I was a boy, my papa owned a farm where he raised corn, pumpkins, and potatoes," Helmut continued. "Every year, Papa would make a scarecrow, its belly made from a pillowcase filled with straw. He installed it in the cornfield to scare away the crows. I don't think it ever scared away a single one," he laughed at the memory, "but I would pretend the scarecrow was my mortal enemy and practice on it with my blade. I believe I became quite good at the technique. I snuck up on the scarecrow quite frequently." He smiled. "That's why the saying goes, '*Übung macht den Meister.*' Practice makes perfect.'

"If you practice anything often enough, as you saw when you and Lily pretended to hide in the butler's pantry, you can become very good at it. I will give you an old pillow to practice with. You can keep it under your bed or in some other hiding spot. Just don't let your momma or Lily see you do it.

"I must confess, I have been very fortunate never to have to use a weapon on a real human being. But now, Hans, I am afraid we have many enemies. And our enemies are not as harmless as an old scarecrow. Germany is at war with the Soviets, who would not hesitate to kill us. And there are the Gestapo, who are our enemies from within. Do you understand?"

The boy nodded his head. He had observed Lily cutting and chopping vegetables or chickens or fish with various sharp knives and developed a great respect for them at Lily's warnings. But he had never given consideration to a knife being used as a weapon. He was more than a little surprised that his gentle grandfather knew about such things. But that made the lesson even more impactful. It was something the ever-observant Hans would never forget.

"Thank you, Opa. I will be very careful with it and treasure it always. And I promise never to tell Momma." They shared a conspiratorial smile.

❖ ❖ ❖

Greta knocked on Hans's door. "May I come in? It is time for your science lesson."

"Yes, Momma, I am ready."

"Hans," Greta cried, "what have you done to your radio?" She stared down at all the components arrayed on his desk.

"Don't worry, Momma," Hans said calmly. "I can put it back together. I just wanted to see how it worked."

"Oh my." She shook her head. "I hope so! I can't imagine how we would have it repaired if you couldn't. I will come back in ten minutes so we can work on your science lesson."

"Yes, Momma."

When Greta returned to his room, Hans was listening to his reassembled radio.

Greta, amazed, said, "How did you put it back together so quickly?"

"It was easy, Momma. I just put it back together the same way I took it apart."

"My goodness," she said. "All right, Hans. Please open your science book to page 74. Can you name the organs in the chest?"

Hans pointed to each one, providing the name and a description of its function.

"Very good, Hans. That's excellent. You must have read the next chapter in advance."

"I did, Momma. I like to find out how things work. I find it very interesting," Hans asserted.

"I am very proud of you. That is very clever." Greta rose. "We will be having dinner in an hour. Why don't you do your mathematics homework before we eat?"

"All right."

Greta closed the bedroom door behind herself, smiling. He truly was an exceptional child. Alfred would have been so proud.

Rather than work on his mathematics, Hans opened his closet door. He would do his homework after dinner. Behind two pair of pants and a jacket, affixed to an old music stand, was the pillow Helmut had given him, its filling protruding from the many wounds it had suffered at Hans's hands. He took the switchblade from his pocket and deployed the blade, the click barely audible.

In a well-practiced motion, he swiftly raised the blade repeatedly into the "heart" of the pillow. Then, he pretended to silently approach the pillow from behind and thrust the stiletto-like blade into the "kidney." Almost every evening, after lessons and before dinner, Hans practiced the upward thrusts and downward stabbing motions Helmut had shown him. *Übung macht den Meister.*

20

NOVEMBER 1943

The unmistakable whine of the air raid siren split the silence of the night. While the Nazi leadership had deliberately evacuated many Berliners to the countryside in anticipation of bombings by Allied air forces, many still remained in their homes. In fact, bombing of the capital had inflicted relatively little damage, and casualties were minimal. Berliners became somewhat inured to the routine—air raid sirens followed by the rush to the shelters; the muffled sound of bombardment in the distance and the comforting response of the antiaircraft fire and buzz of Messerschmitts defending the skies; then the all-clear signal, followed by the smell of smoke and gunpowder and the inevitable return home.

Helmut woke, sitting bolt upright in his bed, wiping the sleep from his eyes. He quickly threw on some clothes and raced to wake the others. There was no need. They were already dressed. Each had donned a warm jacket and boots and stood by the front door. Greta stuffed the Monica Huber papers in her inside coat pocket. Lily had a scarf covering most of her face, and Hans, a wool cap pulled low over his forehead. They all kept their clothing at the foot of their beds. Neither Lily nor Hans had the yellow star affixed to any of their clothing. They had removed them long ago. Obviously, one could not wear such identification when entering a shelter; they would be killed or deported at once.

The family hoped that no one would recognize them or pay them any attention during the mayhem of an air raid. Neither Lily nor Hans had left the apartment for anything except air raids for quite some time, so it was unlikely their neighbors would know their faces. They had rehearsed what to say if they were asked for their papers. Helmut would show his and Greta, hers, and then apologize for Lily, her forgetful, daft old mother, for leaving her identification at home. "She was in such a hurry," Greta would say, and Hans, "You know little boys...lucky he even put on his boots" —all reasonable under the circumstances.

Once inside the shelter, the local air raid marshal, Frederick Werner, herded everyone along. While there had been a fair number of occasions since 1941 when the air raid sirens sounded, only a few Allied air attacks reached Berlin, and all of them had been considered light and did very little damage to residential neighborhoods. Still, Berliners were urged to take air raids seriously.

There was something different about this one, however. Everyone who had descended into the shelter could feel it, could almost touch it. Rumor had it that the Allies had improved their radar technology and were preparing to send a clear message to the Reich.

The bombings of November 18 and 19, the beginning of the Battle of Berlin, resulted in very few casualties, but the earth-shaking concussions from bombs exploding just a few kilometers away were frightening. Berliners emerged from the shelters relieved but shaken. Smoke from fires and the structural damage to some buildings were grim reminders that the war was far from won, despite what Goebbels said.

The longer-than-usual stay in the shelter this time was especially disquieting for Helmut and Greta. While they hunched together in their space, a former neighbor and rabid National Socialist Party member, Otto Gunther, stared at Greta. Helmut was certain he was an informant for the Gestapo. Helmut and Greta avoided eye contact with him, but his attention was unnerving.

Finally, he came over to where they huddled. "You look very familiar, young lady. Do I know you?" he asked Greta.

"I don't believe so," she replied.

"What is your name?" he persisted.

"My name is Monica Huber. I don't believe I have ever made your acquaintance, sir."

He scowled, looked her up and down again before walking back to his spot. Periodically, he looked back at her, clearly not satisfied.

When the air raid marshal gave the all-clear, the shelter's occupants began returning home.

They had almost reached their building when Gunther tapped Greta on the shoulder and stopped her with a menacing stare. "You are Helmut Weber's daughter, are you not?"

Helmut came to stand between them and asserted angrily, "She most certainly is not. Who do you think you are?"

Greta announced, "Helmut Weber is obviously not my father. Anyone can see that. We look nothing alike. But he was kind enough to take me into his home when my husband was killed on the Eastern Front. Here, look, if you must. These are my papers. There is no need to be so unpleasant. We are all in this together, are we not?"

Gunther took his time looking them over, then said unapologetically, "I am sorry, Frau Huber. I beg your pardon." He turned and without another word walked toward his building.

Helmut, Greta, Lily, and Hans walked quickly to their flat more unsettled by the confrontation with Gunther than by the air raid itself.

❖ ❖ ❖

The air raid sirens blared again a few days later. Berliners once again rushed to their bomb shelters. As Helmut descended into theirs, he saw Otto Gunther drive up in a BMW R75 motorcycle and sidecar. Gunther parked it across the street from the entrance to the shelter. Helmut and Greta tried to avoid eye contact with him, but he continued to stare.

The shelling this time seemed to come closer and was even louder. The concussive force of the large bombs exploding nearby shook the walls of the shelter, sending dust and dirt everywhere. The acrid smell of smoke from the fires on the street was nauseating. It filled the nostrils with a stench that would not go away, an uncomfortable reminder of the death and devastation wrought by the war.

Finally, after an almost unceasing barrage from the sky lasting nearly forty minutes, the bombing ended. Air Raid Marshal Werner slowly climbed to the street, then solemnly issued the all-clear. Fires were burning, buildings nearby blasted to dust, craters lay where smoothly paved streets once carried midday traffic. Werner instructed them to be careful, to take inventory of their belongings, and to check on their loved ones when they returned home.

Otto Gunther jumped on his motorcycle and took off, snarling and jabbing an accusatory finger at Greta and Helmut as he passed. It was as if he thought they were personally responsible for the Allied bombing. Helmut and Greta worried that Gunther intended to inform on them, or at least suggest to the Gestapo that they be investigated. They returned home and tried to calm themselves.

Lily prepared a meal of potato soup and bread with jam. Helmut and Greta nibbled their food without appetite, fraught with worry. But Hans was famished and ate with gusto.

Helmut offered, "Lily, you've outdone yourself. Potato soup never tasted so grand." Lily was pleased.

Hours later, the sirens sounded again. It was terrifying. Where was the Luftwaffe to protect them? Was Berlin indefensible? Was there even an ounce of truth to Goebbels's broadcasts? Would the bombing ever stop? Berliners rushed back to their shelters.

Just as Helmut, Greta, Lily, and Hans made it to their usual spot, the entire shelter shook, pieces of the concrete ceiling crumbing around them. Had a bomb exploded directly on top of them? Everyone held each other tightly; families, friends, and total strangers united in fear. Children cried in their mothers' arms and adults trembled, their faces ashen.

When the bombing had finally ceased, Werner had difficulty opening the steel door at the entrance of the shelter. Two soldiers who happened to be on leave and were sheltering in the underground bunker helped Werner crack the door open. A four-story building that once stood across the street had been flattened, many small fires emanating from the rubble. The stench was horrendous.

Helmut and Hans had to help Lily up to the street. She said she was feeling dizzy and was having difficulty breathing. She was rather unsteady on her feet and was bleeding from a cut on her forehead. It seemed a piece of the concrete that had dislodged from the ceiling must have struck her. Werner suggested they get her to a hospital, "if there are any still standing."

Helmut sat her down on a piece of concrete that had once been part of the art deco building which had formerly stood nearby. Helmut noticed Gunther's motorcycle and sidecar across the street, turned on its side. It occurred to him then that he had not seen the man on their last trip to the shelter. Turning his head, he spotted, roughly twenty feet way, Gunther's twisted body lying in the street, his eyes open, blood at the corner of his mouth.

Helmut went over and knelt over his body, putting his fingers on Gunther's throat. There was no pulse.

Werner walked by and shook his head, murmuring something to himself.

Helmut motioned to Hans. "Come here and help me with this. On the count of three, let's push the motorcycle upright."

Seeing their struggle, one of the soldiers who had helped open the door to the shelter helped Helmut and Hans right the motorcycle and sidecar.

"Is this your bike, sir?" the soldier asked.

"No," Helmut replied, "it's his." He pointed to Gunther's body.

"Well, I'd say it's yours now," the soldier responded. "Stay safe, if you can." He tipped his helmet and went on his way.

Seeing that Lily was in no condition to walk, Helmut and Hans ushered her to the sidecar. Helmut hadn't ridden a motorcycle in many years, but some things you never forgot.

Surprisingly, the BMW started almost immediately. That was one thing about German engineering: It seldom disappointed.

"Lily, I am going to take you to a hospital," he said.

"No, Helmut, you can't," she protested. "If you take me to a hospital, they will deport me right away."

"But you are hurt, Lily. You must have medical attention at once."

Greta said, "Papa, Lily is right. We can't take her. Let's see if we can get her home first and then figure out what to do."

Helmut sighed. He didn't want to add what he was thinking—that the building in which they lived could have been flattened just like the ones around them. But he climbed on the motorcycle beside Lily and, when they arrived a few blocks away, discovered that their home stood unscathed. Helmut parked the motorcycle in front of the building and waited for Greta and Hans to join them so they could help him get Lily to their flat.

As a precaution, even though the incidence of vehicle theft was low in Berlin, Helmut instructed Hans to remove the spark plugs from the bike. In the future, Hans made it a habit to take out the spark plugs and put them in his pocket whenever he or Helmut were not riding the motorcycle.

Miraculously, there was no damage to their building or several other surrounding buildings. Perhaps even more amazing, the elevator was still functioning, as was all the electricity. Helmut and Greta helped Lily up to the apartment and settled her on the couch when they arrived. Greta covered her with several blankets and made her some hot tea, but Lily could barely take a sip.

Greta motioned for Helmut to join her in the kitchen, "Papa, we are going to have to get Lily to a doctor. She is burning up with fever."

"I agree she needs to be seen by a doctor, but Lily is right. How can she go to a hospital? They will demand her papers, and within moments she will be arrested and deported."

Greta had an idea. "Papa, do you think it can be true that the Jewish Hospital is still open? I overheard someone in the shelter complaining that 'real Germans' were cowering in bomb shelters while Jews 'basked in the protection of the Jewish Hospital.'"

"I suppose it is possible," Helmut said. "Anyway, I don't think we have much choice."

While Goebbels had insisted that Berlin was *Judenrein* months before, the fact was that several thousand Jews still lived in Berlin. Some, like Greta, who had Aryan features and had acquired false papers, lived in plain sight. Others were hidden by Gentiles, while still others were "patients" in the Jewish Hospital of Berlin. For the duration of the war, the hospital treated Jewish people. By and large, these Jews were married to Aryans, affording them a degree of protection. Others were VIPs who either had converted to Christianity or were under the protection of someone high up in the Nazi party for some reason or another. All the doctors and nurses were Jewish and required to wear yellow stars on their clothing. Throughout the war, many of the healthcare workers and patients were deported to Auschwitz, but the hospital was always staffed by Jewish professionals. The hospital operated under the supervision of the RSHA, the Reich's main security office, under the auspices of Heinrich Himmler.

With the help of both Hans and Greta, Helmut was able to get Lily back into the BMW's sidecar. She was still feverish, passing in and out of consciousness. Helmut had little choice but to find her a doctor; it was obvious she needed medical attention right away.

They drove north on the Friedrichstrasse and passed through

vehicular traffic and a parade of pedestrians: homeless Berliners carting what was left of their belongings through the streets, hoping to find relatives or friends with vehicles to escape what now seemed to be the Allies' primary target.

Twenty minutes later, they arrived at the grounds of the Jewish Hospital, which somehow remained unscathed through the recent bombardments, another miracle. Helmut stopped in front of the main entrance. It was a large complex, with a manicured lawn, so out of place in the streets they had just traveled, a seemingly peaceful island in a sea of madness.

Two Gestapo guards stood at the door. "Papers," one demanded.

Helmut presented his identification papers and Aryan certificate.

The same guard said, "We are sorry, Herr Weber, this hospital is only for Jews. Aryans are not permitted to be treated here."

"Thank you, Obersturmführer," Helmut said carefully, "but I am not here for myself. It is for my partner." He motioned to the sidecar. "Her name is Lily Schwarz…she is my wife. My common-law wife. Here are her papers."

The lieutenant examined the papers. "This is highly unusual. A common-law Jew wife. I will have to consult with my superiors. I shall be right back."

As the officer turned to enter the building, an officious-looking man in a white coat, followed by two orderlies wearing yellow stars and pushing a gurney, approached the doorway.

"Lieutenant, what do we have here?" the man asked.

The officer responded with a note of reverence, as if the man had a higher rank than he, notwithstanding the yellow star on his white coat and his lack of stature. "Herr Doctor Doctor, this gentleman claims to be the common-law husband of this Jew. She seems very ill. What shall we do with her?"

Walter Lustig, who insisted on being referred to as Herr Doctor Doctor to reflect his two degrees—medical and philosophy—was employed by the RSHA as medical director of the hospital. He had converted to Christianity in his youth and was married to an Aryan woman. Lustig essentially made the decisions as to who was treated at the hospital and who was deported to Auschwitz or Thereseinstadt.

Lustig barked orders to the orderlies to remove Lily from the sidecar and take her inside, and he would personally examine her. "Herr Weber," he said, "I will see what I can do. I suggest you go home just in case we suffer another air raid by those villainous Americans and Brits." He turned and began to walk inside.

"Herr Doctor Doctor, if I may be so bold, when or how shall I check on the condition of my wife?" Helmut pleaded.

"You may come back in a day or two to check. Goodbye, Herr Weber." Lustig disappeared behind the doors of the hospital.

Helmut stood next to the motorcycle for a moment. He was still uncertain whether he had done the right thing by bringing Lily there, and now he had left her all alone. He had not been quick or forceful enough to ask if he could stay with her or ask the doctor questions about her care. An overwhelming sadness washed over him. It was too late for him to do any more then, so he sighed, then started the BMW and returned to the flat, where Greta and Hans anxiously awaited news about Lily.

Inside the hospital, Dr. Lustig examined Lily. The wound on her head had become infected, likely causing the fever. He cleaned it and treated it with sulfa. He suspected the patient had suffered a concussion and was suffering from a touch of delirium as a result of the head trauma. She would probably be better in a day or so. The more formidable issue was whether to include her on the next transport or not. He had the unenviable task of fulfilling Gestapo quotas from his inventory of Jewish patients and personnel. Generally, his recommendations were rubber-stamped by the Gestapo officer in charge. It quickly became clear that the patient, Lily Schwarz, was not, in fact, married to an Aryan, so

Lustig could easily make a case for her deportation.

His job was always a difficult one, but it had to be done. He included her name on the list to be deported to Thereseinstadt the next day.

The next afternoon, Helmut rode the motorcycle to the Jewish Hospital. There were different guards at the hospital's entrance now.

"Good afternoon," he greeted them. "My name is Helmut Weber. I came here yesterday and met with Herr Doctor Doctor Lustig. He instructed me to return today for information on a patient. May I speak with him, please?"

A hauptscharführer said coldly, "Your papers, please." Helmut handed them over. "I shall be back momentarily, Herr Weber." He turned on his heels and entered the hospital.

A few minutes later, the master sergeant returned. "Herr Weber, Herr Dr. Dr. Lustig is not available. Would you be able to return next week?"

"I would be happy to wait for him."

"I am sorry, Herr Weber, but he will not be available either today or tomorrow."

It was clear Lustig was avoiding him. Helmut tried another tack. "Herr Hauptscharführer, would you be so kind as to check on the condition of Lily Schwarz? She is my wife."

The master sergeant stammered for a moment, then said, "I shall be right back," and disappeared into the hospital. When he came back this time, he said, "Herr Weber. I have good news. The patient Schwarz was well enough to be released to Thereseinstadt, a transit camp, for a period of rehabilitation and rest."

Helmut's heart dropped. "Hauptscharführer, where is this transit camp located, and where will she be spending the time resting? I am certain she would be much better off doing that at home, with me caring for her. I will go immediately to get her so the Reich may be spared the expense of travel and rehabilitation."

The hauptscharführer replied, "That would be impossible. Good day."

Helmut felt himself becoming extremely agitated. As he took a step toward the master sergeant, the other guard raised his weapon, pointing it at Helmut. The hauptscharführer raised his voice. "Herr Weber, I suggest you leave immediately and not return. Do you understand?"

Helmut was in a state of shock, of total disbelief. What had they done to Lily? Where had they taken her? Thereseinstadt, the master sergeant said. He had heard of it. No one ever returned from Thereseinstadt.

He had no idea what to do. He wanted to strike the man in the head with his own gun. He wanted to slaughter both guards and then find Herr Doctor Doctor and kill him. But he knew he was powerless. He returned to the motorcycle and rode home. He did not recall what route he took, or how he got there. What would he tell his family?

Greta could see that her father was distressed the minute he walked into the flat. "Sit down, Papa," she said, taking his arm. "You look shaken. What happened? Hans, please get Opa some tea."

Helmut explained what had transpired.

"Papa, we must find Lily," Greta cried. "We will go to Gestapo headquarters. They must have records of everyone who is deported."

"Perhaps it would be better if I went alone. What if one of the Gestapo animals recognizes you? And even if they don't, if you appear as Monica Huber, what reason can you give them for asking about Lily's whereabouts? I can at least still insist I am her common-law husband."

"Lily is my momma. I have to go with you…no matter what," Greta insisted.

Helmut thought for a moment, then chose his words carefully. "I understand how you feel, my dear. But I lost your mother. I cannot afford to lose you, too. Hans cannot afford to lose you. I am sorry, but I cannot let you come with me. I will go right away."

She sighed deeply, realizing her father was right. "Oh, Papa, please be careful," she said, hugging Helmut.

"I will. I promise. Hans, take care of your momma."

"Yes, Opa. I will," Hans promised.

It took less than fifteen minutes for Helmut to take the BMW to Prinz Albrecht-Strasse 8. One of the guards in front of the heavily fortified building requested Helmut's papers, then inquired about the purpose of his visit.

Within a few minutes, Franz Karl, once lieutenant, now major, came out, two Gestapo apes trailing him. He offered Helmut a snakelike smile and said, "Herr Weber. So nice to see you again. I am pleased to see you are surviving the war in such fine fettle. It appears that the woman you claim is your wife, the Jewess Schwarz—to whom you are not legally married—was transferred from the Jew hospital to Thereseinstadt. I cannot intercede in any decision made by hospital staff, but rest assured that your 'wife' will be in good hands. I understand Thereseinstadt is a lovely place for elderly Jews. I am sure she will enjoy a restful and relaxing stay."

Helmut said, "Major. I believe Lily would be far better off at home with me. Besides, I can spare the Reich the cost of her expensive accommodations if you can help me bring her back."

Major Karl smirked. "Herr Weber, are you offering me a bribe to find the Schwarz woman? If you are, I want you to know that bribing a Gestapo officer is a serious offense, punishable with a long prison sentence."

"No, sir, I am not doing that at all. I am just suggesting that I can be of service to the Reich by taking care of Lily's rehabilitation and spare the Reich that cost," Helmut replied carefully.

Karl said, "That is very kind of you indeed, Herr Weber. But I am afraid it is out of my hands. Heil Hitler!" As he was about to turn to go back inside, he hesitated for a moment and said, "Oh, by the way, Herr Weber, how is that lovely daughter of yours?"

Helmut knew he was defeated. *Oh, Lily,* he thought, *I only hope to God that you do not suffer…* but he had no intention of accidentally betraying his sense of defeat. "Herr Major, my daughter left the country years ago. When I see her after the war, I will be sure to share with her your interest."

Major Karl smiled. "Good day, Herr Weber."

Helmut returned home dejected. He relayed everything that had occurred to Greta and Hans. Now his poor child had lost two mothers. It was unbearable. But there was nothing either of them could have done to save their dear Lily.

Greta hugged her papa and wept. Then, they turned to young Hans and they both hugged him for a long time.

Hans, as always, showed little emotion, though he seemed even more quiet than usual. Greta thought, *No little boy should have to suffer such unbearable loss again and again.* He had lost his papa, two of his grandparents, and now Lily.

Later that evening, after Helmut and Greta had gone to bed, each aided in that endeavor by several snifters of brandy, Hans repeatedly attacked the pillow in his closet with his switchblade. He pretended it was Major Karl, whose face he remembered distinctly from the visit to Gestapo headquarters with his mother when they were hoping to find information about his father following Kristallnacht, even though that was half a lifetime ago. This was a cathartic exercise for a ten-year-old who had few other outlets with which to process his anger.

Hans was always conscious of the advice his grandfather had given him after his birthday. Anger was a dangerous emotion. It led to irrational thoughts and left one vulnerable. Helmut had told him that to overcome anger, one's best weapon was to have resolve. To be sure of oneself. Certainty of purpose, discipline, self-confidence, and self-respect were the recipes for victory over anger.

It was a hard lesson to grasp for a boy his age. But Opa Helmut was always right. In fact, Opa said if one could harness that resolve, one could even gain an advantage over a much larger and better-armed opponent. Speed, strength, agility, and stealth. Strike when your enemy is most vulnerable. And remember, practice makes perfect. It didn't make a lot of sense, but it stuck in his mind.

Stabbing the pillow helped to exhaust him, but Hans was still very much awake. And distraught. To calm himself, because he knew brandy was not an option for him, Hans had taken to doing calisthenics: jumping jacks, push-ups, sit-ups. The rhythm of the exercises brought him to a state of relaxation. After a while, he lay down and slept, fitfully.

21

The loss of Lily's companionship, humor, and love weighed heavily upon Helmut, Greta, and Hans. Her absence, coupled with the terror of the nearly nightly bombing raids during the next several months, left a palpable, almost indescribable sadness.

Yet they recognized that they were fortunate that following each bombardment, they could return to their undamaged Unterlinden flat. After all, by the end of 1943, more than a quarter of Berlin's residential real estate was uninhabitable. Still, it was a lonely existence. There was no socializing in the shelters. They kept to themselves for fear of leaks to the Gestapo. Following the incident with Otto Gunther, Greta did not venture anywhere except to the shelter during an air raid. Helmut continued to shop for food and supplies with their ration cards. Greta busied herself by teaching Hans his lessons, and the boy grew up quickly in a surreal world. Any semblance of a normal life was gone; there was no Lily to hold things together.

After March 1944, the US Air Force and the RAF bombardment of Berlin subsided considerably, giving the people who remained in the city a respite from the carnage. Instead, the Allies were concentrating their resources on taking back France and Italy, while the Soviets continued to make the German army suffer for every inch they occupied in the East.

By the beginning of 1945, the walls were caving in on Germany. The Allies were closing in from every direction. With the upper hand, the Allied leaders' objective was simple: end the war as expeditiously as possible. Force the Nazis' unconditional surrender. While military victory could still take some time, the Allies reasoned that surrender could be accelerated by breaking German civilian morale. On February 3, 1945, approximately one thousand US Air Force bombers, accompanied by over five hundred fighters, attacked Berlin. The capital's air defenses had been cut back considerably. The Luftwaffe was employing its beleaguered resources primarily on the battlefronts rather than defending its cities and civilian centers. The overwhelming show of force by the US Air Force was met by little resistance.

The air raid sirens blared. Greta, Helmut, and Hans raced down the stairs to the street, wearing winter boots, wool coats, and mittens. They did not dare take the elevator, just in case the electricity went out or a shell hit. Being trapped in an elevator during a bombing raid could be a death sentence. Helmut started the BMW and Hans jumped on the seat behind him, his arms wrapped around his grandfather's waist, while Greta hopped into the sidecar. They rushed to their shelter at the Berlin Zoo and just barely made it inside before the bombs started to fall.

They found their usual space and huddled together, preparing for a prolonged stay. It seemed there were fewer and fewer shelter "residents" with each air raid. Some found shelter elsewhere, some evacuated to relatives in the countryside, and others were killed in air raids before making it to safety.

Helmut was a bit more out of breath than usual as he sat down on the low seat next to Greta and Hans. Rushing to the shelter with one's few important belongings and one's loved ones took its toll. Now in his mid-seventies, he would be the first to admit he wasn't as young or as fit as he used to be. He gratefully accepted Greta's canteen and sipped some water.

Greta fished out some fried potato slices from her small bag and passed them to Helmut and Hans. Greta had, of late, become quite the chef. Considering that she had very little to work with, she had somehow come up with a recipe for crispy fried potatoes that had become a family favorite. Hans devoured them. Helmut had a few, but he had had a bout of indigestion in the last few days, so he was going easy on fried food.

It seemed as if they could hear and feel the impact of each and every one of the massive bombs dropped on the streets of Berlin. While the deep bunker was well protected, the pounding of the bombs was louder and more frequent than ever before. Greta had many a nightmare about being buried alive. She could only imagine the nightmares that woke Hans at night. Remarkably, he didn't complain or show any fear.

Each of them had taken a book from Helmut's library as part of their emergency bag. Hans had a book on automobiles; Greta was reading *Vom Winde Verweht*, Margaret Mitchell's story of Scarlett O'Hara; and Helmut, a biography of Beethoven. Helmut had read the book many times, Greta knew, because it reminded him of Sophia. It seemed to lull him to sleep.

After several terrifying hours of pounding from above and the smell of smoke from the inevitable fires, old Frederick Werner signaled the all-clear. Once again, it was time to take stock of the damage. An uneasy quiet had overtaken the shelter residents. Generally, after a raid, some would chat with strangers about having survived yet another bombing raid. Some would sing softly to themselves, others would quietly gather their belongings, and still others would make the sign of the cross and utter a brief prayer. This time, one only heard the shuffling of feet toward the exit to the street.

Greta put her belongings in her satchel and said, "Come, Hans. Come, Papa. Let's go home."

Hans put his things together and stood. "Come on, Opa, we can go now."

Helmet was still asleep. Greta gently tapped him on the shoulder. "Time to wake up, Papa."

He fell to the floor.

Greta screamed.

Frederick Werner shouted with his megaphone, "Is there a doctor, please? Is there a doctor here?"

"I am a doctor," said an elderly man. He knelt and felt for a pulse in Helmut's wrist. He looked up at Greta and Hans. "I am very sorry, madam. He is gone. A heart attack, I would think."

Greta fell to her knees and threw her arms around her father. "No, no, no. Oh Papa." She wept and shook uncontrollably. Hans knelt down and Greta hugged him tightly. Though he had died peacefully, the loss was overwhelming and impossible to comprehend. "Dear, sweet Papa. Always kind, understanding, and compassionate. How can God take you from us? We need you," she whispered.

"Momma," Hans said, "we will see Opa soon in heaven. He will wait for us there." Hans turned to Helmut. "I love you, Opa. You are my best friend. I will miss you very much. We will see you soon in heaven with Papa, won't we?" Hans, who seldom showed any emotion, wept.

Frederick Werner offered his condolences. "I am very sorry for your loss. I do not mean to interrupt your grieving, but I am sorry to have to inform you that there are strict regulations regarding deceased individuals in the bunker. We will have to move his body to the cemetery for burial. Again, my condolences."

Werner ordered his two assistants to put Helmut's remains on a stretcher. "We will have to take him to the Dorotheenstadt Cemetery. The ground is very hard because it is so cold, but graves are always dug in anticipation of the bombings." He turned back to Greta after preparing a paper and handing it to her. "Please take this. It will identify the deceased. Bring it to the cemetery tomorrow and ask for Dieter Spector. He will perform the burial ceremony. He is a very good man. Again, please accept my condolences."

There would be no time to grieve or mourn. There would be no way to arrange a proper burial for Helmut, to take his body to Halle and lay him to rest next to his beloved Sophia.

Much of the zoo and Tiergarten were obliterated. The ground was littered with massive craters from exploded ordnance. It looked like illustrations of the moon. Buildings throughout the neighborhood were leveled. Fires burned in every direction. Smoke burned the nostrils with every breath. Berlin was on fire.

Incredibly, the motorcycle was still exactly where they left it. It somehow stood unscathed, near the front of the flak tower leading to the shelter. Greta looked at the BMW. *Papa*, she thought, *what do I do now?*

Hans took her hand. "Momma, I know how to drive it."

"Why not?" Greta said at last with resignation. "We should go home. It is cold. Too cold to stand here."

She got in the sidecar and Hans started the bike, then maneuvered it to the Unterlinden. The once-magnificent street was unrecognizable. The buildings surrounding it on both sides were largely destroyed. Their building was almost entirely flattened, with small fires burning inside. They tried scrounging through the rubble, but it was too dangerous. Between the heat from the fires and the instability of the shattered concrete, it was impossible to navigate inside. They could come back in a few days, perhaps, to see if anything was salvageable. They were homeless now. Like so many others.

"We will have to go back to the bunker. We have nowhere to go," Hans said, turning the motorcycle.

They returned to the shelter, and Werner allowed them and any other "patrons" of the shelter to stay there if they had been rendered homeless by the bombings, but he indicated it could not be a permanent arrangement. He was able to direct them to several new locations to obtain rations after others were destroyed during raids.

❖ ❖ ❖

It was a bitterly cold February morning. Hans drove the motorcycle north to the Dorotheenstadt Cemetery. They arrived at eleven o'clock and asked for Dieter Spector, then showed him the tag Werner had given them.

Spector was an elderly man with warm blue eyes and a white beard, bundled up in a long wool coat with fur on the collar, a woolen hat, and mittens. "Ah, yes, Helmut Weber. I am sorry for your loss. Will you follow me, please?"

The cemetery, mostly undisturbed by the recent bombings, was like an oasis in the desert. Spector led them to an area where half a dozen graves had been dug in the frozen ground. Two workers, clapping their gloved hands together to keep warm, stood next to a simple wooden casket that had been placed between the last two graves. "Here we have it," Spector said. "Helmut Weber. You may kneel by the casket and say some final words on behalf of the dear departed one if you wish."

Greta and Hans knelt next to the casket. Her voice cracking, Greta said, "Papa, you have always been my rock. You have been my light in my darkest moments. I don't know how we will go on without you. I promise that you will live forever in our hearts. I love you so much. I will miss you forever." Tears streamed down her face. She still could not believe he was gone.

Hans hugged his mother, then turned to the casket. "Opa, you were my best friend. You were my hero. I hope that there is another world to come so I can see you again. I hope you will be proud of me. I promise to take care of Momma. I love you very much."

They held each other for what seemed a long time before Dieter Spector made a sound as if to clear his throat, signifying it was time to lower Helmut's remains into the earth. He nodded to the workers. Then, they covered the casket with dirt.

❖ ❖ ❖

Greta pulled her woolen hat low over her forehead and drew her scarf completely around her face, leaving just enough bare so she could see. Hans always wore his cap low over his head, but his mother, even on a cold day like this one, rarely tied her scarf around her face. Lily used to tease her about her vanity: "You must be freezing like the rest of us, but I imagine the boys would otherwise not be able to see you."

Greta would throw back her head and snap, "Oh, that's so silly, Lily," even though she knew it was true.

Now, however, the way she tied the scarf was deliberate. From the corner of her eye, as Helmut's casket was lowered into the ground, she'd thought she saw, standing on the other side of the cemetery fence, perhaps 100 meters away, three Gestapo men. She was certain one of them was Franz Karl.

When they got to the street, Hans turned to his mother. As if he were reading her thoughts, he said, "I saw them too. The Gestapo. They were watching us."

Greta's heart sank. Her thoughts raced. How would they know they were there? Could Werner have told them? But why would he? He had seen the family together during countless air raids and never said a word. Had he waited until Helmut died to inform on them? Why would he even suspect Greta was Jewish?

Maybe there was some other reason the Gestapo was following them. Could Gunther have informed on them before he died? Or was Werner simply doing his duty as an air raid warden, submitting the names of the recently deceased to the police? Either way, it did not matter. They couldn't go back to the same shelter next time there was a bombing.

"Hans, I am afraid we will have to go in separate directions to throw them off. You take the motorcycle. Go south, toward the Unterlinden. I know there is nothing but rubble there, but they will have a hard time following you if you are quick. I will go east to the Alexanderplatz and hide in the subway shelter there. There are usually a fair number of people milling around. Hopefully, I can join the crowd and not be noticed. It is noon now. I will meet you right back here at six o'clock. It will be dark then, and they may have grown tired of looking for us."

Hans cried, "No, Momma. I want to stay with you."

Greta cupped his face in her hands. "Dear Hans. You are everything in the world to me. But you have to survive. For me. For Opa. For Lily. For Papa. Here …" She handed him a battered old gray leather wallet. "It holds everything that is important. Go, Hans. Please." She hugged him tightly. Kissed him on the cheek. "I love you. Until six o'clock."

Without a word, Hans started the bike and headed south. Greta walked briskly, parallel to the cemetery fence, heading east.

✧ ✧ ✧

Major Karl heard the unmistakable rumble of the BMW. "Let's go," he shouted, then jumped in the back of the staff car while the two Gestapo officers hopped in the front. It was slow going for the large Mercedes. Navigating the rubble-strewn streets was very difficult and they had to go more slowly than Karl would have liked. Bending an axle or blowing a tire would be a disaster.

When they finally were able to proceed more quickly on a smooth patch of road, the driver shouted, "Major, we have lost the motorbike."

"*Scheisse*!" Karl cursed. "Turn around. Go back to the cemetery. We will interrogate the attendants to see if they can provide anything helpful."

❖ ❖ ❖

The bike came to a halt a block from the building Hans's family once called home. As proficient as he had become at driving, he could no longer navigate the boulder-size rubble that littered what now covered the Unterlinden. He had several hours before he would join with his mother, so he thought he would see now if there was anything he could recover from the building, assuming the fires had burned out.

Hans crawled through what remained, but it quickly became obvious that anything inside the flats had been crushed or burned. He sat down in a crevice between two large hulks of concrete that must once have been parts of the roof. It was a rather cozy spot, he decided after a moment, like a small cave, with the wind and cold blocked. The fires and smoke covering Berlin served to keep the air warmer than usual on a February day, though the acrid smell from the fires that had consumed much of his neighborhood seared the nostrils and was impossible to avoid.

Suddenly, Hans realized how hungry he was. He ate the few remaining slices of Momma's fried potato and took a small sip from his canteen, realizing he would have to conserve what little water he had left.

He would join Momma in a few hours outside the cemetery and, together, they would devise a plan. First, they would acquire some rations and fresh water and leave Berlin. Surely any place far from Berlin and the Gestapo would do, so long as they had each other. There was nothing left for them here.

Hans opened the tattered wallet his mother had given him. It held a ration card. Hans's identification card. A photograph of a little boy he recognized as himself with Momma, Papa, Opa Helmut, Opa Josef, and Oma Bette, all standing in front of a large painting. Happy times he could just barely recall. A piece of folded stationery with the letters "UBS" and an address in Switzerland, followed by a series of numbers and his papa's name, Alfred Sternlicht, neatly typed on it. Lastly, a small wax paper envelope containing a lock of blond hair with the words, "Yours Truly, RH" written on it. He understood the contents of the wallet to be his mother's most valuable possessions. He would keep them safe.

At precisely 6:00 p.m., Hans parked the BMW across from the entrance to the cemetery. Momma was clever. No one would want to be near a cemetery after dark. Regardless, he kept his antenna up for signs of Franz Karl or anyone else wearing a Gestapo uniform.

Hans looked at his watch, a gift from his Opa Helmut. It had belonged to Opa's Papa. It was 6:15. No Momma. Perhaps she had misjudged the time it would take to walk from the Alexanderplatz subway station to the cemetery. It was getting very cold. He walked back and forth to the corner just to keep warm, but still there was no sign of Momma.

It was now seven o'clock. Something was wrong. Momma would never be this late unless something bad had happened. Hans saw that the gate to the cemetery was still open, and the light was on in the small house where Dieter Spector had Momma sign some papers. Hans walked over to the house and knocked on the door. He could see someone look out the window, and then the door opened.

"Hurry and get in," Spector said, quickly closing the door behind Hans. Dieter's right eye was black-and-blue and swollen shut. "Shortly after we buried Herr Weber, the Gestapo came. They were looking for your mother; she is your mother, yes? I swore to them that I had no idea where she went. Still, they beat me. I am sorry, but one of my workmen…he panicked…he is a good soul, but he told them that your momma walked east. They left at once. May God have mercy on her soul."

Hans cried, "Where would they take her? I have to find her!"

"My son, I know she is your momma, of course, but I wouldn't…I mean, the Gestapo…they would…" Spector said, shaking his head.

Hans knew. They would take her to Gestapo headquarters. He knew what had happened to his Papa, and to Opa Josef. "I must go, Herr Spector," he said.

"Wait, son. Here, take some bread and fill your canteen. Get away from here. Save yourself," Spector advised.

"Thank you," Hans said and left the house.

Dieter Spector began to pray.

❖ ❖ ❖

Hans grabbed some broken tree branches near the cemetery's entrance. Though it was dark, he drove back to the same spot near the Unterlinden where he had parked the bike earlier. Then he crawled over the rubble to the cave-like place he had spent the afternoon. The street was deserted and pitch dark. He would have to stay here tonight. With the branches he had gathered, he made a small fire and settled in. *Momma, I will find you.*

At 3:00 a.m., Hans headed to Gestapo headquarters on foot. He could not take the bike. He could not make any noise. He vividly recalled the route to Prinz Albrecht-Strasse 8, where he had walked with his opa years before.

It took him about twenty minutes. Even in the dark, he could see that the building had been badly damaged by the bombing. Hans carefully maneuvered around the perimeter. There were no guards or dogs outside. He could see the faint glare of a single light bulb in the basement.

Hans crawled close to the barred basement window and peered through the filthy glass. There was a man's back directly in his line of vision. He could make out Major Karl standing to the side, his cruel mouth curled in a hideous smile. The man who was obstructing Hans's view moved slightly to the side. He appeared to be buckling his trousers. Hans could now see a woman lying naked on a table, her arms and legs held with restraints, pinioning her to a table, a rag in her mouth. Momma. Hans turned and retched, vomiting uncontrollably. Then he heard the unmistakable sound of a muffled gunshot. He forced himself to look through the window. Karl stood holding a Luger. Blood streamed down Momma's face from her right temple. She did not move and her eyes were wide open. He retched again until there was nothing left inside him.

Hans got up and began to run. He was blinded by tears and tripped over some rubble, landing hard. He scraped his knee and his hands. They were bleeding. He did not feel the pain. He got up and continued to run. It was freezing cold. He ran until he returned to the place where his home once stood on the Unterlinden. He climbed over the rubble to his small cave of concrete and broken glass. Tears were streaming down his face. He was shivering. With more of the branches and small tree limbs he had brought from the cemetery, he made another small fire and sat, rocking back and forth, overcome with sadness. He was now truly alone.

Waves of anguish washed over him. Emotions tugged at him from every direction. One moment he was gripped by heartache, the next by rage. But Opa had warned him that anger was a dangerous emotion. It led to irrational thoughts and left one vulnerable. He sobbed uncontrollably.

Momma told him that she wanted him to survive. But he had nothing now. Nothing to live for. Why survive? There was nothing but death. He was surrounded by it. It had taken everyone he ever loved.

If there was a reason to live, he could only think of one: to avenge his momma's death. But how? He wasn't even twelve years old: strong and mature for his age, but certainly no match for an armed Gestapo major and his minions. Still, Opa had said that under the right conditions, one could gain an advantage over a much larger and better-armed opponent. What was needed was speed, strength, agility, and stealth. Then strike when your enemy is most vulnerable. But how?

For some reason, he thought of the cheetah. In his studies of the animal kingdom, he had developed a fascination with those beautiful felines, the small relative of the lion, the tiger, and the leopard, the big cats. All of them were apex predators that relied primarily on their size and strength to overcome their prey. Arguably, the cheetah planned its kills more carefully than the others. It relied on its intelligence, stealth, and speed to ambush. And, like most successful predators, it sought out its prey when it was vulnerable.

But Hans was not a cheetah. He was a boy, in war-torn Berlin, where the Gestapo ruled, where they were the predators, and people like his momma and he were the prey. Yet, if he was very careful and very smart, perhaps it would just be possible…what else did he have? Momma wanted him to survive. But all Hans wanted was revenge.

First, he needed a plan. For starters, Hans decided he would have to conduct surveillance. He would have to learn Major Karl's routines, his habits, his weaknesses. What time did he arrive at Prinz Albrecht-Strasse? What time did he leave? Did he sleep there? Did he get drunk? Was there a time when the Gestapo goons didn't tag along with him? Realistically speaking, how could a boy not yet twelve kill a grown man? With a gun? How would he find one? Maybe he could douse the staff car with gas siphoned from his motorcycle and set it on fire with the major inside. Could he get that close? Would that just be committing suicide? Did it matter?

Right now, he would have to acquire some food and gasoline. He had seen other children with ration cards when he was in the bomb shelter at the zoo. They sat alone. Their parents had been killed in bombing raids and, occasionally, the ration distributors took pity on them. He would have to collect more firewood to keep warm.

He would take his time. One thing at a time.

He managed to secure the provisions with less difficulty than he had anticipated.

Now he would have to find a place near Prinz Albrecht-Strasse where he could watch it without being noticed. It was almost dawn now. He would have to wait until after dark to scout out a location. Then he would devote considerable periods of time to watching the major's movements…without freezing to death in the process.

On February 26, the air raid sirens blared again. It had been a few weeks since the horrific bombing raid that leveled his building, destroyed the Unterlinden, and seemed to set all of Berlin ablaze. Hans did not attempt to head to the shelter at the zoo, just in case it was Werner who had turned his family in to the Gestapo. He decided to take a chance and stay in his concrete hovel. The Allied bombing might not be precise, but was it likely they would strike the same spot again? Even from the air, he thought the bomber pilots could see the entire area had been flattened.

This time it was a daytime raid. He could recognize the formations flying in from the west. Big B17 bombers accompanied by dozens of Mustang fighters, should the Germans challenge the lumbering flying fortresses. There was very little resistance from the Luftwaffe, and even less from antiaircraft flak towers. Perhaps the Nazis really were losing the war, or maybe they had run out of resources with which to defend civilians.

Bombing raids continued on an almost daily basis now. Many of the raids were conducted during the day, rattling already shaky civilian morale. It seemed quite a number of bombers emanated from the east, meaning the Soviet air force was attacking. The frequency of air raids rendered it unsafe for Hans to establish his surveillance at Prinz Albrecht-Strasse. He could not spend any length of time away from the relative safety of his concrete cave. He only ventured far enough to pick up rations once a week.

While the people on ration lines were chock full of gossip and rumor, sometimes accurate and sometimes not, the consensus was that the Allied forces had broken through from the west and the Soviets were speeding to Berlin from the east. Berliners prayed the

Americans would arrive first; the Soviets were "savages." Many talked about getting out and traveling west, if only the air raids would stop long enough to give them sufficient time. Perhaps, Hans reasoned, revenge would have to wait for another day, or another time and place. He decided he would have to follow his instincts and get away from Berlin; head west, toward the Americans.

❖ ❖ ❖

By the middle of the second week of April, Major Franz Karl and a few other members of the Gestapo began to make plans to evacuate Berlin. Karl's cousin, a captain in the engineering corps under General Gotthard Heinrici, had told him that heavy equipment was being deployed to shore up Berlin's defenses against an imminent onslaught by Soviet forces. While Hitler commanded his forces to fight for Berlin to the last man, Karl had other ideas. His cousin had told him confidentially that Germany was going to lose the war in very short order, no matter what Hitler and Goebbels said. It was now quite clear: Get out of Berlin. Go west and into hiding. It went without saying that things would not go well for a Gestapo officer captured by the Soviets.

Karl would have to abandon his uniform for civilian clothes. He would also have to secure transportation; obviously he couldn't drive out of Berlin in the Gestapo staff car. His mind raced. He had foolishly disposed of his nonmilitary suits and shirts, donating them to a church that handed out clothing and sundries to Berliners made homeless by the bombings. But he thought procuring civilian clothes shouldn't be too difficult. Daily bombings brought with them increasing civilian casualties. He was sure he could find a corpse with clothing in his size. More difficult would be finding and commandeering a civilian automobile or motorcycle.

It was just past dawn on April 16 when Karl started out on foot from the basement bunker at Prinz Albrecht-Strasse 8. During the evening, over one hundred RAF Mosquitos had dropped their payloads inside Berlin, essentially unopposed in the air or by ground fire. Karl hoped some poor soul out for a walk or on his way to the shelter at the zoo had succumbed to shrapnel or the concussive force generated by the powerful ordnance. Best to hunt for corpses early in the morning after an evening of bombing, he'd decided.

❖ ❖ ❖

Unsurprisingly, Hans had found it difficult sleeping through the evening's bombing raid. It did not matter. He had gathered his few possessions and prepared to head west. Where he meant to go, he did not know. Anything would be better than staying in Berlin. In the absolute quiet of the early morning, he heard the echo of jackbooted feet negotiating the rubble of the nearby intersection. Probably on the Wilhelmstrasse, not far from his perch on the Unterlinden. Similar to a blind person's acute hearing, Hans had developed an ability to distinguish potentially dangerous sounds from benign ones. He could hear or sense vehicles approaching from a distance or footfalls on the rubble even a block or two away. He climbed up to the ledge of what once had been the third floor of the building next to his family's. From that precarious vantage point, he could quickly ascertain whether the approaching sound would require an evasive maneuver, like hiding in his rubble cave below.

Hans's heart began to race. It was him. Major Karl. It was unmistakably him. But how had he found Hans's hideout? He put his hand in his pocket to make sure the switchblade was there.

From the distance, he saw Karl bend down, then glance from side to side, as if he was looking to see if he had been followed. It appeared he was rummaging through the pockets of the body of a man who had died during last night's air raid. Occasionally, Hans had seen dead bodies lying in the street. Typically, in the morning, a crew scooped up the bodies in their trucks and transported them for burial.

Hans watched as Major Karl quickly exchanged clothing with the dead man. Very strange indeed.

❖ ❖ ❖

Karl was thinking, *The pants are a little short, but they will have to do.* The shirt and coat fit fine. The shoes would be a bit uncomfortable, but he could manage. The man's dusty fedora lay in the rubble. Karl brushed it off and tried it on. Not bad. He could surely pass as a businessman. He laughed to himself. This is my lucky day. Now, if I can just find a car, or even a motorcycle or a bicycle. Then, he tried to bury his Luger under a pile of rubble. He was unhappy to have to abandon his gun, but if the Allies caught him with it, he was surely a dead man.

Hans watched the scene unfold, not sure what to make of it. It then occurred to him that the coward Major Karl was trying to escape as a civilian before the Soviets invaded Berlin. So, the rumors he had heard in the ration line were true after all. The Soviets could not be far away.

Karl walked a few meters, then stopped. He looked to his left, then to his right. He was sure no one had seen him. He paused and looked back the way he had come. His gaze was stabbed by the glint of metal. It was a motorcycle. Perhaps it belonged to the dead man. It did not matter, as long as it worked. His excitement was building. *My lucky day indeed. This could be my ticket out.* He walked to the bike and tried to start it. "*Scheisse,*" he bellowed. He tried again. Nothing.

Hans, cap pulled low over his forehead, approached slowly. "Hey, mister, is that your motorcycle?" There was enough distance between them, should Karl recognize him, that he could make a run for it through the rubble. He had a predetermined escape route through the labyrinth of concrete rubble and battered buildings, which included precarious hideouts; he knew he could easily evade Karl. In any case, Karl and his Gestapo goons had been so intensely focused on Momma at Opa's burial, it was unlikely Karl would recognize him.

Karl hesitated. "Yes, my boy, it is mine. I just can't seem to get it started. Perhaps the bombing last night did something to it."

"Maybe I can take a look at it," Hans offered. "I am handy with motorcycles."

Karl, recognizing he had little choice, said pleasantly, "That would be wonderful if you can."

Hans approached cautiously, noticing not a hint of recognition in Karl's eyes, only the desperate desire to get the motorcycle working so he could get out of Berlin. Hans pretended to examine the bike, then tried to start it, knowing it would not work. "Ach," he said, "I think I know what is wrong. I can fix it."

"Please proceed, thank you," Karl said, beginning to become impatient.

Hans knelt next to the motorcycle, appearing to concentrate on the repairs.

Karl bent forward over Hans and said, "How is it going? Can you work a little faster?"

He was so anxious to leave that he didn't hear the click of the switchblade. Nor did he realize before it was too late that Hans had thrust the blade into his midsection, below the rib cage, directly into Gestapo Major Franz Karl's heart, then withdrawing it quickly, just as he had practiced.

The Nazi's lifeless body rolled onto the ground, his eyes wide open, a look of utter shock plastered on his face. Hans wiped the blade clean on Karl's coat. Then he closed the blade and slipped it into his pocket.

For a brief moment, Hans felt triumphant. Then he took the

spark plugs from his pocket and reinstalled them, turned the ignition key, and started the bike and headed west.

Hans was fortunate. Had he gone south or east, he would have arrived at the desperate efforts of German forces to build defenses to thwart the fast-approaching Soviet army. He would likely have been captured or killed by them.

April 16 signaled the beginning of the final assault on Berlin by Soviet forces from the east, north, and south, battering Berlin with an unceasing barrage of rockets, while the RAF engaged in tactical bombing from the air. During the next two weeks, the Soviet army encircled Berlin, forcing its surrender. Hitler, hiding in the Führerbunker, committed suicide on April 30, 1945. The death toll for Berliners and the Soviet army was staggering.

As Hans rode west, he passed the infantry and panzer formations of General Walter Wenck's Twelfth Army. The battered Twelfth stood on the eastern side of the Elbe River and west of Potsdam and Berlin. The American Ninth Army was encamped on the western side of the Elbe. When the Soviets fully encircled Berlin on April 27, Wenck knew any further efforts to save Berlin were futile. So, he enabled civilians and soldiers to retreat to the Elbe and surrender to the American Army, which they much preferred. The Germans surrendered unconditionally on May 8, 1945.

Hans endeared himself to the American soldiers almost immediately. He could speak English, knew the terrain, and could fix almost anything. For the most part, anything he could take apart, he could put back together while diagnosing the problem and correcting it. He was able to fix radios, motorcycles, and even Jeeps. The Americans were astounded that he was Jewish and somehow had managed to survive the war in *Judenrein* Berlin. They marveled at his story and treated him like a mascot. But the war was now over, and soon, the soldiers would disperse and go home. Not yet twelve, he would have to face the prospect of building a life on his own.

Hans had no family anymore. The Sternlichts were all gone. There were no Webers as far as he knew. He had nothing and no one. But he also did not have the luxury of feeling sorry for himself. Hans was not the only displaced orphan in Germany. He had to move forward. With the help of his new American soldier friends, he was settled in the Düppel Center, an all-Jewish Displaced Persons camp located next to Lake Schlachtensee, in the American sector of Berlin.

22

THE BRONX

May 8, 1945

"Walter, Walter, did you hear?" Paula Remer shouted excitedly from the kitchen. "Just now on the radio. The Germans surrendered! The war in Europe is over!"

He gave his mother a celebratory hug, and they danced and whirled around the kitchen. "Papa should be home any minute. This is so exciting! Maybe Sam and Janet can come by and we can have a celebration tonight!"

"That would be great, but Janet and I already have plans for tonight. I am going to meet her when she gets off her shift and then we are going out to dinner and dancing at the Copa," Walter said.

"Young people." She smiled, "Always having a party. Well, if you get home early enough, we'll be up."

"Thanks, Momma," Walter said. "I bet everyone in Manhattan will be having a party tonight! I'm going to put on my uniform and head into the city."

Walter was still officially a soldier on duty. He held the rank of captain, and the tall, blond officer looked splendid in his uniform. Yet he was self-conscious about his hands and wore officer's dress gloves to cover the scars and stumps. It had been almost six months since his last hand surgery, but he still suffered considerable pain and soreness. The lack of dexterity would be with him forever. The doctors assured him that the pain would diminish in time and he would recover some use of his fingers.

Janet's shift ended at eight o'clock, and she met Walter at the bar at the Copacabana an hour later. They embraced and kissed like lovers who hadn't seen each other in months, although they had just gone out on Sunday night.

Jules Podell, the nightclub impresario who now managed the Copa for Frank Costello, immediately recognized the young couple, who had become regulars at the club. "Happy VE Day, kids!" he exclaimed. "Drinks on me! I saved you guys the best seats in the house. Come on."

He dragged them over to their table, and just before the show started, another round of drinks was delivered to them. From the bar, Ralph DeLeo raised a glass in Walter's direction. Then he made a gesture, pretending to punch himself in the jaw, and grinned broadly. Walter smiled sheepishly and raised his glass in acknowledgment.

Podell and most of the staff were well aware of Walter's status as a war hero; his gloved hands and Purple Heart attested to that, though none knew anything of the nature of his mission or his affiliation with the OSS. Most, however, recalled his marvelous piano playing before he left for Europe.

For the patrons and staff at the Copa that night, seeing the handsome war hero on VE Day was electrifying. It was as if he were the star of the show, a true celebrity. It was as if Sinatra had walked into the club. The band, most of whom had played with him when he occasionally filled in at the piano, gave him a standing ovation. Walter blushed. Patrons rose and applauded. After the show, five of the Copa girls ran out from the back and almost mauled him, a dizzying display of hugs, tugs, and kisses. His hair was a mess, and he had lipstick all over his face. Even Janet had to laugh. She dutifully wiped it off with a handkerchief, pretending not to mind.

❖ ❖ ❖

Brooklyn

Before he left the woman's apartment, the police officer asked if there was anything else he could do for her. Even for a hardened veteran of the New York Police Department, he had difficulty holding back his tears. He had had the unenviable task of delivering the shocking news that the woman's beautiful daughter-in-law had been murdered, made even worse by the fact that it was the morning after VE Day, when most of America was in a joyous mood, celebrating the end of the war in Europe.

He had handed her a bag containing the girl's personal effects. A pocketbook, a lipstick, a hairbrush, a watch, and her wedding band. A cursory examination had suggested the cause of death was strangulation. The policeman did not describe the gruesome details, but the photographs taken at the scene revealed the bruising and the finger marks left on her neck by the powerful hands of the killer. There did not appear to be any bloodstains on her clothing, but the police would hold her sweater, dress, and undergarments for evidence and forensic scrutiny.

Seeing how distraught the woman was, he elected not to tell her that the girl was sexually assaulted. The poor woman was in a state of shock. She literally didn't have a second to process what had happened with the baby screaming in the other room.

Sandra Mills was no stranger to grief, but life never seemed to afford her the time to mourn properly. Eleven years earlier, the police had come to her door to inform her and her then-nine-year-old son, Philip, that her husband had been murdered by mobsters from Murder Incorporated.

Her late husband, Joseph, was a good man. A well-intentioned man. He worked eleven-hour days as a presser in a dress factory.

But he'd had a problem with gambling. His debts mounted, and he borrowed more and more money to cover them, looking for that one big hit to cover the losses and, perhaps, enable him to buy a car and a nice house out on Long Island for his young family. He was in way over his head, notwithstanding the repeated warnings from his creditors. His body was found in a field near the Brooklyn Navy Yard.

It was difficult being a single mother. Sandra worked ten-hour days, six days a week, sewing lace onto dress collars. It was monotonous piece work, but it paid the bills.

Sandra's son, Philip, married Dana Wolofsky, his high school sweetheart, soon after they graduated in 1943. Philip was able to secure a job as a longshoreman, and Dana was hired as a secretary at a small accounting firm in Manhattan. And several nights a week, she worked as a dancer at the Copacabana to earn extra money. She didn't care for the job, the late hours, the ogling men or their wandering hands, but the tips were very good. The couple lived with Sandra to help with the rent and hoped to save some money so they could eventually buy a house.

Shortly after his eighteenth birthday in late December 1943, Philip received his draft notice. After basic training and before he shipped out in early May 1944, Dana gave him the wonderful news that she was expecting. According to the doctor, the baby was due on January 1, 1945. A New Year's baby—although Sandra, who couldn't wait to be a grandmother, knew such precision was unlikely. Philip ached for his tour of duty to end before it even started so he could be home when his baby was born. As hopeful as he was, at that time the war showed no signs of ending quickly. The way things were going, there was a good chance he would even miss the baby's first steps.

Sandra would never forget the exact moment, on June 8, 1944, when her doorbell rang: 1:34 a.m. The doorbell never rang in the middle of the night. Sandra quickly threw on a robe and ran to the front door, her heart beating like a bass drum. She froze at the sight of the uniformed Western Union man. He handed her a telegram and began to cry even before she read it. Dana sleepily padded to the front door. She took one look at her sobbing mother-in-law and the Western Union man hanging his head and fell to the floor. Philip had died on the beaches of Normandy, a distant place that neither Sandra nor Dana had ever heard of.

Now Dana was gone. In an instant, Sandra Mills had become her grandson's mother. Poor, poor Teddy.

PART 4

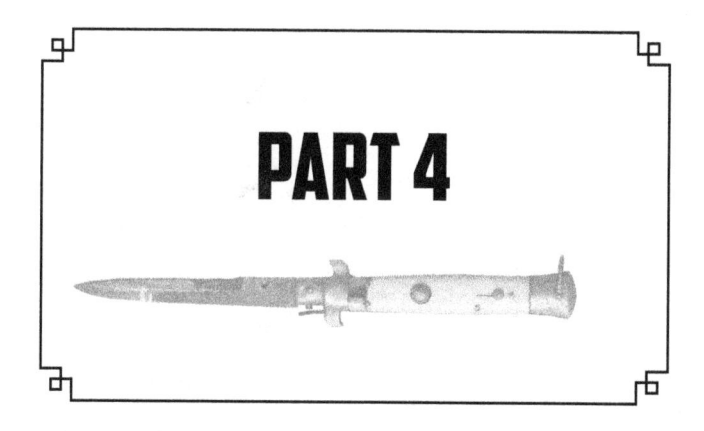

23

MANHATTAN

September 2018

The way veteran detective Tony Rosario would describe it, to become a successful detective in the cold case squad of the NYPD Special Investigation Unit, one had to possess the four Ps: Patience, Persistence, and the Passion for solving Puzzles. Of course, if there were no women present, Rosario, would add a fifth P: a big Pecker. Anything for a laugh. "Well," he would say, "back in the day, it would get a laugh. No one laughs no more."

Tony was an ex-Marine, not a politician. Being politically correct wasn't his job or part of his skill set. But he was an excellent detective. He had helped close twenty-nine cold cases in his nineteen years in the unit. Tony was indefatigable, detail-oriented, and hardworking. He led by example. He worked long hours and would never give up so long as there was a shred of evidence, or the possibility of obtaining one, that might lead to the resolution of a cold case.

Rosario was not a physically imposing figure by any stretch of the imagination. He was fifty-four years old with a receding hairline and stood about five-foot-seven with shoes on and lifts in them. He had put on a few extra pounds around the midsection since becoming a detective, but he had a certain no-nonsense presence that commanded respect, a keen intelligence, and a knack for finding leads when there didn't seem to be any.

After offering his canned opening remarks to the newest member of the team, Tony introduced the new kid to the cold case squad, as was his custom. In order of seniority, Detective Tim Sweeney, Sergeant Alberto Padilla, Detective Ann Sunking, and Detective Cal McPherson, all longtime veterans of the unit. The new member of the team, Detective Doug O'Connell, had transferred to cold case from the counterterrorism unit. He had served in the CU for a few years but suffered PTSD-related nightmares from his two tours of duty in Iraq and Afghanistan. The police psychiatrist suggested he move to a unit that would remind him less of the horrors of war. Something more analytical. Something that might offer a little more job satisfaction and a little less stress.

In the military, O'Connell had been with Special Forces. He was frequently deployed behind enemy lines and participated in one too many assassination missions, many at close range. O'Connell put down a lot of bad guys, but he lost some good friends along the way. He was a shade under six feet tall, good-looking, with close-cropped dark hair and a physique reminiscent of Ben Grimm of Marvel Comics' Fantastic Four.

When Tony Rosario escorted O'Connell to his new office, Sweeney turned to McPherson and whispered, "How many different ways do you think that guy could kill you with his bare hands?"

McPherson cracked, "If he drinks your shitty coffee, you might just find out."

"O'Connell," Rosario started, "good to have you. We're a pretty close-knit group. We work independently for the most part, but there's a lot of experience here to share, so never, ever be afraid to pick our brains. We all do it. Padilla will take you through the dos and don'ts. He'll show you our online tools, the DNA databases like GEDmatch, 23andMe, and Ancestry, and other resources. We'll also get you access to some extraordinarily talented genetic genealogists. They do amazing work. And he'll introduce you to our counterparts at the FBI and take you out to the Queens forensics lab so you get to know those folks. They're worth their weight in gold, let me tell you."

"Looking forward to it, Captain Rosario," O'Connell said.

"The name is Tony. No ranks here, O'Connell. First or last names make the grade."

"Roger that. Will do. Question for you, Tony…who is the old guy sitting at the desk over there? Is he part of the team?" A gray-haired man sat in a cubicle, staring at a computer.

"Oh, that's Ted Mills. I'll introduce you. He's actually a fixture here. Retired about six years ago. He's got to be pushing seventy or more. Got an interesting story…like everyone else, I suppose. He was born toward the end of World War II. He was raised by his grandma. His pop was killed during the Battle of Normandy, before he was born. His mom was a dancer at the Copacabana nightclub. She was a looker, I guess.

"The story is that on VE Day—that was May 8, 1945, I think—she never made it home from the show. Cops found her body in Central Park, not too far from the club. She was strangled, her neck broken. A bloodless killing. Photos are in the file. If that wasn't enough, she was raped too. Just horrible. Ted became a cop, as he tells it, to find his mother's killer, get the creep off the streets and make him pay. Believe it or not, he's still looking for a lead to put the case to bed. The poor bastard has spent his whole life trying to get closure. It's a freaking shame. His mom's clothes are still in a bag in the evidence room. He's very protective of the stuff."

O'Connell interrupted. "Did forensics run all the clothes?"

"Oh yeah," Tony said, "a long time ago. Found a hair sample in her sweater and another under her fingernails. It was a good sample, actually. She must have yanked it from the guy's head, because there was some hair root. A hair follicle wouldn't help to conclusively identify the guy, but nuclear DNA found in the root is good shit. Problem is that we never found a match in the database. Mills comes here every freaking day, hoping a match will miraculously pop. It happens, but given the amount of time that has passed, it's highly unlikely. If the murderer is still alive, he'd be in his freakin' nineties. How's a guy in his nineties gonna commit a felony and leave a new DNA sample? Never going to happen unless he's a freakin' homicidal Methuselah. Ted's only shot is that if the old dude is still alive, he's into finding his roots and decides to do 23andMe or Ancestry. I wouldn't bet my salary on that."

"Dumb question—I'm pretty green at this forensic stuff—but did they also find a semen sample? You said she was sexually assaulted. I mean, if the semen DNA matched the hair sample, that would at least positively ID the killer, right?" O'Connell asked.

Rosario sighed. "That's a good question for sure from a newbie. Well, this is going to sound ridiculous, but it took a long time for Mills to let anyone near the underwear. It's his mother's. Some weird psychological shit, right? I guess I understand it. Admittedly, its creepy shit.

"Anyway, a few years ago the lab guys convinced him that semen samples are good for like a hundred years, so it would be worth his while to pursue it. So, we finally ran it, and it turned out the semen was from someone completely different from the hair. The semen itself wouldn't conclusively prove the 'donor' was the murderer anyway. I mean, it's possible she had consensual sex with some guy earlier that day, or the rapist didn't penetrate or soil her panties. No way to know for sure. Needless to say, it certainly could have been, but we can't prove it. And you can't even talk to Mills about that. So, he's convinced that the hair dude was the killer. Problem is, there are no matches on any of the DNA databases for either sample. So, he's got this vigil going for as long as I've known him, looking for a DNA match to pop up."

"That's really sad. I feel bad for the guy."

"Yeah, we all do. Anyhow, Ted is 100 percent sure the hair-sample guy did it. He sort of has this image in his head of his mom desperately trying to fight off the killer, kicking, punching, yanking on his hair, the works. Maybe…at the end of the day, this is probably one of those cases where the murderer kicked the bucket years ago. Just no way to know. Look, Ted's a decent-enough guy. So we let him hang out and look at the DNA database. That don't hurt nobody. And, occasionally, he helps us out on other cases. But that's off the record, capisce?"

O'Connell nodded his head in agreement.

"Come on. I'll introduce you to him," Rosario said.

24

MERRICK, NY

October 2018

Seeing the two police cars, one New York City and one Nassau County, as well as an unmarked black Chevy Impala parked in front of his dad's small house on Olive Road, Alfred Sternlicht quickly stopped his car and rushed in. Hans Sternlicht sat on his frayed sofa in the living room, surrounded by a detective and two officers engaged in conversation. They stopped and turned as Alfred opened the door.

Hans said, "Come on in, Fred. Meet my new friends. This gentleman is Detective Martin Golden, from the NYPD, but he said to call him Marty. This is Sergeant Ron Fleming, also from the NYPD, the Seventy-Seventh Precinct in Crown Heights, and Officer Tom Glover from Nassau County, Seventh Precinct over in Seaford. Did I get that right, fellas?"

Even at eighty-five, Fred's father's mind and memory were still sharp as a tack, attention to detail his hallmark. He also was physically fit and light on his feet for his age. In fact, Monday and Thursday mornings he would almost always be given the honor of hagbah, lifting the heavy Torah in his synagogue, primarily because he could do it with grace and certainty. The younger congregants never ceased to be amazed by his strength and agility.

"Yes, Mr. Sternlicht, spot on," Detective Golden said. "And you must be Hans's son?"

Unlike his wiry, five-foot-nine-inch, blue-eyed, light-haired father, Fred was six foot tall, heavy set, with brown eyes and dark hair. He ran an eponymous investment advisory firm headquartered in Great Neck, Alfred Sternlicht & Company. "Yes, Alfred Sternlicht. But everyone calls me Fred. I don't mean to be rude, but what's going on here? I saw police cars in front of the house and my heart almost leaped out of my chest. I can't even begin to tell you the thoughts running through my head."

Golden said, "Understood, for sure. Your dad's fine. In fact, he's kind of a hero. He saved someone's life. Why don't you take a seat, Fred? You're shaking like a leaf. Hey, Ron, you mind getting Fred here a glass of water?"

"I'll get it. Anyone want anything while I'm up?" Hans asked calmly.

"No, thanks, Mr. Sternlicht," Golden said. "Let me sort of cut to the chase. Last evening at about 9:45 p.m., a young Orthodox Jewish woman whose name we're going to keep confidential, was walking between Albany and President Streets in Crown Heights. It's a couple of blocks from 770 Eastern Parkway, Chabad World Headquarters. Given the history and mix of the neighborhood, we have a lot of surveillance cameras set up there. Anyhow, a creep wearing a hoodie grabs the woman from behind and pushes her into an alley. She screams. He punches her hard in the face and knocks her to the ground. He holds a knife to her throat. He covers her mouth with the other hand and then proceeds to attempt to sexually assault her. Literally within seconds, a man wearing a driver's cap pulled low over his face, almost like he knows he's on camera and doesn't want to be identified, enters the alley. He slaps one hand under the rapist's chin and with a swift, upward thrust, stabs the perp expertly through his lower back into his heart and withdraws the blade in one motion. Kills the guy instantly. He calmly takes the blade, wipes it off on the hoodie, drops it in his jacket pocket, and with some difficulty pushes the dead rapist off the girl and walks away."

Fred, his hands shaking a little less violently, interrupted. "I'm sorry. You've lost me. What does this have to do with my father?"

"Well, Fred, when we checked out the surveillance video, we were able to follow the man with the cap for half a block. At approximately 10 p.m., he got into an old Volvo, license plate YKM5984, and drove home, to Olive Road, Merrick. So, here we are," Golden said.

"What? You can't be serious. There must be some mistake."

"It's no mistake, Fred. It was definitely your dad in the video. Stuck the rapist right through the heart, like a pro. It was like watching something right out of the movies. Don't feel sorry for the dead guy; the piece of garbage had a rap sheet a mile long. He was also packing a loaded, unregistered handgun. He'd been arrested at least two dozen times in the last five years, but nothing sticks nowadays. Attempted rape, attempted robbery at gunpoint, knifepoint, you name it."

"This is all so far-fetched. My dad just turned eighty-five, for heaven's sake. He's not a killer, he's a retired mechanic. A Holocaust survivor! There must be some mistake. Dad?" Fred said, his voice rising as Hans came into the room carrying a bottle of Poland Spring and four plastic cups.

Detective Golden chose his words carefully. "Fred, before your dad answers, there are a couple of things you should know. You're right, he's not a killer. He's an angel. And no, it's not far-fetched. Maybe you don't know as much about your dad as you think you do. But I'll leave that to him to tell you. In the meantime, even though he did a great mitzvah, saving that girl from being raped or worse, he did kill someone, and he left the scene of the crime. So, while I would bet money the grand jury won't indict him, we'll have to dot the Is and cross the Ts."

"What exactly does that mean?" Fred asked.

"In these crazy times, when—well, I'm going to try to be as politically correct as I can—when a white person kills a person of color, justified or not, it often becomes a media event. Some folks—I'll call them political opportunists—and our friends in the media occasionally like to paint even the act of a good Samaritan as being racially motivated. In this case, they would have no leg to stand on. But if they can make it fit their narrative…you know. Anyhow, we have the video and testimony from the woman, but you have to be prepared for the worst. Do you know what I mean?"

"Go on," Fred said, while Hans calmly listened.

"Well, first thing this morning, we viewed the video with the district attorney and an acquaintance of mine who happens to be a criminal defense attorney. By the way, this conversation is strictly off the record. We watched it three or four times, actually. The DA thinks that when the grand jury hears the witness testimony and sees the video evidence, it will be unlikely to indict, and the case will be dropped. The attorney, David Solender of Solender, Ostrowsky and Solender, said the same thing. Solender will be coming by in a few minutes to chat with your father. He said it would be his pleasure to represent him and will take his case pro bono if he is indicted."

"Isn't Solender the lawyer who defends the Mafia?" Fred interrupted.

Golden laughed. "We don't call it the Mafia anymore. We refer to it as 'organized crime.' Yes, that's him. He said he wants to be with you before any charges are leveled or an arrest is made. He'll be here shortly, so we'll wait for him before we say anything else."

"Okay." Hans spoke up. "Where do we go from here, Marty?"

As Detective Golden was preparing to answer, a man knocked on the half-opened screen door and let himself in. It was Solender; Fred had seen him on a couple of true crime cable shows. The man was right out of central casting: tall, trim, with beautifully coiffed white hair, a Caribbean tan, bright blue eyes, a navy suit, a starched white shirt, and a dark tie. Solender must be in his mid-fifties, and Fred imagined his mere presence would give a defendant confidence. He introduced himself and, having heard Hans's question, took the liberty of answering it.

"Hans, Fred, it is my pleasure to meet you both. Let me explain what you can expect. Officer Fleming will read Hans his rights and arrest him. He'll be arraigned this morning before Judge Arlen Cohn. He's a good guy. He will read the complaint against him and he'll plead not guilty. Then Judge Cohn will refer the complaint to the grand jury. I think they have arranged for it to be heard by the grand jury on Friday morning. Hans, the woman whose life you saved is eager to testify to clear you, and the jurors will be presented the video evidence as well. The jurors may ask the DA questions or they may not. Then, they'll vote on whether to indict. In the unlikely event that they do indict, we'll arrange bail and map out our strategy. My staff has already done some very preliminary work, just in case. But let's take one step at a time.

"I would like to say this will be a no-brainer, but in this day and age, jurors are very sensitive to what could be perceived as a case of vigilantism, where a white person confronts and kills a person of color. The fact that you are eighty-five and the perp was a well-armed twenty-two-year-old with a record a mile long should help but is no guarantee. What is most problematic is that you left the scene before the police arrived, so we can't be certain how the grand jury will see things. In other words, it is plausible that the panel will wish to press charges if they perceive an armed vigilante is walking the streets. So, it likely will boil down to whether, after hearing the woman's testimony and seeing the video, the grand jury believes you to be a vigilante or a good Samaritan. Hans, can I ask you a question? What were you doing in Brooklyn that late at night by yourself?"

"One night every week, I go to a *shiur* at 770 Eastern Parkway."

"Excuse my ignorance," Solender said. "I'm a lapsed Jew. A *shiur*?"

"A *shiur* is a class in Talmud." Hans sighed and then drew a deep breath, as if he were about to unload a burden that had been chained to his back for a millennium. "I grew up in Berlin during the war. My parents were not religious, so I had no Jewish education. But the Nazis didn't care how religious they were. They killed my family anyway. They beat my father to death with a truncheon because he was a Jew. The irony is, he didn't even grow up Jewish. His parents, my grandparents, converted before he was born. I watched the Gestapo rape and kill my mother."

Addressing no one in particular, Hans told the story in detail. "It was a major miracle, with a little luck thrown in for good measure, that I managed to kill the Nazi bastard who murdered my mother. I stabbed him with the same blade I used on this rapist and felt the life leave his putrid corpse. It's funny in a way. When you kill someone with a knife, you actually feel them die. You feel their heart stop and they cease to breath. It is different killing with a gun. That's more like playing a video game. It's one thing to see someone die and another to feel it. It changes you. At any rate, I didn't derive any satisfaction from killing either of them or anyone else. It was just a job that had to be done."

Hans paused for a moment. Then he looked directly at Detective Golden. "Have you ever killed a man, Marty?" It was a rhetorical question; he already knew the answer. He could tell by looking in the man's eyes.

Golden looked down at his hands and replied quietly, "No. I never have. I guess, fortunately."

"Good. I hope you never have to." Hans continued, "I think that killing someone destroys part of your soul. Of course, I am certain not everyone feels that way. You know, when I was a kid, it seemed like almost every day we were running to the air raid shelter, sometimes just making it inside before the bombs made the earth tremble. I thought to myself, 'Does the pilot feel anything? Is it just a job to him? Does he know that he destroyed my house? Did he know that old Mrs. Engels, who once made delicious apple pie, didn't make it to the air raid shelter in time?' Now her head is on one side of the street and her legs on the other. It's just a job, right? Maybe like the Mafia guy—I stand corrected—the organized crime assassin, who follows his victim into a restaurant and shoots him three times in the head while the victim is eating spaghetti with marinara sauce. Then, the killer goes home and watches his kid at soccer practice. Just something he had to do. Just a job.

"Anyway, when the war ended, I spent more than two years in a DP camp in the American Zone in Berlin. I attended high school classes and learned to read Hebrew. I learned about Israel, a homeland for Jews. The camp grew pretty quickly and was full of refugees from all parts of Europe. The refugee kids in my class were from all different countries and spoke different languages, and they sort of stuck together, depending on where they were from. It was kind of cliquey. Almost none were from Germany. I can't say I had any real friends my age.

"Soon after the Soviet blockade of Berlin in 1948, they closed the camp down and I made my way to Israel. It didn't take long to discover that, like the Jews in Europe, the Jews in Israel were surrounded by people bent on killing them. So, a few years after I arrived, when I was eighteen, I joined the Army. I was always good at fixing things: motorcycles, radios, jeeps. So, the Army placed me as a mechanic in the motor pool.

"One day, an armed terrorist entered the Army base through a hole he dug under the barbed wire fence. I was coming out of the motor pool after dusk, having just fixed a jeep's transmission. I saw him shimmy under the fence. I couldn't believe it. He had a long gun of some sort and a sling of grenades. He approached one of the barracks that had its lights on. My guess is he intended to kill whoever was inside. I followed him, and just as he reached for the door handle, I thrust my left hand under his chin from behind and stabbed him through the lower back directly into his heart in one motion with my Opa Helmut's switchblade and yanked it out quickly. He died instantly.

"All kinds of excitement ensued, sirens, you name it. After the commotion died down, the guys in my unit hoisted me up in the air, taking turns dancing with me on their shoulders, singing

'Chaim Melech Yisrael,' which means Chaim—or Hans—the King of Israel. It was a play on words for a song about King David, 'David Melech Yisrael.'

"After that night, the base commander found I had a knack for something other than fixing motors. Killing. During the wars, and in between them, I killed many of the enemies of Israel. On the battlefield, in Europe, and behind enemy lines. It was a job. Something that had to be done. Those I killed or helped kill, like this garbage who attacked the young woman in Crown Heights, deserved what they got. I derived no pleasure or satisfaction from it. I did what had to be done. I have never mentioned this to anyone before, not even my son."

Hans, still speaking to no one in particular, took a deep breath. "But with each killing, I started to feel something strange. I can't really explain it, but it was like I was playing Russian roulette with my soul. Killing had become too routine. I knew deep inside that there was something wrong. This wasn't normal. It wasn't the way to live.

"On March 11, 1978, Palestinian terrorists hijacked a bus in Israel, killing thirty-eight innocent civilians including thirteen children, wounding many more. I can't explain why, but for some reason that day changed everything for me. It just hit me. I felt as helpless as I had when the Gestapo scum fired a bullet point-blank into my mother's head. The futility of it. Even if I did my job well, it didn't matter. It would never end. Wherever we go, whatever we do, they will still come to kill us just because we are Jews. They will kill our babies, just because they are Jews. We can win Nobel Prizes and eradicate diseases, but they will keep coming to kill us. So, I quit my *job*, packed my bag, tied up some loose ends, and left Israel a week later for New York. I sublet a one-bedroom apartment in Brooklyn.

"I found work as an auto mechanic in Crown Heights. This may sound strange to you, but people who came in the shop often talked about this very special rabbi in Brooklyn. He had developed a cult-like following around the world. At first, I thought it was just nonsense. But I was told that he really helped people. He believed everyone had a soul…a *neshama*…and every *neshama* can be redeemed. Even mine. He too had survived the Nazis. He escaped Europe in 1941, one step ahead of the Nazis. I figured if anyone could understand me, he could. So I sought his council. His name was Menachem Mendel Schneerson. He was known as the Lubavitcher rebbe. He was a very wise and brilliant man. People waited in long lines to see him. He advised me that I needed to find closure for my many open wounds. He quoted the Talmud from Sanhedrin 37A, 'Whoever saves a single life is considered to have saved the whole world.' That included those I saved, and myself as well. He said, through *teshuvah*, *tefilah*, and *tzedakah*, or repentance, prayer, and charity, I could be whole. I could repair my damaged soul. I could save myself and then help others. My life could have purpose, even as a simple mechanic. I no longer needed to live for revenge or to avenge the Jewish people. Shortly thereafter, I met my beloved wife, Fred's mother, Sarah. And then I started a new life.

"You know," he digressed, "I visit her almost every Monday and Thursday morning at Godwin Nursing Home in Northport. I go there early to make a minyan, although they usually have ten men without me. But none of them can lift the Torah for hagbah, so it's become my job. Then I visit with Sarah for an hour or two. I hold her hand. We have lunch. Unfortunately, her mind was lost to Alzheimer's disease a few years ago, though I know her soul is still there. I was lucky to have her for as long as I did. She does not recognize me any longer. Maybe one day she will. For years I have attended the *shiur* at 770, hoping that teshuvah, tefilah, and tzedakah will give me peace. Whatever happens, happens. If your people want to put me in jail, my soul has already been there. It does not matter. I have no apologies to make except to my children."

Fred was dumbfounded, tears rolling down his cheeks. No one in the room could speak.

Hans looked directly at his son for the first time. "I am sorry, Fred. You do not deserve to learn about my past this way. I have always wanted to shield you and your sister from it. I am truly sorry."

Fred came to hug his father. "Papa, I had no idea…you never …" He whispered, "Does Gila know?" His younger sister had made Aliyah to Israel a few years before.

Hans shook his head.

No one spoke.

At last, Detective Golden broke the awkward silence. "Mr. Sternlicht, were you in the Mossad or something?"

"Something like that. A lifetime ago."

Then Solender spoke. "Typically, the defendant—you, in this case—doesn't testify before the grand jury, nor is he required to. But I would like you to, in light of the story you have just told us. The DA will ask you to describe what happened. You will describe it without embellishing. 'I heard a scream, saw a woman being attacked, and came to her rescue.' I happen to know that the DA will ask you, then, why you risked your life without conscious thought and acted as you did. Could you then tell the jury, in detail, the story of your mother being raped and murdered by the Nazis in front of your eyes as a child?…If you can't or won't, I understand. But if you can, it would be very valuable."

"Yes, I will. Perhaps it is time I did."

"Excellent," Solender said. "Hans, Ron is going to read you your rights now."

Fleming proceeded to Mirandize Hans. After he finished he added, "Mr. Sternlicht, we're going to need you to give us the alleged weapon and a DNA sample, just to make sure you have no other outstandings."

Hans removed the switchblade from his pocket.

Fleming held open an evidence envelope and Hans dropped the switchblade in. Fleming sealed it.

"Papa," Fred said, "I have never seen that before. How long have you carried that around with you?"

"My opa, my momma's father, gave it to me for my tenth birthday. It has come in very handy over the years. When will I get it back?" Hans asked.

"Let's just take care of the legal stuff first," Golden replied. "Can you come with us, please?"

25

BROOKLYN

A tiny article buried on page 26 of the *New York Times* described the death of an "alleged rapist," who was killed in the act by a good Samaritan in Crown Heights. There were few details, except that the alleged rapist had a long rap sheet and was armed with a knife and an illegal handgun. The other major news media didn't pick up the story at all. Perhaps that was why there was no crowd in front of the courthouse when Hans was arraigned. He pleaded not guilty, and the district attorney referred the complaint to the grand jury.

In an amazingly short time, the Brooklyn grand jury heard the felony complaint against Hans Sternlicht at 360 Adams Street. They listened to the emotional testimony of the Orthodox Jewish woman whose black eye was on full display. It was hard for some of the jurors to look directly at her, and they had no questions for her. They watched the video and gasped as the alleged rapist brutally punched the woman and threw her to the ground. Then they saw a figure quickly come into the frame, violently grasp the man's chin with one hand, and thrust a gleaming instrument into his back, then just as quickly withdraw it. With considerable difficulty, the figure, with a cap pulled low over his head, pushed the assailant off the woman, then walked away.

After the video, an assistant district attorney, Ty Sherman, called in the defendant, Hans Sternlicht, who appeared with his attorney. Sherman asked the defendant to describe in his own words what occurred in the alley. In a barely audible, accented voice, Hans Sternlicht described precisely what happened. Some of the jurors looked as if they wanted to stand up and cheer. Then, just as David Solender had said, Sherman asked Hans why he had acted as he did. Hans took a breath and briefly described how he had survived as a Jewish boy in Nazi Berlin. He told them that he saw his mother chained, naked, to a table in the basement of Gestapo headquarters, raped, then shot by an officer. He explained the series of events that took place thereafter, including the way he had used the same switchblade to kill the Nazi.

Later, Solender said that many of the jurors had tears streaming down their faces, and some were shaking their heads in disbelief. Sherman himself seemed to be struggling to retain his composure before he could ask the jurors if they had any questions. There were none. He instructed Hans and Solender to leave the room, then formally presented the charges to the grand jury and instructed them to begin their deliberations. Fifteen minutes later, the foreperson called in Sherman to reveal their decision as to whether to indict or dismiss.

Shortly thereafter, Sherman gave Hans, Fred, and Solender the news: The charges had been dismissed unanimously. Solender thanked him, as did Hans and his son.

"Can I go home now?" Hans asked.

Sherman smiled. "Yes indeed. Just do me a favor. I would be grateful if I never see you again in this courthouse. Let the police take care of enforcing the law next time."

Hans gave what Fred thought was a noncommittal nod.

"Before you leave," Sherman said, "you can pick up your knife from Detective Golden. He's in the building."

"Sometimes the good guys win. Have a good day, Mr. Sternlicht."

Hans retrieved his switchblade from Marty Golden, who congratulated Hans on his "victory." As they were leaving the courthouse, Hans and Fred thanked David Solender profusely for his help.

"It was my pleasure, but I didn't do anything, really. As Ty said, sometimes the good guys win. But I was thinking," Solender suggested gently, "it might be cathartic for you, Hans, and helpful to you, Fred, and your sister, if you told your story to the Shoah Foundation. Let me know if you do."

26

MANHATTAN

"Tony, Tony," Mills screamed. "Look at this. Holy shit!"

Rosario rushed out of his office and sprinted over to the cubicle where Ted Mills was standing, waving his hands. O'Connell, Sweeney, Sunking, and Padilla were right behind him. "What's the matter, Teddy? You okay? Should we call an ambulance?"

Mills was grinning from ear to ear, his face flushed with excitement. "Sorry, sorry, I'm fine. Look at this. Nearly a 25 percent match! Gotta be a grandson, a half brother, or a nephew!"

Rosario relaxed. "Slow down, Kemosabe. What are you talking about?"

"A GEDmatch. Just came up. I'll be damned. Just came up, for the fucker who killed my mother. A 25 percent match. Gonna need some help tracking him down. What do you say?"

"Definitely worth running down the lead," Rosario said. "I got a perfect idea. O'Connell, good time to get your feet wet. Why don't the two of you have at it?"

Ted looked a little disappointed that Rosario wasn't offering up a more experienced cold case veteran from the team, but then said, "Sure, that would be great."

Rosario knew that a 25 percent DNA match based on a hair root sample would lead to nothing conclusive. Certainly no guarantee that the sample belonged to the murderer. This probably would be nothing more than a wild-goose chase. But it would be a good experience for O'Connell as his first investigation in the unit, and his first attempt at breaking down a family tree. At best, Ted and O'Connell might be able to come up with some additional evidence and another trail. And if it somehow gave poor Mills some closure, if only illusory, it would be worth it.

❖ ❖ ❖

Merrick

Fred Sternlicht sat at his father's small kitchen table. "So, Papa, are you ready for the Shoah interview?"

"Ready as ever, I suppose," Hans said.

If push came to shove, he would concede that Jesse and Sam, his twin grandsons, and not his looming mortality, drove Hans to agree to sit for the Shoah Foundation video testimony. They were only three years old, but when he looked into their playful, innocent eyes, he knew some day they would want to know his story. He had not told his own children before now and felt enormously guilty about it.

The Institute for Visual History and Education, the project founded by Steven Spielberg, had conducted over fifty-five thousand testimonies from Holocaust survivors. A professional interviewer had scheduled a preliminary conversation with Hans to establish the guidelines and to complete the forty-page questionnaire from the Shoah Foundation's website. Once the pre-interview process was complete, a two-hour video testimony would record his memories—some shocking, some poignant, and some pedestrian—for future generations.

Hans, ever the introspective, analytical, and cautious man and former Mossad operative, printed out the questionnaire to prepare himself for the interviewer. Some of his life would remain secret, in accordance with the oath he had taken when he joined Israel's most secret service, at least to the extent that such stories remained classified. After all, some of his old comrades were still alive and, indeed, so were some of their targets or, as he referred to them, "missed opportunities." Retribution never aged or took a holiday.

Fred, named after Hans's father, Alfred, had only just heard him talk about how he had survived his first dozen years in Berlin. In fact, the intake person he had spoken with on the phone had suggested Hans's story was a rare one. He could be counted among seventeen hundred Jewish Berliners who survived the war in plain sight. In fact, they were the subject of a documentary made by Claus Räfle, *The Invisibles*. The interviewer would surely be most interested in that.

More important, though, he hoped his grandchildren might one day benefit from learning his story. How he survived. The life he led. The mistakes he made. His redemption.

"I still can't believe what you went through as a kid. You never breathed a word. Did Mom know?"

"I told her a fair amount. She knew pretty much everything, but we agreed to shield you and your sister from it. I came to America to bury my past, not to relive it. In retrospect, I know that was a mistake. When I saw the look on your face when I was telling the cops about my momma..." His voice trailed off. "I felt like I betrayed you by not telling you the truth. I saw the hurt. It was not fair to withhold it from you. It was selfish on my part, even if was painful to talk about it. That is not the legacy I wanted to leave you. It is important for you and your kids to know where you come from.

"And I think I will FaceTime your sister and bare my soul to her after I speak to the Shoah folks. Between the time difference and her crazy hours, I'll have to see when she is available. So do me a favor, if you speak with her by some chance, don't say anything. I want her to hear it from me," Hans said.

"Dad, Jesse and Sam may be too young to understand right now, but someday I know the video will mean a lot to them. I am sure Gila will feel the same but be equally surprised. You know, I've been dying to know more about what happened after the war and before I was born."

"You mean after I came to the States and met your mother? Well, you know, I came here in 1978 and met your mother in 1979, got married, and we had you in 1980."

"No," Fred interrupted, "I mean when you were a boy. Right after the Nazis surrendered. You said you were in a DP camp. I can't imagine what that was like, after suffering the way you did during the war. Then to have to stay in a DP camp afterward …"

"I see," Hans said, and began to tell his son what had happened after he escaped Berlin. "The DP camp wasn't so bad. You know, for the first time in a long time, I had a solid roof over my head. I lived in a bunk that had heat! It wasn't like building a fire to keep from freezing to death in the rubble of my building on the Unterlinden.

"My bunk housed almost entirely orphans. At the very beginning, there were only about fifty kids, but by the end of 1946, there were something like three thousand people at the camp, and of that, a thousand were kids. Lots of Polish and other Yiddish-speaking refugees. They stuck together.

"The authorities set up a school, a synagogue, a theater, and a hospital. It was like a little Jewish city within a city. Like I told you when we met with the cops and Solender, they taught us Hebrew and all about Israel. The land of milk and honey. More importantly, I heard that Israel was where Jews fought for themselves and weren't afraid of anybody. That's when I decided I wanted to go there.

"But let me tell you the most amazing story. I witnessed the first real miracle of my life at Schlachtensee. It was the beginning of April, and we had a large influx of Poles. They brought in more adults from other places to help in the commissary, to dole out food. But they still needed healthy volunteers from the camp itself to help out. There was this pretty Polish girl—I don't know her name to this day—but I figured that being a volunteer handing out food would be a way to get to meet her, to impress her. So that's what I did.

"I walked into the kitchen, and as God is my witness, I almost stopped dead in my tracks. My mouth dropped to the floor and there I was, staring at Lily. Lily Schwarz. My beloved second momma. The woman who had raised my momma and me! We ran to each other and hugged and cried like babies. To me, it was what it must have been like when the Jews saw Moses coming down from Mount Sinai holding the Ten Commandments! It was as if she had risen from the dead.

"Incredibly and unbelievably, after my opa left Lily at the Jewish Hospital after she suffered a head wound in the bomb shelter, she was held at the sammellager to be deported to Theresienstadt. Just as she was getting in the truck, her name was called, and she was pulled out of the line and escorted back to a room in the hospital.

"It turned out that a big shot SS general, Martin Becker, saw her name on the list for deportation, and he personally went to the hospital to seek out the director. He ordered the man to get her back and give her a private room and extra rations until he was told otherwise. Becker came to her room the next day, after confirming that her husband was Arthur Schwarz. Lily's late husband had saved Becker's life at Verdun during the First World War. Arthur took a bullet meant for Becker. He visited her every month until the war ended. He brought her chocolate!

"The Soviets eventually liberated the hospital, and Lily was released. She went to the DP camp in the American sector of Berlin, hoping someday to go to America.

"I have to give the Soviets some of the credit for expediting my moving to Israel. After the Soviet blockade of Berlin in the summer of 1948, they closed the camp. I was almost fifteen by then, and with the help of some people from the Jewish Agency, Lily and I went to Israel together."

Manhattan

Mills stood over O'Connell as he referenced recent arrest records that would have predated the GEDmatch by a week or so. The DNA sample was obtained from a criminal arraignment in Crown Heights. Within a very short time, the case had appeared before a grand jury. Incredibly fast.

Mills mumbled, "The accused must have had connections. Things never happen that quickly. The records were sealed because the grand jury declined to charge him. Damn it. We won't be able to see the testimony or why they dropped it. But it doesn't really matter. We just need the guy's name and address, and we can pay him a visit ourselves. Let's you and me take a ride over to Crown Heights and check with some of the guys at the precinct."

Merrick

Fred was mesmerized. "So, you and Lily arrived in Israel in the summer of 1948?"

"We actually arrived in Israel late in 1948," his father continued. "The Jewish agency placed us in a small farming community near Jerusalem. I learned how to do everything, from planting vegetables to harvesting wheat to picking cotton. I went to school and bettered my Hebrew. The adults took turns guarding the fields while others worked them. We were under constant threat from infiltrators, the *fedayeen*. In May 1951, two *fedayeen*, armed to the teeth, used wire cutters to penetrate the fence just after dusk. They were professionals, trained in Egypt. Before they were apprehended and eliminated, they tossed a live grenade into the nursery. A nursery! A twenty-four-year-old nurse, an old woman in her eighties, and two babies were killed. The old woman was Lily Schwarz. Sweet, dear Lily."

Hans did something Fred had never seen his father do before. He started to cry. And he could not seem to stop. Fred sat next to his father and put his arms around him.

At last, Hans pulled himself together. "You see, Fred, I can cry now. I have to credit the Lubavitcher rebbe for that. I truly have found my soul. It took a long time.

"As you can imagine, after Lily was gone, I was heartbroken. But I wanted revenge. As far as I was concerned, Israel's Arab neighbors were no different from the Gestapo. They took joy in killing innocent Jews. But not if I could help it. I volunteered to do night patrol. It was a few months before my eighteenth birthday. I was put through some training with a variety of weapons. During my time with the American Ninth Army, some of the soldiers showed me how to use an M1 Garand semiautomatic rifle, so I had a pretty good idea how to shoot. But I took a class to hone my shooting skills. And I was already pretty adept at using a knife. When I was ready, I patrolled at night at every opportunity. All I wanted to do was kill terrorists. But as luck would have it, we did not see additional infiltrations. As soon as I turned eighteen, I joined the Israeli Defense Forces.

"After basic training, as I told you and the cops, I was first assigned to the motor pool because I was mechanically inclined. After I eliminated the terrorist on our base, the commander decided there might be a better place for my skills, and they assigned me to a unit that did reconnaissance work. Training was intense. I learned more about killing in the next three months than you can imagine. Once I graduated the course, much of the time I was involved in clandestine operations. I'll just say I conducted surveillance, fixed equipment as necessary, and eliminated targets. I proved myself in some missions that were not publicized for obvious reasons and came to the attention of Ariel Sharon. In 1953, he was tasked by Prime Minister Ben-Gurion to create a group, Unit 101, expressly designed to retaliate against the *fedayeen*. It had, I would say, mixed results, and created a lot of controversy. During one operation, a fair number of terrorists were eliminated, but so were a lot of civilians. Sharon suffered a great deal of criticism, and there was political fallout. The unit was terminated, I think, something like five months after it was created, folded into the Paratroopers Brigade.

"I remained with Sharon for a while. But given what he called my 'tool kit,' he pushed me to transfer to the Mossad. I guess because I spoke several languages fluently, had blond hair and blue eyes, and could easily pass for a European or an American, that was where I fit best. I can't tell you specifics, but I can say that much of what you read in books or see in the movies about the Mossad is somewhat exaggerated.

"Operations like the Wrath of God, for example, which was intended to eliminate the terrorists who masterminded the murder of our athletes at the Munich Olympics, took years to plan and execute. It didn't happen in ninety minutes on a big screen, with the assassin giving the victim a ten-minute speech before pulling the trigger. Months of time-consuming and, often, boring electronic and visual surveillance, cultivating and paying informants, infiltrating terrorist organizations and meticulous planning were the critical elements that made for a successful operation. The assassin or assassins who fired the twelve shots into the terrorist in a hallway, or the bomb that blew up when the terrorist started his car were somehow, to me, at least, anticlimactic.

"I spent months at a time in Europe. There was no time off for sightseeing. It was strictly business. Long, lonely hours. Lots of watching and waiting. Then, finally, the culmination of the operation. Assassination, followed by time spent in a safe house and exfiltration. Needless to say, it was an existence that did not lend itself to fulfilling relationships. It would be fair to say that we were discouraged from marrying and having families."

The phone rang. "Let me get that, Papa." Fred rose. "Must be the Shoah people saying they are running late."

"No, this is his son," Hans heard Fred say. "What is this in reference to?" Fred was listening to the caller and seemed perturbed. "Look, I think my father has answered enough questions from the police," he said and hung up.

"What was that about?" Hans asked.

Fred was just finishing up explaining when the phone rang again, and this time Hans answered it.

"Hello?"

Doug O'Connell perhaps was more surprised than pissed off to be hung up on. All he'd done was identify himself and indicate he had a couple of questions for Hans Sternlicht. Now, he said, "Hello, Mr. Sternlicht. This is Detective Doug O'Connell from the NYPD Special Investigation Division. Please don't hang up."

"This is Hans Sternlicht. What can I do for you, Detective? My son didn't mean to be rude, but as you can imagine, we've been through a lot recently."

O'Connell said calmly, "I fully understand, Mr. Sternlicht. Look, maybe I was the one who came off sounding rude. I apologize to you and your son. I wasn't calling in connection with your case in Brooklyn. That was closed and you were fully exonerated. The reason I am calling is that when your DNA was run through GEDmatch, we discovered a close match with a sample from an old crime scene."

Hans raised his eyebrows with a look of genuine surprise on his face.

Fred whispered, "Just hang up."

Hans waved him away. "What do you mean, an old crime scene?"

"Nothing to do with you, Mr. Sternlicht. But it's possible some relative of yours many years ago might have been involved."

"Look, Detective, if you spoke to Marty Golden, you know I am a Holocaust survivor and have no relatives. Both my parents were killed by the Gestapo during World War II. My grandparents died during the war as well. I was an only child and so were my parents, so I think you are barking up the wrong tree," Hans said.

"Is it possible you have relatives you don't know about? In the United States? The case I am referring to goes back to the war era. Could you have an aunt or uncle or cousin you didn't know about who lived here then? Is it possible your parents had other children? Or that you were adopted? Generally speaking, DNA doesn't lie."

Fred could see that his father was becoming more and more agitated. "Papa, just hang up the phone."

Hans gestured to Fred to be quiet. "Detective, it is not possible. At least I don't think so." He had, of course, read stories about people discovering long-lost relatives after sending DNA samples to 23andMe or Ancestry.com, but he'd never expected to be involved in such a thing himself.

Perhaps O'Connell had noticed curiosity in Hans's voice; he certainly didn't seem to be willing to end the phone call just yet. "Look, Mr. Sternlicht, I don't want to give you agita. I tell you what—let me give you my phone number. My division handles old cases, what we refer to as cold cases. Sometimes DNA and genealogical evidence help us crack them. If you're interested, give me a call, and I'll come to see you one day. No obligation." The detective rattled off his number, and Hans found a piece of paper and a pen to write it down.

"Let me give this some thought and maybe I'll give you a call. I've got your number."

The doorbell rang.

Fred looked exasperated. The nerve of that detective, bothering an old man who'd already been through so much. He collected himself and then rose and went to the door.

A short woman in her early forties, with curly brown hair and large, black-framed glasses, introduced herself to Hans and Fred as Amanda Bomzer and handed Hans her card.

Fred extended his hand, "I am Hans's son, Alfred Sternlicht. Please call me Fred. Is it all right if I stay?"

Bomzer said in a respectful but no-nonsense fashion, having been asked this question many times before, "Generally, I prefer that a child not be involved during the intake or filming sessions. We don't want the subject to feel inhibited in any way. Sometimes memories are painful and emotional but are always very valuable. In other words, we don't want your father to hold back. Is that okay?"

"No worries at all," Fred replied, a little disappointed. "I've got to get some work done, so I'll be off."

After Fred left, Hans offered Ms. Bomzer coffee or tea. He read and signed the release before they began.

"Mr. Sternlicht, I am truly looking forward to our interview. While I have conducted quite a few interviews over the years, you are one of the few 'survivors in plain sight' I have had the opportunity to meet. I want you to feel at ease. I know that retrieving and coming to terms with some memories will be difficult. Anytime you want to take a break, don't hesitate to ask. Don't worry about the questionnaire. I know it can be daunting, which is why we do the intake in person. We will make things as conversational as possible. If you want to come back to a subject at any point, don't hesitate. There is no time limit, and if you don't remember exact times and places, don't be concerned. Once we complete the preliminary interview session or sessions, we'll schedule the videotaping. And in between, if there are any documents, photos, or anything else you would like to share, please feel free," she said.

Ms. Bomzer was an excellent interviewer. She jogged Hans's memory when it seemed necessary but for the most part allowed Hans to answer questions and add information as it came to him. She never interrupted. And Hans's superb memory and attention to detail, due in part to his Mossad training, made the time fly. They had started at about one o'clock and it was 6:30 before either of them glanced at the time.

"Oh my," she said, "where did the time go? I am sorry, Mr. Sternlicht. I didn't realize it was so late. You are terrific! You have an amazing memory and your story is remarkable."

"I must confess, I found it heartbreaking and comforting at the same time," he said. "It brought back lots of memories. It was actually nice to reminisce about my papa and his parents. I was only five when Papa died during Kristallnacht, but I remembered more about him than I had thought. I think I never had the time to miss him. Does that make any sense?"

Ms. Bomzer nodded. "Yes, it does."

"I have never gotten over the horrible irony that my Opa Josef and Oma Bette left everything they worked so hard for in Berlin only to be killed in London during the Blitz. It was almost like being killed by the Germans twice. So sad. It amazes me how much I remembered." Hans shook his head.

Then he stood a bit shakily, crossed the room, and opened a drawer in the buffet where Sarah kept her china and flatware. He came back to the interviewer holding the tattered gray wallet his momma had thrust into his hands before they parted outside the cemetery in Berlin so many years before.

He opened it and took out the photograph, which he gave to her. "This is my momma and papa, my Opa Josef, my Oma Bette, and my Opa Helmut…and me, of course. I was a little shorter and much younger," he joked.

"That's an amazing photo, Hans," she said. "Where was it taken?"

"In my Opa Josef and Oma Bette's flat on the Unterlinden. They had two apartments in the building and their store was on the ground floor. We lived in the flat above theirs."

Ms. Bomzer examined the photo carefully. "Hans, I am not an art specialist, but I would wager that painting is a Renoir."

"Yes," Hans recalled. "They were pretty well off and had a lot of artwork. But they lost everything after Kristallnacht. Imagine the Nazis forcing Jews to pay for the damages they themselves caused."

"Did you file for reparations? Or try to trace the artwork?"

"I get a few hundred dollars every month."

"I don't mean just that. I mean the Commission for Art Recovery. You should contact them to see if they can assist you in getting back your grandparents' artwork," she said. "I'll get you the information. And I'll get back to you about when I can return with the videographer. Thank you again for all your time and for telling your amazing story!"

Hans showed her to the door. "Thank you so much, Amanda. I wish I had done this sooner."

After she left, Hans stood holding the gray leather wallet. Other than the switchblade his opa had given him, this was the only physical remembrance he had left of his childhood. The family photo, the stationery with his father's name typed on it followed by the letters UBS, an address, and a series of numbers—he had learned years ago that the information would lead him to a Swiss bank account that probably would have made him a wealthy man, if he cared about money; still, he made up his mind to tell Fred about it—and the small wax paper envelope containing a lock of blond hair and the faded words, "Yours Truly, RH." He had forgotten the Steiff elephant that once belonged to his father until this moment, and now his heart ached for it, vividly recalling his Oma Bette giving it to him as a reminder of his father and his solemn oath to care for it. Tears welled up in his eyes as he realized he had let his grandmother down. The poor stuffed animal had been buried in the rubble of their building on the Unterlinden. In their rush to leave the flat when that last siren sounded, he had left it behind. The little elephant had died a hero's death, he thought.

Hans put down the wallet, his focus turning to the phone number he had written down just before Amanda Bomzer arrived. Detective Doug O'Connell, Special Investigations, Cold Case Division. A DNA match from an old World War II case. He had to admit the call had piqued his curiosity. Hans, fascinated with science even at a young age, had read enough since to know that O'Connell's emphatic statement was correct: DNA didn't lie.

He picked up the phone and dialed the number.

27

BERGENFIELD, New Jersey

Every member of the band was chilled to the bone. Standing in formation in the high school parking lot on a windy fall afternoon was no one's idea of good time. They'd been out there rehearsing for hours. Now the sun was starting its slide into night, painting the clouds a mélange of orange, red, and yellow, removing what little warmth there had been. The same time next week it would be dark, after the clocks were turned back for Daylight Savings Time.

"Hold on, hold on, cut, cut," Richard Rimes, the band director, shouted. He paused, then placed his hands over his ears in mock horror, doing his best impression of Edvard Munch's "The Scream." "Hey, trumpets…don't take this the wrong way, but that sucked," he said, more seriously than in jest this time. "The song is 'Santa Claus Is Coming to Town,' not 'Santa Claus Is Tone Deaf.' Folks, we have just weeks left to get this right. You've got to get it together. I don't want us to be the turkey at the Macy's Thanksgiving Day Parade. Let's take it from the top."

With that, Rimes turned, tapped his baton on the music stand in front of him to get everyone's attention, and collapsed to the ground.

At first, some of the kids started to laugh. Rimes was known for his offbeat theatrics. He would do almost anything to reduce the tension when things sounded hopelessly awful, especially before a big performance. Pratfalls, a brief tap dance, or even dropping his pants to reveal a pair of bloomers he'd borrowed from the theater department were Rimes classics. They'd endeared him to many a student over the years. He was much loved by Bergenfield High School marching bands for the past two decades, and somehow he always managed to get the most out of them when it came to crunch time.

But this time it was no gag. He didn't move.

"Mr. Rimes, you okay?" The first trumpet, closest to Rimes, said. "Oh shit, somebody get the nurse."

Within six minutes, an ambulance had arrived and rushed him to Hackensack University Medical Center.

❖ ❖ ❖

"Overhead page Dr. Strassman, would you, please? He seems to be coming to," Dr. Feldman said, turning to the nurse beside him. She nodded and entered the page.

Rimes looked up quizzically as a man in a white coat and a surgical mask came into focus. Out of the corner of his eye, he could see tubes running into his left arm from a bag suspended above him and another tube taped to his right wrist. Annoying tubes in both nostrils were delivering oxygen to help him breathe.

"Ah, Mr. Rimes, I see that you are back with us. I'm Stuart Feldman, chief resident at Hackensack Medical. You've been in the hospital for a few hours now. Believe it or not, I recognized you right away. Like ten years ago or something like that, I was third clarinet in the B Band."

Richard tried to smile. His head and vision were starting to clear.

Dr. Mark Strassman entered and asked Dr. Feldman how Rimes was doing. He could see for himself that the patient was regaining consciousness. Without waiting for an answer, he continued, speaking directly to Rimes. "My name is Mark Strassman. I am a hematologist connected with Hackensack. Can you hear me?"

Rimes nodded.

"Good, good. Mr. Rimes, earlier today you collapsed and were brought here in an ambulance. You've been in the hospital for about three hours. We ran some tests, and you have a condition known as myelodysplastic syndrome, better known as MDS. Basically, MDS is a type of blood cancer where the cells in your bone marrow become abnormal. Right now, we are giving you a blood transfusion to replenish your platelets, at least temporarily, and some fluids to help you get your strength back. I have to tell you, this is a very serious condition. Fortunately, you are fairly young—I see from your chart, sixty. For patients under say, seventy, the treatment regimen is to administer a stem cell or bone marrow transplant, preferably from a donor with a strong match. Do you have any closely related family members? A brother? A sister?"

Richard's mind was racing, fear overtaking him, "I'm not following you. What's going on?"

Strassman took a breath before continuing. "I am sorry, Mr. Rimes. I know you're just waking up and I am throwing a lot of information at you. Waking up in a hospital bed is disorienting for anyone. You were at band practice today and passed out. You were rushed to Hackensack University Medical Center. We ran extensive tests and you have a condition called myelodysplastic syndrome, or MDS. To get better, you will need a bone marrow transplant from a close match. And, generally, time is of the essence."

Clarity of thought began returning to Rimes. He realized this was no joke and started to understand the severity of the situation. "A stem cell transplant? What if that doesn't work?"

"Let's take one thing at a time, Richard. May I call you Richard?" he asked without awaiting a response. "Do you have any close relatives?"

"Just my father, but he's in a nursing home. He's in his nineties."

"Well, that's a bit too old to provide stem cells for a marrow transplant," Dr. Strassman said gently. "Anyone younger? A brother or sister, a son or daughter? Even a cousin?"

"No. I have no children and I'm an only child. I am actually, well, gay, but I never had a special partner or any children. My mom passed away years ago, and she was an only child as well. So, no cousins. As for my dad, he was adopted, so, quite honestly, I have no idea if I have any blood relatives on his side."

Strassman thought for a moment before he spoke again. "Well, we will try to find as close a match as possible from the donor pools if there are no relatives. Let me ask you, did you ever do a 23andMe or Ancestry.com test? Did your father?"

"I never did, and I'm sure my father didn't either. He never had any interest in that sort of thing. I think he just accepted that he was adopted, and that was that."

"Well, I'd like to run some DNA samples from you and your father," Strassman said, partly addressing Richard and partly articulating his treatment strategy to the nurse's assistant who was taking notes. "You never know what may pop up, especially when there's been an adoption. I don't mean to speculate, but maybe your dad had another child somewhere along the line. Naturally, we'll run the marrow donor pool database."

Strassman paused for a moment and then asked, "By the way, any chance you're an Ashkenazic Jew on your mother's side? The reason I ask is that there are several sizable marrow registries for Ashkenazic Jews."

"Yeah, my mom was. Her surname was Silverstein. My grandparents on my dad's side were too. Not that it matters, because they adopted him. But they came from Germany, and I'm guessing they adopted him there...I just don't know if the birth parents were Jews or not. Actually, my real name is Richard Remer, not Rimes. I changed it after college. Back in the day, when I came out, it wasn't the norm to admit you were gay. To some families, it was a source of embarrassment. I decided to change my name so as not to bring shame to the parents. Ridiculous, isn't it? Anyway, yes, my mom was 100 percent Ashkenazi."

"Ashkenazis seem to share a fair amount of DNA. That might broaden the pool. There is an organization, Ezer Mizion in Israel. I think it was established in 1979 to create a registry. Israeli recruits have their cheeks swabbed and their data is entered. There have been a fair amount of donor success stories as a result. That said, the best donor is generally a close relative. I think you're young enough and in good enough condition to benefit from a bone marrow transplant, so, I'd like to get moving on identifying a donor as soon as possible. Where did you say your dad lives?" the doctor asked.

"The Godwin Home in Northport, on Long Island. He lives in the assisted living section, not the nursing home."

"Does he have his faculties? I mean, will he be responsive if we were to ask him to give a sample?"

Rimes chuckled and then coughed, the tubes in his nostrils irritating him. "My dad is in better shape than you and me put together. He's as sharp as a tack. He just started using a cane recently. He won't even call it a cane. He calls it a 'walking stick.' Says canes and walkers are for old people. He's ninety-six! I've always said, Walter Remer will outlive us all."

Rimer added, "During World War II, he suffered a severe injury that messed up his hands. With my mom's help—she was a nurse—he was able to adapt. But now he needs help doing more things. Almost anything requiring even a hint of dexterity. Arthritis has really done a number on him. Before the war, he was an aspiring pianist. Good enough, I've been told, to play with the Philharmonic or the best jazz bands. Sorry, I'm running at the mouth."

"No, this is interesting. What happened to him?" Strassman inquired.

"He never spoke much about it. Neither did my mom. All my

dad would say was that he was on a mission for the OSS behind enemy lines, and it was classified. Silly; that was seventy-five years ago now, for heaven's sake. I wish he would talk about it before it's too late, but the guy is stubborn as a mule. Anyhow, some of his fingers are missing, and he suffered a fair amount of nerve damage. So, he had to abandon the piano altogether. I inherited the music gene but was never in his class. That's why I'm a high school music teacher, not a concert pianist.

"But he was successful in business. My dad worked with my grandfather in his fruit brokerage business after World War II. Grandpa died in the 1970s and then my dad grew the business into a fairly big company. He eventually sold it to a large distributor. Must be over seventeen or eighteen years ago now. About the same time my mom died.

"Much to my surprise, he agreed to take a look at assisted living. I think in part because he knew over time he would need help and partly because he gave quite a bit of money over the years to Godwin, and I think he knows they will always take good care of him.

"I'll call him and let him know where I am and what happened. I don't think he was ever too interested in identifying his birth parents. I always got the impression he believed they abandoned him. But I'm sure if it might help save my life he would give a sample. We've always been on pretty good terms."

When he paused, the doctor explained the next steps. "We'll be able to release you once you regain your strength, probably in the next day or two. But your platelet count can drop like a stone again, with no warning, so no driving. No extra stress, so no band rehearsals. Like it or not, you'll have to take some time off teaching. Is there someone who can look in on you at home? Run errands for you?"

"Yeah, sure. My next-door neighbor. She's a doll. We bring in each other's mail when one of us is away. She's on my list of emergency contacts. Why?"

"With MDS, you can collapse if your platelets drop suddenly. So, if you need to be rushed here for another transfusion, it's good to keep someone apprised of your condition. Before we release you, I'm going to give you a shot of Procrit to help stimulate your bone marrow to produce red blood cells."

"So, you haven't talked about what happens if the marrow transplant doesn't work."

"Full disclosure, Mr. Rimes." Strassman hesitated momentarily. "Some people are helped by taking Procrit. And I have seen some have success with a drug called Inqovi. But marrow transplant, if it takes, is your best hope. Some, sadly, develop AML, acute myelogenous leukemia, which can limit life expectancy."

Rimes shook his head. "This is crazy, Doctor. One day I'm prepping the band for the Macy's Thanksgiving Day Parade, and the next I'm fighting for my life! I'm having a hard time comprehending it all."

Strassman said with great sympathy, "Let's be optimistic. We'll get the DNA sample and take things from there."

28

MERRICK

The doorbell rang at precisely 10:30 a.m. Hans appreciated punctuality; perhaps it was his German upbringing. He looked through the wide-angle peephole in his front door and saw two men and a woman outside. Out of habit, he put his hand in his pocket and clutched his switchblade.

"Who is it?" Hans asked.

"Mr. Sternlicht, it's Detective O'Connell, Detective Mills, and Dee Dee Moller from NYPD Special Investigations Division."

Hans opened the door. A late-model Chevy Impala, standard NYPD detective wheels, was parked in the street in front of his house.

He showed them into the living room and asked if they wanted something to drink to be courteous. O'Connell said they appreciated the offer, but they had stopped off for breakfast on the way.

O'Connell sat on the couch next to Mills, and Moller took an armchair next to it, while Hans sat down across from them in his old, oversized chair, the one Gila referred to as the Archie Bunker chair. Hans smiled at them. It was funny, but even though he had stopped working for the Mossad almost forty years before, his training, so deeply embedded in his psyche, forced him to observe their movements, their microexpressions. And, of course, his mind sped through options on how to disable them. Even on his best day, taking down O'Connell, who looked like he might once have been in an Army Special Forces unit, would have been a difficult task, though not impossible.

His initial instinct suggested O'Connell was a sincere, honest cop with a military background. He could tell O'Connell was relatively new at this job. Moller seemed eager, genuine, and resourceful. But Hans suspected something wasn't completely right with Mills.

"Thanks so much for agreeing to meet with us, Mr. Sternlicht. So, I'm Detective Doug O'Connell. We spoke on the phone. This is retired detective Ted Mills and this is Dee Dee Moller. She's a genetic genealogist."

Hans smiled broadly, nodding at each of them as they were introduced, noting that O'Connell said Mills was retired and that Moller had no official police title. "Nice to meet you all. So, I'm sure you are all good at what you do, but I'm not sure what this is about and even less sure how I can help you."

Mills was about to speak, but O'Connell cut him off. "I will explain what we do and what led us to you. But I've asked Dee Dee, who is an expert on exploring DNA matches and building family trees, to explain the details. She has been instrumental in helping us crack cold cases and can explain how that works better than I can. Dee Dee makes the science of DNA simple enough so even I can understand it. She'll explain why we wanted to talk with you and how you can help us."

"All right," Hans replied, a clear note of suspicion in his voice. "The floor is yours."

"Thanks, Mr. Sternlicht," O'Connell continued. "So, first, a little background on our department. The cold case squad reexamines cases, usually homicides, where we've previously exhausted all investigative leads. Since there is no statute of limitations for prosecuting homicides, we could conceivably work on a case that occurred decades ago. Thanks to advances in technology, particularly with regard to the forensics of DNA evidence, we can resurrect and solve those cases. Believe it or not, we've had a fair amount of success in identifying and convicting murderers many years after they occurred. And, occasionally, DNA has been used to exonerate someone who has been in prison for a crime they didn't commit. Quite honestly, this is in large part thanks to the advent of GEDmatch, 23andMe, and Ancestry.com. Their popularity has enabled the DNA repository to grow almost exponentially."

Dee Dee Moller interrupted on cue. "As Doug said, between forensics and genetic genealogical tracing and good old police legwork, we're able to break cases that would otherwise have remained cold forever. What we do is find relatives whose DNA is in common with the suspect. We often start by building out a family tree of a person who uploaded his or her DNA data to GEDmatch.

"Police investigators do a great job harvesting DNA samples by collecting blood, semen, or hair samples from victims at crime scenes. On top of the forensic evidence, of course, they do their best to run down every conceivable lead. But sometimes, even with their robust tool kits, they still come up empty. It could be that the killer didn't leave any trail. Or maybe he hasn't committed any other crimes, so there's no physical evidence to match it to.

"But as Doug said, we now have a tremendous pool of DNA to reference. If we're persistent and a little lucky, we can sometimes trace a killer back to an innocent relative's family tree. Let me give you a real-life example. If I'm getting too gory or gross, let me know. Everyone has different sensibilities and I want to respect that."

Hans said, "Please continue."

"A murder case that took place around thirty years ago remained a mystery until recently. The victim, a woman in her early twenties, was found in a wooded area in Rockland County. She was beaten and raped and buried in a shallow grave. It turned out that she lived alone in Manhattan on the Upper West Side. Her remains were found by a Boy Scout troop hiking in the woods a few days after she was reported missing. The police investigators swept the area, but there was a nor'easter the night and day following the murder, so any footprints were wiped clean. Investigators recovered blood samples from under the victim's fingernails and there was a semen sample, but nothing in the system identified the killer. The police conducted dozens of interviews with neighbors, coworkers, friends, family members, and ex-boyfriends, but eventually all leads were exhausted.

"About three months ago, there was a hit on GEDmatch. Roughly 20 percent shared DNA. In plain English, that translates into the possibility that the person who contributed to the DNA pool could be a grandparent, grandchild, aunt or uncle, niece or nephew, first cousin, or even a half sibling of the killer.

"We contacted the match, and she was willing to talk with us. She was a college student from New Jersey who got 23andMe for her nineteenth birthday. We helped her build out her family tree. Often, we have to do a lot of digging. Depending on how far back the case goes, we look at military records, ship manifests, employment records, speeding tickets, real estate, you name it. Painstaking work, but eventually it often pops. But in this case, it was fairly easy. The DNA trail led right to an uncle. It turned out he was a loner who she and her parents had little contact with. When we were certain he was our man, we still had to get a current DNA sample from him to confirm and make the arrest. He worked at a gas station up in Orange County, and the cops who were surveilling him were able to get a sample from a cup of coffee he tossed out in the garbage can.

"It turned out to be a match. He had apparently known the victim. They had grown up in the same town in Rockland, attended the same high school. He happened to meet her in a bar one evening in Manhattan. He eventually confessed he was going home to

Rockland County, where her parents lived, and offered to drive her home. I'll pass on the grisly details, but the police got him, and he was later convicted."

Hans nodded, understanding and admiring both the technique and the advancements genealogical tracing offered. He figured the Mossad had already incorporated this method of search in their tool kit. "Very interesting, Ms. Moller. So, how do you think I can help you?"

"Mr. Sternlicht," she started earnestly, "we think your DNA profile might help us solve a cold case."

"With all due respect, I think you've all wasted your time coming to see me. I realize DNA doesn't lie, as Detective O'Connell so eloquently told me, but maybe you got mine mixed up with someone else's. I am a Holocaust survivor. I was an only child, and so were both of my parents. I have no blood relatives except my children. The Nazis saw to that," Hans said dispassionately.

"We double-checked the sample to make sure," O'Connell interjected. "We found more than 25 percent shared DNA with a person of interest from a cold case that dates back to 1945. May 8, 1945, VE Day."

Hans said wistfully, "Ah, yes, I remember that well. I was with troops from the American Ninth Army. It was the greatest celebration I had ever seen. They even got me drunk!"

"Mr. Sternlicht, based on the shared DNA, the sample we collected from the person of interest in the homicide, by genealogical definition, would have to be either your grandfather, uncle, nephew or half sibling," Moller said emphatically, disrupting his reverie.

"Look, Ms. Moller, I am sure you're a great expert, but my grandfathers both died before 1945. My grandpa Josef Sternlicht was killed in London during the Blitz and my grandpa Helmut Weber died of a heart attack before the war ended and is buried in Berlin. I had no uncles, or nephews, or siblings," Hans said, visibly upset. "It would seem to me that someone mixed up my DNA sample with someone else's when they uploaded it to the system."

Moller, red-faced, said, "That isn't possible, Mr. Sternlicht."

Hans saw this was going nowhere. "I am sorry, but I cannot help you."

Mills was about to jump out of his seat, and Hans wondered if he would grab him by his collar and shake him. O'Connell, who also sensed Mills's anger, put a firm hand on the retired detective's knee.

"We're not asking you to do anything," he said. "Do you mind if we check records with our German counterparts to see if there is any data that might help us from their end? Maybe your mother or father were previously married and had a child. Maybe, after we leave, something or someone will come to mind. Anything is possible, don't you think?"

"Do whatever you want to do, Detective. That is your business," Hans said dismissively, indicating that the discussion was over.

"Thank you for your time, Mr. Sternlicht," O'Connell said as he got up to leave.

"I'm sorry if I upset you, Mr. Sternlicht. That wasn't my intention," Moller said as she shook his hand.

Mills said nothing, mumbling to himself as he less than subtly brushed past Hans, who was sure the man thought he was covering up something. What a strange, paranoid man!

Hans hadn't planned on getting Fred involved. He had elected to follow up with Detective O'Connell to satisfy his own curiosity, nothing more, nothing less. But, for whatever reason, something didn't feel right. It was instinct. Hans had spent his entire life trusting his instincts, and they mostly had been spot on. His gut had saved him more times than he could remember. Now, he decided to call Fred to fill him in. Get his son's opinion, and see if he was missing something. Besides, he didn't want Fred taken by surprise should O'Connell, Moller, or Mills contact him.

Also, after his cathartic outpouring to his son and Amanda Bomzer from the Shoah Foundation, he wanted nothing of his past hidden. He was going to share everything with Gila as well.

"Maybe you should report them to the NYPD. Not a very professional way to act. Did the old guy really act as if he was going to push you? Disgraceful. He should be put up on charges," Fred said angrily.

"I think he was definitely a bit off, but he didn't hurt me," Hans assured him. "I just thought he acted as if he wanted to."

"Like you said, Papa, they must have mixed up your DNA sample with someone else's. Stuff happens. Anyway, your entire family died in the war. I don't think they get that. They ought to read a history book, for God's sake, or better yet, go to a Holocaust museum. It's getting to the point where the Holocaust is just a historical footnote. I hate to say it, but I'm afraid once all the survivors are gone, the revisionists will be able to make up their own story of the past. What was it you said you learned from Goebbels? 'If you tell a lie big enough and keep repeating it, people will eventually come to believe it'? The next generation won't have any idea what the truth is and probably won't care."

"That might be going a bit too far. But that is one of the major reasons I decided to do the Shoah interview. Maybe someday future generations will be forced to watch old guys like me on video tell them what really happened. That's the only way to educate them so it never happens again," Hans said hopefully, though unconvincingly.

"I hope you're right. You know, the more I think about those cops, the more pissed off I get. After everything you went through, they should have just left you alone. It's pretty obvious that somewhere along the line someone made a mistake uploading your DNA information. And there's no way they're going to have any luck finding a murderer from seventy-five years ago no matter whose DNA they think they have. What's the chance the guy is still around? Just for argument's sake, if they did find him, what good would it do them? They're going to slam the shackles on some hundred-year-old guy in a wheelchair who can't remember his own name? It seems more like an obsession to prove something rather than to put a dangerous criminal behind bars. Sounds like the cops are wasting time and resources to me. Anyway, it's a shame they got you upset." Fred changed the subject, "Would you like to come over and have dinner with me and Ellen and the kids? Maybe it will take your mind off this stuff."

Manhattan

O'Connell drove back to the City with Dee Dee Moller sitting in the passenger seat and Mills growling in the back.

"The little fuck is lying. I can feel it. He's holding back, that shit. He's protecting the killer," Mills sneered.

"Are you freaking sick? What is wrong with you, Mills?" O'Connell said angrily. "If I wasn't driving, I'd punch you in the nose. That little old man is a Good Sam, for Christ's sake. Didn't you hear what Ron Fleming said? That guy has been through a lifetime of hell. And even so, at eighty-five, he risked his life to save that girl in Brooklyn. He's a freakin' hero. What the hell have you ever done?" O'Connell meant it, having examined Mills's less than impressive accomplishments during his career. Still, he instantly regretted saying it. After all, O'Connell grew up in a loving family raised by both his parents. Mills hadn't had that luxury.

"Listen, tough guy, that little prick knows something. He's holding out. I can smell it. Harboring a murderer is a crime, just in case you didn't know," Mills snapped.

"You don't know what the hell you're talking about," O'Connell shot back.

"Guys, guys, come on," Dee Dee Moller jumped in. "Stop. This is ridiculous. Both of you need to cool off."

"First off," O'Connell couldn't help himself, "the guy was freaking twelve years old in a DP Camp in Berlin when your mother was killed. He didn't come to this country until he was forty-five, and up until then, he didn't think he had a blood relative in the whole world! And until the NYPD ran a familial search and then went to GEDmatch, there's no way he would have known he shared DNA with anyone except his own kids. So where the fuck do you come up with this 'harboring a murderer' shit?"

Mills spat, "Listen, smart ass. The guy worked for the Mossad, for Christ's sake. He probably knows all kinds of secret shit. I'll bet you he knows everything about his relative that killed my mother. If you paid any attention, you would have noticed he didn't flinch when we told him he shared DNA with a killer. He just denied it. He could have been in this country with diplomatic immunity many times to cover it up. Those Israelis are masters at cover-up. He probably knows more than we'll ever know. He probably helped the guy change his identity or something. I'll bet he's been protecting the killer for years."

"You really aren't making any sense, dude," O'Connell said. "You're off the freaking deep end. Maybe you should take a Valium."

"Enough, you guys. I'm sorry, but this is really unacceptable," Moller said. "I have to work with your department…you guys are making me feel very, very uncomfortable…I don't want to have to report this."

They drove in silence the rest of the way to the NYPD office. When they pulled up to the security post at the garage, Mills quietly said, "I'm going to get out of here." He left the car and walked away.

O'Connell parked the car, and he and Moller took the elevator up to the squad room. They walked in and were met by Rosario. "So, how'd it go?" he asked, already sensing that something had gone awry. Intuitively, he followed up before anyone answered: "Why don't we take this into my office?"

Dee Dee described the day's events, quoting verbatim where

she could, O'Connell nodding his head in agreement with her recollections.

Rosario sighed. "First, do you think old man Sternlicht is going to report anything? Brass never wants to be surprised by unprofessional conduct letters, especially from a Good Sam. I don't know how I'd explain allowing a retired cop to be involved in conducting an investigation."

"I don't think so," Dee Dee offered. "He seemed a little annoyed, but nothing serious. Mills didn't accuse him of anything; he just was acting, well, unpleasant. And we were just doing our job."

"Good," Rosario said. "I don't need my ass in a sling at this point in my career. Where did Mills come up with this harboring-a-criminal shit? I'll have a word with him next time I see him."

"He looked pretty pissed when he left," O'Connell said. "I don't think he's gonna want to see me for awhile."

"He'll cool off in a week or so and bring you a doughnut and a cup of coffee and kiss and make up. Don't worry. Look, the guy has searched for his mother's killer for over seventy years. It's become an obsession. Now, in his head, he thinks he's on to something. Wacky for sure, especially 'cause no one could prove the hair sample is sufficient to ID the killer anyway, no matter what he thinks. But he's obsessed with it. Definitely one for the psychologists to figure out. And no matter what, Mills is going to need Dee Dee's help to build a tree for him to link the old man to the hair sample. So, my bet is he'll be as sweet as a pussycat next time you see him," Rosario said.

❖ ❖ ❖

Ted Mills walked to the subway. He picked up his pace as he realized how stupid he had been to lash out at O'Connell. First off, he would probably still need his help finding the killer. He certainly needed

Dee Dee's help. She was a magician when it came to tracking down hard-to-find DNA matches. And, of course, he knew he needed to stay in Rosario's good graces if he were to be allowed to come to the office and have access to resources. The last thing he needed was to be shut down at this point. He had waited so long.

He had to cool off and think of a way to make it up to O'Connell. He hated to apologize, and being a loner most of his life, he'd almost never had to. He would have to suck it up and just do it. Besides, he couldn't have O'Connell pissed at him. The guy was the detective officially assigned to the case now, after all.

Hopefully, he could make it good with O'Connell. Ted almost laughed out loud for a second, accepting that the confrontation with him definitely had been a bad idea. You didn't have to be Einstein to figure out that O'Connell could beat the crap out of him. And he'd heard he had PTSD or something. He didn't need to piss off a crazy bastard like that. Yeah, back in the day, he reminisced, he could go toe-to-toe with a guy like O'Connell. When he was a young cop, he was as strong as a bull. Now, though, at seventy-three, a few too many beers had rolled his soft middle over an already loosened belt. It was stupid to get a bruiser like O'Connell hot under the collar.

It was just that now that the case was live again, with legitimate evidence from the DNA match, he had a pretty good feeling Rosario would take it to the end, no matter what. This was such a close match to his mother's killer, it was just a matter of time before they would be able to track him down.

As he hopped on the Q Train to Kings Highway, he couldn't help but think about that little shit Sternlicht again. Mills had been in the business long enough to know when someone was lying. There was no doubt in his mind. It was so obvious. Sternlicht never would have called O'Connell back to set up the meeting unless he thought they were on to him. Probably wanted to see how much they knew so he could cover the trail. The little creep must have used his Mossad contacts all along to cover up and protect his uncle or cousin or whoever it was who killed Mills's mom. How many times had he imagined his poor mother, fighting back with all her strength, ripping the son-of-a-bitch's hair out of his head before he killed her? Now, he was close to getting even.

Okay. He'd call Rosario as soon as he got home, admit he was a bonehead, and tell him he would come back into the office in a week or so, enough time to let O'Connell cool off. He'd do the mea culpa dance and set things straight. He'd apologize for his conduct to Dee Dee Moller as well. He wanted to be there when she finished the tree and identified the match.

Then the light bulb lit up. Now that Sternlicht knew they were on to him, like any creep harboring a criminal or covering up evidence, he would try to cover his tracks. Mills's investigative juices were coming back...he'd surveil the old guy. Follow him. *I think I might just tail the old bastard for the next few days.*

Great Neck

After dinner, Ellen and Fred cleared the table while Hans played with Jesse and Sam. Three-year-old fraternal twins, they were a handful. But they were the cutest things ever. He wished Sarah could have gotten to know them. Fred brought them with him to visit her at Godwin, but she didn't know who they were. She would smile at them and pat their heads, then turn her gaze to the window. It was heartbreaking.

"Okay, guys," Ellen said, "time for bed. It's nine o'clock, way past your bedtime."

"No, no," Jesse squealed.

"Just one more ride on the Grandpa choo-choo train," Sam shouted.

"I think the train has arrived at the station. Last stop, everyone," Ellen said.

Hans let Sam roll off his back onto the carpet, then gave them both hugs and kisses. "Next time, guys. The grandpa express will be back, making all stops. I promise."

Ellen led them off to bed.

"Don't you think that's a bit much, Papa?" Fred said.

Hans smiled. "As long as my heart beats, the grandpa express is here to stay. Those kids...I could eat them up."

"Let's FaceTime Gila, before she goes to work. I texted her earlier in the day, and she said she would be available at 4:00 a.m. her time, which is like now. Crazy hours she has."

Gila never really told them what she did, but she was always too busy to talk for very long and kept weird hours. Hans could tell, given her generally evasive answers, that she was either with the Mossad, Shin Bet, or Unit 8200, the secretive cybersecurity unit. It didn't pay to ask; she wouldn't tell him anyway.

She picked up on the first ring, smiling into the phone. "Hi, Abba," she said. "How are you? I see you're with Fred."

"Gila, good to see you smiling," Hans said. "Not bad for 4:00 in the morning." He laughed. "How much time do you have?"

"For you, Papa, all the time in the world," she said.

"Good. I'm not sure how much Fred texted you, but I've got a little story to tell. It's been a busy couple of weeks, to say the least." Hans proceeded to summarize the past few weeks in a succinct, former-Mossad-operative-like fashion. He understood that regardless of what she said, Gila would have a time constraint.

Her expressions changed from concerned when he discussed the Brooklyn incident, to somber when he told her the never-before-revealed details of his life in Germany, to annoyance at the recent visit by the Special Investigation detectives. Yet if she was shocked by any of it, neither Hans nor Fred could tell. That was Gila...very much like her father. Observant, analytical, and largely unemotional. She was slim and had blond hair and blue eyes, just like he did. Fred, on the other hand, had dark hair and a thicker frame, like Sarah.

"Wow, Papa. I am truly speechless. Well, I'm glad you finally decided to tell us. I can't believe what you went through as a kid." If she was surprised, which she probably wasn't, about his career in the Mossad, she didn't show it. "Do me a favor, though: no more rescuing damsels in distress, okay? Might be a good idea to retire the switchblade while you're at it."

Hans smiled, then held up the photograph from the tattered gray wallet. "I'm not sure if you can see this on the FaceTime, so I'll have Fred scan it for you, but this is the only photo I have left of my family. The lady from the Shoah Foundation loved it." Fred looked at it for the first time. Hans pointed out each of the people in the crumbling photo.

Fred gasped. "Dad, this is truly amazing. Why'd you hide this away? We've got to preserve it. It's incredible. I've never seen a photo of Grandma and Grandpa, or either of their parents. Why didn't you ever show it to us?"

"I am sorry, children." Hans seemed troubled. "I don't know why. I have always kept it with me as, well, as an amulet of sorts. This wallet was the last thing my momma gave me before we were forced to split up in Berlin. Whenever I looked at the picture, it made me depressed. But as long as I had the wallet and the knife Opa Helmut gave me, I also felt safe. And I'm not sure why I felt I had to show it to the lady from Shoah. She said the painting in the photo behind us, which hung in my Opa Josef and Oma Bette's flat, was a Renoir. I guess I'm not surprised. They were very well off before the Nazis seized all their belongings after Kristallnacht. She thinks I should try to post some kind of a claim, but I can't be bothered with such things. Besides, I have no proof it belonged to them."

"There are lawyers who do that sort of thing," Gila said. "We should look into it."

"What else do you have there, Papa?" Fred asked, seeing the crumpled paper and the small wax paper envelope.

"I don't know," Hans said disinterestedly.

Fred unfolded the paper. "This appears to be a numbered Swiss bank account for Alfred Sternlicht. That we should definitely check into. And this?" He pointed to the envelope.

"Beats me," Hans said. "It's a lock of hair. On the envelope it says, 'Yours truly, RH' in German. I have no idea who RH is, or whose hair it is. I'm not sure who put it in the wallet. For that matter, I don't know if it belonged to my momma, or to Papa or one of my grandparents. But my momma kept it with the things she said were most important to her, so I've been holding on to it for over seventy years."

29

BROOKLYN

Halloween. Not a good day to tail old Sternlicht, Mills thought. With all the kids and their parents marching around, an old man cruising around in a beat-up 2002 Toyota Avalon would stick out like a perv. Best to try the next day. No matter; Mills was an early riser. He'd get up at 4:30, as usual, and get to Merrick before 5:00. Going against traffic on the Southern State should be a breeze. Going the other way, toward the City, ugly.

Actually, it could be kind of fun. He hadn't been on a stakeout since he retired. He still had the old Nikon with the telephoto lens, and his Zeiss binoculars. Fill one thermos with coffee and another with Campbell's Chunky Chicken Noodle soup. The best.

He would make good use of the day. He would go in to the office now and apologize to O'Connell and Moller. He would pick up doughnuts and coffee for the whole office, then acknowledge what a jerk he had been and ask them to forgive him. They would understand if he said it the right way. All these years and being so close to finding closure about his mother had set him off. Dee Dee was a woman. She was soft. She'd understand for sure. O'Connell might be more of a challenge, with his PTSD and all. But, hopefully, the coffee and doughnuts would do the job. He took the Q train into Manhattan.

Merrick

Sternlicht's house was on the north side of Olive Street, between Whitcomb and Hamil Avenues, south of Sunrise Highway. Mills parked on Whitcomb, east of Olive. From his vantage point, he would know immediately if the old man left his driveway and in which direction he went. He could easily follow him north on either avenue. Mills could change it up every day or so.

Mills took a sip of coffee from his thermos and spread the *New York Post* on the steering wheel. Just like old times. Then, before he got comfortable, he saw Sternlicht's door open. He pulled his driver's cap low over his face and continued to "read" the paper. The old man never saw him.

❖ ❖ ❖

It was a Thursday morning. Hans left the house at 6:45, as usual, carrying a small bag containing his tallit, tefillin, and a peanut butter and jelly sandwich. He would attend the morning service at Godwin's small synagogue at 8:30, visit with Sarah, and have lunch with her before returning home. While he hoped and prayed Sarah would recognize him again one day, he knew it was not likely. The doctor had told him that while Sarah might have a moment or two of lucidity, or even draw an old memory from a certain part of her brain that still retained such things, there would be nothing more.

❖ ❖ ❖

Mills followed Sternlicht's Volvo up Whitcomb to Wantagh Highway, heading north. He stayed in the right lane and tried to maintain a distance of three or four car lengths between them.

Sternlicht took the Northern State Parkway East to the Commack Road North exit, traveled north on Commack Road several miles, and then turned left on Jericho Turnpike, heading west, for a mile or so. Then he made a right turn into the Godwin home.

Mills continued to drive west for about a mile on Jericho Turnpike so as not to be noticed.

❖ ❖ ❖

Within seconds of leaving his house, Hans had noticed the Toyota Avalon parked across Whitcomb at the southeast corner of Olive. He immediately recognized "retired" Detective Mills behind the wheel, his hat pulled down over his forehead, pretending to read the newspaper. Hans, who had once taught a surveillance course to new Mossad operatives, was both annoyed and amused at the detective's amateurish attempt at tailing him. What was his problem? Did he really think Hans was hiding something? Absolutely ludicrous.

Godwin had strict rules for visitors to the nursing facility. All the security personnel at the front desk knew Hans, Fred, and Gila were the only visitors permitted to see Sarah. They would never let that character, or anyone else, for that matter, see her, so he wasn't concerned about Mills upsetting her. Just to make sure, though, he would double-check the procedure with security prior to going to the synagogue. Could Mills be so stupid or so cruel as to try to interview Sarah? Badger her for information that didn't exist? Perhaps, Hans thought, he was getting a bit carried away, reading too much into this foolishness.

❖ ❖ ❖

Mills made a U-turn at the first light a mile down on Jericho Turnpike and drove back. He conveniently found a strip mall diagonally across from Godwin. There was a deli, a toy shop, a dry cleaner, a hair salon, and ample parking. Perfect. He could hang out there for as long as necessary, then follow Sternlicht to his next destination. Surveillance was generally boring work, but it could be rewarding if you stuck it out.

He took out his iPhone and Googled the Godwin home. It was a big place. A nonprofit containing residences for those age fifty-five or older, assisted living, and nursing facilities. Bingo! Mills thought; it seemed it also housed his mother's killer. Though before he got too carried away, he realized he would have to surveil Sternlicht for another few weeks, gathering as much insight and intel as he could, just to be sure. He couldn't just barge in and follow Sternlicht to the killer's room. He was retired, so he had no credentials to get him through security. And he had no warrant. He had come too far and waited too long to do something stupid now.

But it made perfect sense. The old man was visiting the killer. Probably telling him how close they were to nabbing him. For a moment he panicked; what if the murderer was senile? No matter; after so many years of pain, someone had to pay. Mills just needed a name and a room number.

For a second, the anguished child's voice inside Mills's head told him to just ambush Sternlicht at gunpoint, get him to give up his mother's killer's name. But the adult, the detective, reminded him to calm down. He would get the name, approximate age, and maybe even the room number once Dee Dee Moller had completed the family tree and confirmed the identity. It couldn't be more than a matter of weeks. Once in a while, she hit a brick wall, but most of the time, she was a magician. Just in case, though, he would continue to keep a close watch on Sternlicht.

❖ ❖ ❖

Hans left Godwin with assurances that no one but his immediate family would be permitted to visit with Sarah. The security personnel and nurses were on the case. Just for the sake of his peace of mind, though, he took a moment to visit with Arlene Weinstein, the chief medical director of Godwin, before he left. Hans had known her for several years, and a more caring person would be hard to find. Her reassurances regarding Sarah's privacy were comforting. Just to be sure, he gave her a description of Mills.

He left Godwin around 1:00 p.m., after lunch. He fed Sarah some soup and applesauce and told her how much he loved her. She smiled and looked flattered. She might not have any idea who he was, but she seemed to enjoy the soothing words.

On his way home, Hans noticed the gray Toyota pull out of the strip mall kitty-corner to Godwin. For a moment he thought about losing Mills, but what was the point? The idiot probably had nothing better to do. He'd likely tail him for a few days until he realized he was wasting his time.

The next morning, Friday, Hans left his house at 6:45 again, but this time, as he did every day except Monday and Thursday, when he drove up to Godwin, he attended morning services at the Ohav Shalom Synagogue on Marcy Avenue. Afterward, he stopped in to Stop and Shop to get some provisions and then went home, where he stayed for the rest of the day.

On Saturday, Hans left home at 8:30 and walked to the synagogue nearby. He spotted the Toyota immediately, and Hans decided to wedge a tiny leaf in his front door before he closed it, just in case the fool broke in to search his house. Then, Mills would have gone too far. Hans laughed at his own paranoia, part of his old skill set. Just the same, he would give this charade a few more days before reporting Mills to the Merrick PD or placing a call to his new buddy, the attorney Solender.

Brooklyn

Mills had been tailing Sternlicht for almost two weeks. An easy mark, for sure. Same pattern. Too bad that when Mills was an active detective the bad guys weren't this easy to track.

On Saturdays Sternlicht walked to a synagogue and then back home, presumably after morning services. He didn't go out again. On Sundays, Tuesdays, Wednesdays, and Fridays, he drove to the synagogue in the morning. He did his Stop and Shop gig on Fridays right after.

On Wednesdays, at 7:00 p.m., probably after dinner, the old guy drove to Crown Heights. He somehow managed to find a place to park, which in itself was kind of a miracle, and then went into the Lubavitcher World Headquarters building at 770 East Parkway. A little over two hours later, he emerged from the building, got into his car, and drove home. Mills lived in Brooklyn, so he just headed back to his apartment at 1901 Avenue P. No sense in following Sternlicht back to Merrick and then making a big U-turn back to Brooklyn.

Like clockwork, on Mondays and Thursdays, Sternlicht headed out at 6:45 in the morning to the Godwin home in Northport. He did his business there, then drove back home.

Easy enough to follow the old liar. Well, no matter. Mills had positively ID'd the location where Sternlicht visited his mother's killer. Had to be. Now he just needed a name and a room number. Knowing Dee Dee Moller, she'd be able to construct a family tree in no time. Even if she had to reach across the Atlantic to her German contacts, she'd be able to unravel the identity of the killer. One thing about the Krauts, they kept good records.

30

HACKENSACK, NJ

It was almost exactly two weeks, just as Dr. Strassman had predicted. Richard Rimes called his neighbor, sounding disoriented. She quickly dialed 911 and the ambulance took him to Hackensack University Medical Center, where the ER doctor on duty immediately paged Dr. Strassman. When he arrived, Rimes was already receiving fluids and a transfusion and looking far more alert than when he arrived.

"How are you feeling, Richard?" Strassman asked.

"Better now. Well, Doc, I know we have an appointment this afternoon at 2:30. I guess I'm a little early," Rimes joked.

Strassman half smiled. "I am sorry, but this is how MDS works. But I have what I hope will develop into some good news for you. While we haven't found a great marrow stem cell match in the pool yet, we did find a reasonably close DNA match. Not sure how old the subject is, but we'll be contacting him. If he is a good match, hopefully he will be a willing and able donor. I don't have a name yet, but he's in Merrick, on Long Island, near Jones Beach. Not too far away."

Merrick

Hans answered the phone on the third ring. "Yes?"

"Is this Hans Sternlicht?"

"Who should I say is calling?" he responded warily. He'd seen "Hackensack University Medical Center" on his caller ID.

"My name is Dr. Mark Strassman. I'm a hematologist with Hackensack University Medical Center in New Jersey. I'm calling because we have discovered that a Mr. Hans Sternlicht shares a substantive percent of DNA with a patient of mine who requires a bone marrow stem cell transplant. In cases where there is shared DNA, it's possible one might be a suitable stem cell donor, in a position to save someone else's life. Is this Mr. Sternlicht?"

"Yes, it is. So, could you explain how you found me and why you think I might be able to save this person?"

"Well, Mr. Sternlicht, you have a sufficiently similar DNA profile to my patient, so somehow you must be related. My patient suffers from a type of blood cancer, called MDS, myelodysplastic syndrome. MDS patients are essentially unable to produce normal bone marrow and require frequent blood transfusions. In many cases, without a stem cell or marrow transplant, they will die. Generally, we look for a healthy donor, age sixty-five or younger, who shares a specific protein marker, known as HLA, human leukocyte antigens, with the patient," Strassman said. "Relatives or people who share DNA tend to be good donor candidates."

"I am sorry, Doctor. I would like to help," Hans said, genuinely disappointed, "but first, I am eighty-five. Second, I don't know how I could possibly have similar DNA to anyone other than my own children. I am a Holocaust survivor and have no other relatives. Perhaps this is a mistake."

It was clear now that whoever uploaded his DNA sample had mixed it up with some other person. Here was confirmation that the visit from the cold case cops was a function of that mix-up. He would have to try to clear this up, have whoever was responsible correct their information.

"That's too bad, Mr. Sternlicht." Strassman was persistent. "A mix-up is possible, but just in case, would you be willing to give us a cheek swab? That way we could independently confirm if it is or isn't your DNA. I think you're correct, however. You would likely be too old to help us regardless. But you said you have children?"

"Yes, I have a son who lives nearby and a daughter who lives, umm, out of town," Hans said.

"Would you mind if I sent swab kits to your son and daughter? Even if your DNA match is due to an input error, one never knows if your children's HLA might be a match. It would be a great mitzvah, Mr. Sternlicht."

"I'm always up for a mitzvah, and I know Fred is as well," Hans said.

"I'll FedEx you a few swab kits with overnight return boxes to your Olive Street address? Or I could send them directly to your kids?"

"No, that's okay. Send them to me. I will have to explain it to Fred before I give it to him."

"Will do, Mr. Sternlicht. I would be grateful. Time is of the essence, I'm afraid," Strassman said.

"Thank you."

"Goodbye, Dr. Strassman."

Hans hung up the phone and immediately dialed Fred, who was just finishing up a phone conversation and promised to return his call.

Hans's phone rang a few minutes later.

"Hi, Papa, what's up? How's everything?"

Hans relayed the conversation with Strassman as best he could.

"Strange with this DNA stuff. We'll have to figure out how to correct what the cops and GEDmatch has on their sites. Perhaps it's as easy as submitting a new DNA sample and having them correct it in their systems. I'll call them to find out. At any rate, I'll come by tomorrow to take the swab test. If they send an extra, Ellen can do it as well. You never know. To save a life is like saving an entire world." Fred smiled at the Talmudic reference his father so often quoted.

Northport

Fred drove out to Godwin to have lunch with Hans and his mom, as he had done once a month for some time. He was grateful his mother still smiled at him when he came into the room with his father. She obviously didn't know who he was, but she seemed genuinely pleased with the company. Sometimes, though, it was unbearable. She had his mother's outer shell, but the inside was empty. *Alzheimer's—the greatest scourge of our time,* he thought.

As they prepared to leave, Hans's cell phone rang. They were standing next to Fred's Volvo. "Hackensack University Medical Center" scrolled across his phone. He answered on the third ring.

"Good afternoon, Mr. Sternlicht. This is Dr. Strassman from Hackensack University Medical Center."

"I didn't expect to hear from you so soon. But you're in luck; my son is here with me. I'll put you on speakerphone."

"Great. Gentlemen, I hope you're sitting down," the doctor said, clearly excited. "So, some great news. While I'm afraid Mr. Sternlicht Senior is too old to be a donor, as he and I discussed, Mr. Sternlicht Junior's HLA is a match. We think if he donates his stem cells, my patient's chances of survival are good. Interestingly, both your DNA samples indicate a fairly close relationship to him. As I said, I hope you're sitting down. Hans, your DNA is a pretty close match to my patient's. In fact, even more interesting, you are roughly a 25 percent match with his father, who resides in a nursing home on Long Island. The father could be your half brother or an uncle. We would need to do some genetic genealogical tree building to ascertain exactly how you are related, but we may have discovered a close relative you never knew you had."

Hans was dumbfounded, "It can't be possible, Doctor."

Fred's mouth was wide open in shock.

"But it is, Mr. Sternlicht. I realize it's a surprise, but DNA doesn't lie," Strassman said, repeating the words Hans seemed to have heard so often lately.

There was silence on the other end of the phone as Hans and Fred absorbed the doctor's assertion.

"I'm sorry," Strassman said. "I realize this is a lot to comprehend and probably a shock. But as I explained, the sooner we can harvest stem cells from Mr. Sternlicht Junior, the sooner we can try to save my patient's life."

Fred said, "All right, Doctor. Count me in."

He and the doctor discussed setting up a meeting in New Jersey as soon as possible, and Strassman briefly explained the process of an allogenic transplant. "We'll just do a blood test first to make sure everything is in order. Then, we'll administer a general anesthetic, and the sample will be drawn by syringe from your pelvic or hip bone. You'll need to remain in the hospital for a few hours, if that's all right."

Hans volunteered to go with Fred, and then said, "Dr. Strassman, did I hear you correctly? Did you say your patient's father could be my uncle or half brother? And he's in a nursing home on Long Island?"

"Yes, Mr. Sternlicht, on both counts. He could be an uncle, a half brother, a nephew or a grandfather, but given his age, I would rule out the latter two. My patient's father also provided a DNA sample, which is how we figured out the proximate relationship. He is in his mid-nineties but has all his mental faculties. He lives in an assisted living facility. The Godwin home in Northport."

Hans and Fred were stunned. "That's where we are right now! My wife is in Godwin. She has Alzheimer's."

"That's quite a coincidence! Truly one for the books," Strassman exclaimed. Then he demurred, "Due to confidentiality, I'm not permitted to give you his name until I can have my patient clear it with his father. But I'll call him right after we hang up. May I give your names to the patient? I can have him contact you if you wish. If you'd prefer not, we can certainly maintain your confidentiality."

"It's okay with me, Dad," Fred declared.

"Same here. I can't believe it. For the life of me, I can't fathom how we are related," Hans pondered.

"I'm no genealogist, but my patient did say his father was adopted," Strassman offered.

31

MANHATTAN

"You didn't have to do this," O'Connell said, taking a cup of coffee and a doughnut from the tray Mills held in front of him.

"Yeah, I did. Peace offering. I was a jerk. Got carried away. I'm sorry," Mills said with as much faux sincerity as he could muster. Maybe not an Academy Award–winning performance, but good enough. He had called O'Connell and Moller a week before, after confessing to Rosario about his poor conduct after the interview with Hans Sternlicht. Mills had apologized to them then as well. But a mea culpa in person, dispensed with coffee and doughnuts, usually really did let bygones be bygones.

"Roger that," O'Connell responded.

Mills offered the tray to Dee Dee Moller, who was focused on her computer. "Oh, no, thanks. On a diet. But I'll take the coffee black, if you have it."

"Sure," he said, selecting a plain black coffee and handing it to her from the tray. "Dee Dee, listen, I just wanted you to know I was sorry for the way I acted."

"No worries, I understand," she said, still engrossed in whatever it was she was looking at on the computer screen.

Just like he thought…women were soft. He walked toward his desk. O'Connell and Sweeney were still munching on their doughnuts, and Rosario had come out of his office to grab a cup of coffee and a snack. "Hey, any chocolate ones left, or did you freaking diabetics finish 'em all?" Rosario asked.

"Well, I'll be a son of gun," Dee Dee said in a surprised yet excited tone. "Look at this!"

Rosario was the first to come over and look over her shoulder, followed by O'Connell, Sweeney, and Mills. "What you got there?" Rosario asked.

"A 100 percent match," Miller said. "I was scrolling through GEDmatch and bang, there it was. This data was just uploaded to the site. Amazing! We'll have to make a request to them for the suspect's name and location. I'll check with some of my buddies at the FBI to see if we can expedite it. As soon as we get a name and location, we can go pay a visit to the so-called person of interest."

Mills already knew the location…he just needed the name!

❖ ❖ ❖

Great Neck

Ellen, Fred, and Hans were attempting to convince Jesse and Sam to sit at the table for dinner, both at the same time. Ellen said, "It's like herding cats."

Fred laughed. As it was, he was already in a good mood, elated at the prospect of donating his marrow to save the life of a relative he never knew he had. "I can't believe the whole thing. I'm dying to know how we're related. By the way, Papa, I scheduled another FaceTime with Gila for Sunday night to fill her in."

"It must be a special occasion. Speaking to Gila twice in a decade! A miracle." Hans laughed at his exaggeration.

Just as they were about to sit down to eat, Hans's phone rang. Caller ID said "Unknown caller."

He answered cautiously, "Hello?"

"Hi, am I speaking with Hans Sternlicht? My name is Richard Rimes. I'm Dr. Strassman's patient. I believe he spoke with you about me."

"Yes, Mr. Rimes. Hold on a second; let me put you on speakerphone. Mr. Rimes, I am Hans Sternlicht and I am here with my son, Fred, his wife, Ellen, and my grandchildren, Jesse and Sam. It is nice to meet you."

"Please, call me Richard. I'm more thrilled to meet you than you can imagine."

"Richard, this is Fred. So great to speak with you. If you're up to it, would you like to FaceTime?"

"Great idea, but please excuse my appearance. I'm in the hospital," Rimes said.

Fred initiated the FaceTime call on Hans's phone, and they were all on.

"Wow, Hans. You have my dad's blue eyes," Rimes said. "I can't believe I'm looking at you all. First, I want to thank you, especially Fred. I'm so blessed that you're willing to donate your stem cells to me. I can never thank you enough. I can't wait until the surgery."

"It's my greatest pleasure. I hope and pray it will be 100 percent successful," Fred said.

"Thank you. Quite ironic that my MDS comes with a special bonus: relatives I never knew I had."

"We can't wait to hear more about you and your family," Fred said excitedly.

"Of course. And I'd love to hear all about you. I'm a bit weak right now, though, so, I'll just give you the highlights. Hopefully, if I'm cured, we can get to know each other a lot better. I am a music teacher in Bergenfield, New Jersey. Both my parents were only children. To make things more complicated from a DNA standpoint, my dad was adopted as an infant. His name is Walter Remer. He was born in Germany in 1922. Oh, I changed my name to Rimes years ago. I'll explain more when we meet."

Hans interrupted. "I know the name Remer from someplace."

"Yes," Rimes said. "Hans, Dr. Strassman told me that your wife lives at the Godwin home in Northport. There's a wing there called the Herbert and Paula Remer Assisted Living Residence. My dad named it in memory of his parents. You may have seen the dedication plaque. My dad has lived there for several years. He's ninety-six."

"That's so nice," Fred said. The Remers must be very wealthy to have an entire wing dedicated to them at Godwin, he thought.

Rimes was saying, "But there are no official records of his birth. No birth certificate. It's odd, I guess, since the Germans have always been sticklers for keeping records. We always speculated that his birth mother was too young to raise him and his father abandoned them. Or maybe he was whisked away, or stolen from his crib and sold to my grandparents, who couldn't have children. We really have no idea. What we do know is that my grandparents, Herbert and Paula Remer, adopted him when he was an infant. Soon after that, they came to live in America. Anyway, Dr. Strassman says Hans must be a very close relative of my dad— either his uncle or a half brother."

"Richard," Hans said, "is there any chance I can meet him? I visit my wife at Godwin twice a week."

"As a matter of fact, Hans, I spoke to my dad today. I told him what's going on, and he's very grateful that Fred's willing to donate stem cells to me. He definitely wants to meet you. Given his age, he has very few friends left. Maybe when the two of you get together, you can figure out exactly how you're related. I'll give you his phone number. You're best off calling him first and arranging the visit in advance."

It was obvious Rimes had reached the point where he needed to end the call. He gave Hans his father's cell phone number, thanked Fred again for agreeing to donate stem cells to him, and said, "I can't wait to meet your whole family. I hope this is the beginning of many family reunions to come. God bless you all."

"All the best," Hans said, and Richard hung up.

"Papa, call Mr. Remer right now. Dinner can wait. The guy is ninety-six," Fred said, only partly in jest.

"Sure, why not?" Hans said and dialed the number Richard had given him.

Walter Remer answered the phone on the first ring, "Hello," he said in a surprisingly strong voice.

"Hello, Mr. Remer, I mean Walter. My name is Hans Sternlicht and I'm here with my son, Fred, and his family."

"I've been expecting your call, Hans Sternlicht. Nice to make your acquaintance, and your family's. Thank you so much for trying to help Richard. This is a great mitzvah you're doing!"

"Walter, I would love to come to see you. My wife lives at Godwin. She's in the nursing home, and I visit her twice a week. I'll be driving Fred to Hackensack on Tuesday morning to donate the cells. Would you be up to a visit on Wednesday or Thursday?"

"How about Wednesday morning? I've got a bunch of tests scheduled for Thursday," Walter said.

"That would be great," Hans said. "I'm not sure if Fred will be up to coming. I imagine Tuesday will be a bit taxing for him. But I'll come myself and you can meet the rest of the family another time. I also have a daughter who lives in Israel."

"I'll let them know at the desk that you're coming," Walter said, and when they settled on a time he repeated it out loud, probably so he would better remember it. "I'm really looking forward to meeting you, Hans. Truth is, I don't get many visitors anymore. I can't wait to bore you with all my stories," he said with a laugh.

After the kids were in bed, Fred tapped his iPad to FaceTime Gila. It was the middle of the night in Israel. He'd never figure out how she kept such ungodly hours.

"Hey, Fred, hey, Papa, how's it going?"

They filled her in on everything that had transpired since they last spoke.

"That's marvelous. First, Freddy, it's really wonderful of you to donate your stem cells to this man you never met. I'm very proud of you. To save someone's life as an organ donor is the greatest gift you can give."

"Thank you, Gila. He seems like a really nice guy. I hope things work out for him."

"And Papa, I can't wait to hear about your visit with Mr. Remer."

"I'm really looking forward to it. He's a very old man, but he sounds like he's still got all his marbles."

"I have something to tell you two. After we last spoke, I did a little digging on my own," Gila reported. "Apparently, a day or two ago, Walter Remer's DNA popped up on GEDmatch. It seems Richard Rimes's doctor was able to get samples from him and his father and uploaded the data to try to find a DNA match for them. Here's where the police enter the picture: The NYPD Special Investigations unit reopened a cold case when your DNA signaled a close genetic match to a sample found at the scene of a 1945 homicide."

Gila explained what she'd learned about the murder on VE Day.

"So, that crazy guy associated me with a person he thinks may have killed his mother," Hans deduced. "That's why he's been following me. Mills thinks Walter is the killer and I'll lead him to him."

"Yes, Papa," Gila continued. "First, when your DNA sample popped up on GEDmatch, the similarity to the one found at the homicide scene triggered their interest in you and effectively reopened the investigation. They thought you would either have information about a person of interest, or they thought you could provide enough information to construct a family tree and, thus, lead to that person. Then, purely by coincidence, when Richard Rimes and his father took DNA tests to establish a potential genetic donor match, Walter's DNA lit up like a Christmas tree. Literally, a 100 percent match to a sample they've had since 1945."

"So, my newfound relative could be the man who killed Mills's mother?"

"The answer to that is no. The police report and the photographs of the crime scene indicated the killer strangled the victim, leaving a full handful of finger marks on her neck. The murderer couldn't have been Walter Remer because he lost most of his fingers. They were either severed or mangled during the war. Evidently, he was captured by the Gestapo on a mission behind enemy lines. He was tortured, and many of his fingers were ruined. The saddest part is, he was a promising pianist before that. So, even though he may have known the dancer in some way, he couldn't have been the one who strangled her. It would have been absolutely impossible."

"Do the police know this, Gila?" Hans queried.

"They're about to. Once the FBI hears about this, they'll convey it to the NYPD team," she answered. "It seems that everyone present at the club that night was interviewed by the cops after the murder. In the police report, they interviewed a 'Janet Silverstein and her boyfriend,' a war hero—it didn't mention his name for some reason—perhaps just quick or shoddy police work, or they didn't think it important enough to report—were seen with the deceased earlier in the evening at the nightclub, but they left together and were not witnesses to the murder, nor did they see anyone who they could say was a potential assailant. Janet's boyfriend, and soon-to-be husband, was Walter Remer."

"May I ask how you found out all this?" Hans asked, though he didn't expect a straight answer.

"Let's just say a little birdie told me and leave it at that. I suspect in a couple of days, you'll get a phone call from O'Connell or Moller, letting you know that you and your DNA match relative are no longer suspects in the Dana Mills cold case. But here's the most interesting thing we found: It seems Herbert and Paula Remer set sail on a luxury liner, the *SS Resolute* from Hamburg, Germany, in September 1922, destination, New York. They had two cabins. The ship's manifest lists the Remers, a Bella Ginzburg, who we guess was either a relative or a baby nurse, and a baby, Walter Remer. Are you ready?" Gila paused. "Their first-class fares were paid by Helmut Weber of Berlin. Also, a sum of fifty thousand dollars was wired from a UBS account from Helmut Weber to a Bank of New York account in Herbert and Paula Remer's name. A fortune in those days."

Hans froze. "Opa," he whispered. Then there was a pause while his brain processed the facts. He looked up, as if he were searching the heavens. "Momma."

"Yes, Papa. Your momma must also have been Walter Remer's."

32

MANHATTAN

"How about this. Walter Remer? That's the name from GEDmatch. He lives at the Godwin home in Northport," Moller announced to no one in particular.

"What did you say?" Mills's ears perked up.

"Walter Remer. R-E-M-E-R," she repeated, then spelled it for emphasis. "That's the guy's name. He's a resident at the assisted living home at Godwin."

A small group had gathered. Rosario, O'Connell, and Sunking were hovering around the cubicle Moller used when she worked in the office. "And get this: The building is named the Herbert and Paula Remer Residence, dedicated by their loving children, Walter and Janet Remer."

Rosario said, "Well, I think you guys should make an appointment to interview Mr. Remer as a person of interest. Amazing. A fresh lead after seventy years!" Rosario stressed the term "person of interest" so as to drill home the point to Mills—Remer might be a suspect or a witness, but certainly not the definitively accused. He didn't want another embarrassing incident. Imagine if this wealthy, ancient guy got shoved around by a retired detective Rosario had permitted to attend their meetings. He'd be demoted to a street beat instantly.

"Roger that," O'Connell said. "End of this week or beginning of next, I'll make it happen."

"I would love to be there for that," Moller added.

Mills nodded. "Jeez. Count me in."

If Rosario or O'Connell were surprised by Mills's subdued response, they didn't show it. Perhaps, for Mills, this was anticlimactic. Or it finally had hit him that this was just a lead to follow, not proof they had identified his mother's killer. Mills was a weird dude.

❖ ❖ ❖

"Hey, O'Connell," Moller shouted from her cubicle. "I just got off the phone with my buddy at the FBI. More intel on that old man, Remer. Where are the chief and Mills? Got to let them know too."

"I'm coming, I heard you," Rosario said as he walked out of his office. "What's up?"

O'Connell was already standing beside Moller. "Mills isn't in today. Probably tomorrow or Friday."

Moller said, "It turns out that while the hair sample belongs to Remer, he's not a suspect in the cold case."

"How so?" Rosario asked.

"The murder took place the night of VE Day, so everyone all over the country was partying. Mills's mom was a dancer at the Copacabana nightclub."

Rosario interrupted, "The Copacabana. Yeah, I know, the Barry Manilow song."

"The cops interviewed everyone who was at the club that night, including Janet Silverstein and her boyfriend, later husband, Walter Remer. He'd come back from Europe months earlier as a war hero." Moller explained the details. "The FBI recently received access to a previously classified file detailing Remer's mission.

Before Remer joined the OSS, he was a student at Columbia and a promising piano player. In fact, he played at the Copacabana on occasion, so everyone there must have known him. So, good chance the dancers and musicians all gave him a big hug when they saw him for the first time since he came back from overseas. That's probably where the hair sample came from. If you recall, the police report said Dana Mills was raped and strangled by very powerful, masculine-size hands. The finger marks were all clearly evident. The police concluded that Remer couldn't possibly have killed her." Moller explained Remer's injury. "He also had an alibi from his soon-to-be wife."

Rosario said, "Holy crap. That's some story. I'll give Mills a call later and tell him. I'm sure he'll be bummed out that the hair sample ain't from the killer."

Brooklyn

He had to laugh at the irony. Retired Special Investigations detective Theodore "Ted" Mills had spent his entire adult life upholding the law as a New York City cop. When he turned twenty-one, in 1966, he became one of New York City's Finest. He still remembered the swearing-in ceremony vividly, his grandmother, Sandra, beaming as he recited, "I do solemnly swear that I will support the Constitution of the United States and the Constitution of the State of New York, and I will faithfully discharge the duties of the office of police officer, according to the best of my ability."

Now, he was on his way to commit a murder. Well, technically you could call it a murder. But Ted didn't see it that way. To him, it was a fully justified act of retribution. Scratch that. Not retribution. It was redemption. He was simply going to eliminate a killer. He knew the law wouldn't do it. Courts were soft. No way they would incarcerate and convict a wealthy ninety-six-year-old codger in a nursing home. Mills could, and would, make it right after all these years.

In his mind, Mills finally had the conclusive proof, without the shadow of a doubt, that after all these years, he had identified his mother's killer. Walter Remer. He shivered at the thought of the scum choking his mother to death while she fought back valiantly, ripping Remer's hair from his head in a fight for her life.

The question was how to get past the Godwin security. He had his old badge and a revolver with a shoulder holster. The badge alone might work, but just to be on the safe side, he'd looked through his file drawer and removed a blank arrest warrant signed by Judge Harold Kantor…a judge he knew when he was on duty years back. Kantor was long gone, but it was unlikely that anyone at the front desk would know that. He filled it out…cold case…suspicion of murder…DNA evidence. Mills would tell them that he was not there to physically arrest the man, just question him about a cold case in which his DNA had identified him as person of interest. It was all true.

Finally, he made sure he had a syringe filled with the barbiturate-and-anesthetic cocktail he had lifted from the track, where he once arrested a veterinarian who used the stuff to illegally euthanize horses.

Remer was ninety-six. They'd never do a full autopsy. He had it all figured out. He'd jab the old man and then, after he was sure he was dead, run out in the hallway and get the nurse, yelling that the guy had died…before he could even question him. The guy must have keeled over just before he got there. Or, if there was a brief struggle, he'd just say the old guy freaked out when he presented the warrant, realizing he was finally caught after all these years. Heart attack on the spot.

Mills had all his bases covered. Besides, he figured, ninety-six-year-olds probably crapped out a dozen times a week in a place like Godwin. They'd be used to it.

He had no worries about running into the Sternlicht creep. From Mills's surveillance, he knew the guy only seemed to visit Remer on Mondays and Thursdays. In his mind, Mills figured if he could jab him with the euthanasia drug too, he would be doing mankind a service. He smiled to himself.

Northport

Hans went to the security desk at Godwin's Herbert and Paula Remer Assisted Living Residence Center. They requested a photo ID. He signed his name, and the security guard countersigned and entered the time: 9:30 a.m.

An attendant showed Hans to the apartment. Walter was sitting in his living room in a large chair, adjacent to a small couch and a cocktail table. He had wisps of light hair combed neatly over his head. He looked quite dignified, wearing a crisp, buttoned-down white shirt and an expensive cardigan sweater. There was an array of coffee, tea, water, fresh fruit, and assorted pastries on the table.

"Have a seat, Hans," Walter said. "Excuse me for not getting up and shaking your hand, but ..." He held out his gnarled fingers. "War injury. Long story."

"No need to apologize for anything. I think we both have some long stories. Can't wait to hear yours."

"Richard was right," Walter said. "You and I share the same blue eyes. Amazing."

"We share something else, Walter," Hans said, getting straight to it. "We had the same mother. We are brothers. Half brothers."

Walter was stunned. "What did you say?"

"I don't know why you were given up for adoption. We can speculate, of course. But we had the same mother and different fathers. I knew both my parents. They were married. I was born on September 25, 1933. You, in 1922. By my calculation, Momma must have been fifteen or sixteen when you were born. Too young for a family, I suppose."

"Incredible...I always thought it must have been something like that. I gave my parents a really hard time of it when they told me I was adopted when I was a boy. Later, I felt bad about it. They gave me such a great life, such a loving home," Walter said.

"Once your DNA posted as a result of Dr. Strassman's inquiry for Richard's marrow transplant, my daughter and her acquaintances somehow discovered you were adopted by the Remers and left Germany for America soon after you were born. She found the ship manifest with all your names on it. The voyage was paid for by Helmut Weber. He was my grandfather. My mother's father. I knew him well. He was my best friend in the whole world. He gave me this." Hans showed Walter the switchblade.

"That's a beauty," Walter said sincerely.

"Not only did he pay for the tickets, he deposited fifty thousand dollars in an account at the Bank of New York for the Remers. Those are the facts. My guess is that my grandfather didn't think my mother was old enough or responsible enough to raise you and, instead, gave you to the Remers. We have no idea who your father was. But I can tell you about my momma, Greta, your birth mother, and my grandfather, if you want."

"This is utterly fantastic, Hans. I can't believe it. It's right out of a movie or something. Please, please continue."

Before they knew it, it was after noon. "Ah, Hans, where has the time gone? Would you like me to order something for you for lunch?"

"Thank you, but I'm going to have lunch with my wife next door. I usually come on Mondays and Thursdays. Not that she knows the difference, I'm afraid. But I'll tell you what. I will go have lunch with her and come back here afterward, if that's okay."

"That would be great," Walter replied. "I just can't get over this. You couldn't even write a book like this."

Hans beamed. "You bet, my brother!"

"Brother," Walter said wistfully. "All right, I'll see you after you have lunch with your wife. What is her name?"

"Sarah," Hans said. "I'll be back around two?"

"Great," Walter said excitedly. "I can't wait to tell Richard all this. Hopefully, all will go well with the transplant and we can all get together soon."

"Amen," Hans said. "See you in a few." He put his hand tenderly on Walter's shoulder, then left the apartment. On his way to see Sarah, he told the security guard at the desk that he would be back after lunch. He couldn't wait to tell Sarah everything, even though she would have no idea what he was saying. But she would smile and nod.

After he left Sarah, Hans went to his car to retrieve some photos of Gila, Fred, Ellen, Jesse, and Sam to show Walter. He would probably love to see his newfound nieces, nephew, and great-nephews. He grabbed the envelope from the passenger seat and started to walk back toward the assisted living residence entrance.

Something wasn't right. Hans's instincts were seldom wrong.

He stopped and looked back. There it was. He recognized it right away. It wasn't there when he entered the nursing home building to see Sarah. Mills's battered old Toyota Avalon. Oh my God. *Walter.*

Hans hurried to the entrance. The automatic doors opened and he rushed to the security desk. A new guard was on duty. "Walter Remer, please."

"Do you have an appointment?"

"Yes. I was here all morning. Here's my signature." Hans held up his driver's license.

"Sure, Mr. Sternlicht. I'll have an attendant show you to Mr. Remer's apartment, but he already has company. A detective had a warrant to speak with him about some cold case. I had to let him in. He had a warrant," the guard said somewhat defensively when he noticed the expression on Hans's face.

He bolted toward Walter's apartment.

"Hey, wait a minute!" the security guard called out.

Hans was gone before the guard phoned for an attendant. "Ms. O'Malley, please go to Mr. Remer's apartment, STAT."

The door was locked. Hans removed a small tool he kept in his pocket from his Mossad days, out of habit, and quickly picked the lock. From behind him, he heard a woman—perhaps Ms. O'Malley—shout, "Hey, you can't…"

Hans rushed in. Mills was on top of Walter, knees pinning the old man down, one hand over Walter's face, while the old man flailed his arms helplessly. The other hand was plunging a syringe into Walter's arm. He dropped it and reached for his revolver.

Hans's switchblade clicked open. There was a gunshot, and there was suddenly blood everywhere.

The woman screamed. A security guard came running, firearm extended. Nurses and doctors came running from every direction. Sirens pierced the air.

33

The first Suffolk County PD officer at the scene had been called to Godwin a few times during his tenure on the force. Beyond the occasional Alzheimer's patient wandering the hallway or parking lot naked, it was pretty tame. In all his years on the force, he had never seen, much less imagined, anything like this. He commanded everyone in the room not to touch anything and called for backup. "CSI will be here in a few minutes."

When the CSI team arrived, a doctor was holding a shaking, weeping woman who turned out to be Godwin's chief medical director. Another woman—Ms. O'Malley—was explaining to a detective that she was the first on the scene, followed by the security guard and the doctor, but it was too late.

Photographs were taken, the room cordoned off. Detectives swept the apartment for evidence. The sign-in book was impounded, as were Mills's Toyota Avalon and Hans's Volvo. Godwin employees were questioned, as were members of the NYPD's Special Investigations division. Next of kin were notified.

Autopsies would show that ninety-six-year-old Walter Remer died from a lethal injection of barbiturate and anesthetic, the pathology report suggesting it was enough to kill a horse. Theodore Mills had died instantly from an expertly administered knife wound to the heart. Eighty-five-year-old Holocaust survivor, mechanic, and, perhaps, former Mossad operative Hans Sternlicht died of a gunshot that pierced his carotid artery.

The next day's *NY Post* headline read, "Crazed Former Police Detective Invades Nursing Home, Kills Brothers."

EPILOGUE

After a thorough investigation by Internal Affairs for the NYPD, Captain Tony Rosario of the NYPD's Special Investigations Division was relieved of his duties and suspended from the force.

Richard Rimes of Bergenfield, New Jersey, recovered fully as the result of a lifesaving stem cell transplant from his cousin, Alfred Sternlicht. He was too weak to attend his father's or his uncle's funerals. But Fred Sternlicht, his wife, Ellen, and children, Jesse and Sam, along with Gila Sternlicht, who flew in from Israel, attended the funerals of Walter Remer and Hans Sternlicht. Remer was buried next to his late wife, Janet Silverstein Remer. Hans Sternlicht was buried next to them at the Beth Moses Cemetery in West Babylon, New York.

Gila and Fred and his family visited Richard Rimes frequently as he recovered from his transplant and became close.

With the aid of the Commission for Art Recovery, under the Holocaust Expropriated Art Recovery Act of 2016, the Sternlichts opened an investigation and filed for the recovery of artworks stolen from Josef and Bette Sternlicht by the Nazis. One painting in particular, a Renoir for which they had photographic evidence, was held by a private collector who claimed to have purchased the painting legally, and would not relinquish it. The case is pending.

Alfred and Gila Sternlicht also sued UBS to access numbered accounts belonging to their grandfather, Alfred Sternlicht. This case, too, is still pending.

Gila Sternlicht's contacts established that the strands of hair in the wallet given to Hans by his mother belonged to the architect of the Final Solution of the Jewish question, the premeditated murder of all the Jews in Europe, Reinhard Heydrich. Further analysis discovered that he was Walter Remer's biological father. Richard Rimes, Alfred Sternlicht, and Gila Sternlicht agreed it was best their fathers never lived to learn the truth.

AUTHOR'S NOTE

Kill Brothers is a work of fiction.

Actual historical figures, battles, and incidents were employed for context. For example, there are accounts, often disputed, that after reading his brother's papers prior to Reinhard Heydrich's funeral in Berlin, Heinz Heydrich endeavored to use his printing presses to arrange false papers to save Jews.

Janet Schenck was the founder of the Manhattan School of Music and Dora Zaslavsky, a much-loved teacher there. They never encountered a prodigy named Walter Remer.

Arthur Flegenheimer, known by his nom de guerre, Dutch Schultz, was indeed an infamous Bronx gangster known for his horrific temper and gruesome murders. Chances are he never befriended a fruit monger in the Bronx.

Charles "Lucky" Luciano was one of the leading figures in organized crime in the United States. The Office of Naval Intelligence solicited his help during World War II, and the collaboration was known as Operation Underworld.

Camp X, the spy training school, located in Whitby, Ontario, Canada, trained many OSS operatives for missions behind enemy lines during World War II. The big boss, William Stephenson, who is from Winnipeg originally, was friends with Roosevelt and

Churchill. William Fairbairn, better known as Dangerous Dan, was a British Special Operations close combat instructor there.

The Austrian Resistance was led by the Austrian Roman Catholic priest Heinrich Maier. He collaborated with Franz-Josef Messner and Walter Caldonazzi, who succeeded in providing information to the Allies through Allen Dulles in Switzerland. All were eventually captured, tortured, and executed by the Gestapo. Barbara Issakides, the talented pianist, was also arrested in early 1944 and remained in Gestapo custody for eight months but survived the war.

The Blitz and bombings of Berlin were real events and no doubt far more horrific than depicted in this book.

The simple descriptions of the Einsatzgruppen and Nazi killing machine do not do justice to the vulgar, inhuman, and despicable Holocaust inflicted on the Jews and other innocents at the mercy of the Nazis.

The Jewish Hospital of Berlin did, in fact, treat Jewish patients throughout the entire war, even though Goebbels had announced that Berlin was *Judenrein*.

Other characters are occasionally loosely based on individuals who are familiar to the author but in no way are meant to represent them.

ACKNOWLEDGMENTS

I am eternally grateful to my wife, Michele, who is both my biggest fan and most gentle critic.

I would like to thank GMK Writing and Editing, Inc. for all they do. They are truly amazing. Special thanks to Gary Krebs and Katie Benoit for shepherding my manuscript to publication. I cannot thank Randy Landenheim-Gil enough for her remarkable editing. I am exceedingly fortunate to have worked with the best editor on the planet. Thank you to Josh Rosenberg, copyeditor extraordinaire, for a job well done. Also, many thanks to Libby Kingsbury for her fantastic artwork. Special thanks to Alesha Peluso of True Living. And, of course, thank you to my amazing publicist, Deborah Kohan.

I would like to express my appreciation to Bruce Black, Lou Oppenheim, and Kay and David Krebs, who read early versions of my manuscript and offered many constructive suggestions.

Thanks also go to Leib and Chava Moscovitz, Evan and Susan Krebs, and Gary and Liz Krebs for their positivity and encouragement. And thanks to Sylvie and Max Librach and Sarah Moscovitz for their love and support.

ABOUT THE AUTHOR

Steven D. Moscovitz is an American author and artist. His fascination with the use of DNA to solve cold cases and his intense interest in World War II and the Holocaust inspired him to write this debut novel. He is a husband and father with two daughters, a son-in-law, and two cats. He lives in Long Island, New York.

Visit Steven D. Moscovitz at www.stevendmoscovitz.com

CPSIA information can be obtained
at www.ICGtesting.com
Printed in the USA
LVHW051451120623
749513LV00005B/190